What Happened To Mary Faye Hunter?

Brad Golson
Glenda Yarbrough

Copyright © 2019 golson&yarbrough

All rights reserved.

ISBN: 9781080117307

This work, although based on a true story, is fiction. Characters, events, organizations portrayed in this novel are either products of the authors' imagination or used fictitiously unless stated otherwise. No part of this book may be copied or reproduced in any form without the authors' permission.

DEDICATION

For Mary Faye, who loved God, family, church, friends, and her piano.

ACKNOWLEDGMENT

On June 10, 2019, retired state investigator, Robert E. "Bob" Hancock passed away at the age of 87. Over the course of a two-year investigation, I spent several hours with Bob painstakingly discussing the details of Mary Faye's case. I am grateful to have had the opportunity to work with such a dedicated individual in the pursuit of justice. Without Bob's perseverance and guidance, I would not have been in a position to finish what he had started in 1967.

Rest in peace, my friend.

PREFACE

Mary Faye Hunter was a devoted Christian woman who still lived at home with her parents. She was regarded by her family and peers as responsible and considerate, almost to a fault. She held a full-time government job and was an accomplished pianist. Mary Faye's social life was a different story. She had no close friends, nor had she ever had a boyfriend. On May 6, 1967, Mary Faye Hunter walked into downtown Decatur, Alabama, to have her hair styled. On her way home from a nearby supermarket, she disappeared on a residential sidewalk. Five months later, her skeletal remains were found in the backwaters of the Tennessee River. What happened to Mary Faye Hunter? The book that you are about to read is based on facts and circumstantial evidence collected during a two-year investigation, but written as a novel. **Most of the names used in this book are real, but some names were changed for legal purposes or to respectfully protect the families of the accused.** Keeping that in mind, as you read this novel, remember that Mary Faye Hunter was a real person who had her own secrets.

God, Family, Church, Friends, Work, Music
Until…

Chapter 1

May 2, 1933

Etolia Hunter wailed in agony. Her clenched fists ripped at the bedsheets. Sweat poured down her face. She prayed the last push would finally produce her first newborn. Etolia was still recuperating from the surgical removal of her appendix and tonsils only a few months earlier at the Baugh Infirmary. This time, she was in the mother's ward at Benevolent Society Hospital. In 1944, the hospital would expand and be renamed Decatur General Hospital.

The pain ripped through Etolia's hips. Moments later, the sound of a baby crying filled the small space.

"It's a beautiful baby girl," the doctor told Etolia Hunter.

He smiled at the young mother and placed the infant in her arms. The baby cried and trembled.

"Nothing more beautiful than a young mother holding

her baby for the first time."

The nurse who cleaned the baby raised an eyebrow at the doctor. Her eyes questioned him, but he shook his head and waved her away. He wasn't going to spoil a precious moment between a young mother holding her newborn.

The truth could wait.

"Have you picked out a name for her yet?" the nurse asked.

"Oh, yes. She's going to be named Mary after her aunt." She kissed the baby. "Mary Faye Hunter. My sweet, sweet, beautiful baby girl."

Etolia gently tugged at the blanket. She counted each finger, kissed the baby's hands, and stroked her arms. Gently, Etolia pulled again at the wrap. The baby began to cry. She pulled Mary Faye closer to her.

Suddenly, Etolia stared in horror. Her eyes turned to the doctor. Her face shrouded in shock and filled with disbelief.

"We need to talk," the doctor said. His voice was soft and compassionate.

-2-

Etolia Hunter lay in the hospital bed, pillows propped behind her. Webb Hunter sat on the bed beside his wife, his fingers caressing her hand.

"It's going to be all right, Etolia."

She didn't answer.

"It could have been worse," he said.

"I know that...I know, but it will always—"

"No. Just wait and see what the doctor says."

It seemed like forever, but only twenty minutes had passed when Dr. Stone came into the room.

"This is not as bad as you think," said the doctor.

"But—" Etolia began.

"No buts. Sometimes it happens, but it's not something

that will drastically affect her life." He moved closer to the bed, but his eyes were on Webb. "She's a beautiful, healthy baby."

"Tell me what can be done to correct this," said the young father.

"She will need to be fitted for a dental prosthetic. Yes, it will affect her speech, but not seriously. Don't consider this as something horrible. Many babies are born with a cleft palate. She will be fine."

Etolia pulled at the bed covers and fought back tears.

"Take care of your daughter. Don't ever make her feel like she has a handicap. Her speech will be fine. Maybe different, but fine." He stroked Etolia's hand and smiled. "And yes, she has all her fingers and toes."

Webb laughed.

The doctor added, "Young parents always count them."

Etolia glanced from Webb to Dr. Stone. "She will be all right, won't she?"

Both men nodded. Etolia was not convinced, but she managed to return the nod.

Chapter 2

Summer 1938

"You talk funny," six-year-old, Henry, told five-year-old, Mary Faye.

"No, I don't," Mary Faye replied. Her voice had a nasally sound.

Henry's family had just moved in next door to the Hunter family on Fourth Avenue. Mary Faye rode her new tricycle into the backyard. Henry ran after her.

"Mary Faye! Mary Faye! Can I ride your tricycle?"

"No." Her small feet pushed the pedals hard as if she was attempting to get away from the young boy. Mary Faye didn't really want to escape. She enjoyed playing with Henry but didn't like his words. Other kids had made hurtful remarks, but most of the time no one had said anything.

"Mary Faye, you're my friend. I want to ride with you."

She stopped and surrendered a smile. "All right. Get on

the back."
Henry hopped on behind Mary Faye.
"Hold on." Mary Faye pedaled as Henry pushed with one foot. Together they circled the backyard. Henry squealed with pleasure. Mary Faye beamed over her shoulder at her new friend. For a moment, fear of judgment melted away.

Chapter 3

Spring 1943

Mary Faye's fingers tingled with anticipation. The piano nourished her spirit just as water cleansed her body. The notes she played provided a deep meaning that satisfied her soul. The piano was her true love. It gave her the attention, approval, and amazement that she desired. Music was one with her. When Mary Faye performed, her mind placed her center stage before a vast audience that adored her.

"Mary Faye." Etolia leaned against the doorway that separated the kitchen and living room. "That's so pretty."

"Thank you, momma." Her fingers continued to play. "When I grow up, I'm going to be a great pianist playing all over the world."

Her mother smiled. What foolishness. Her daughter needed a college education, but not for such nonsense as a concert pianist. There's no way she would allow her baby girl to travel all over the world playing the piano.

"You have a beautiful talent, baby."

Etolia went back into the kitchen. Mary Faye was delicate and unique in so many ways. God had blessed her with a musical talent, but there was no sense in encouraging her to think of it as a stable career.

Etolia removed pans, sugar, cocoa, and flour from the cabinet. She placed butter, milk, and eggs on the counter. She wanted to bake a chocolate cake to have after supper.

-2-

September 1951

Mary Faye was stretched out across her bed. The pediment frame was solid cherry with four tall posts and a spindle style headboard. A light knock came from the door before her mother entered the room.

"Mary Faye." Her mother sat on the edge of the bed. "We need to talk."

Lying on her stomach across the bed, Mary Faye glanced over her shoulder at her mother.

What on earth was wrong? Momma never approached me this way.

"I know you're eighteen, and starting college next week."

"What is it, momma?"

"I don't really know how to say this," Etolia's eyes moved away from her daughter.

"Momma?"

Etolia laughed nervously and patted her daughter's leg.

"Oh, it's nothing bad. It's just...Mary Faye, don't ever let some boy take advantage of you." She gave her another gentle pat. "I know you're a young woman now. You know about sex, but I just want you to be careful since you're going off to college."

"Momma... really?" Mary Faye planted her face into

the mattress.

Etolia straightened her back. "I'm just going to put it plain. Don't you ever let some boy lay between your legs without marriage."

"Oh, momma!" Mary Faye could feel her face turning red. Never had her mother mentioned sex to her. She didn't know what to say.

Etolia gave Mary Faye's head a quick pat as she got off the bed. Mary Faye could not look at her. Etolia turned, but stopped when she reached the door.

"Supper will be ready soon. Your daddy will be home from the store shortly. Thought we'd have pork chops tonight."

The lesson in sex had passed. Both mother and daughter were glad it had.

Chapter 4

April 11, 1966

"If you would," Leland Mitchell said as he strutted among the rows of desks, "lend me a few minutes of your time. Thank y'all for coming in from the warehouse too."

The warehouse workers stood at the back of the room.

"I know everyone is busy, but this won't take long. When I started working at Redstone Arsenal in 1941, the idea of retirement was just a day somewhere in some distant future, but—" he chuckled, "after 25 years, it's here."

Everyone applauded.

"Are you clapping because I'm leaving or because I survived 25 years?"

Several people chuckled.

"As you know, Friday week, April 22, will be my last day. There's a young man from another department who will take over for me. His name is Adam Fletcher. He's been at the Arsenal for two years and a veteran of the

Korean War. Young men who serve our country during wartime should have our deepest gratitude. I know y'all will make him feel welcome."

Leland Mitchell had been too young for the First World War, but had been prime draft age for the second one at age 36. Nevertheless, he had not been required to go. Being married with children did not keep a man out of the military during the war, but being a farmer did. Because of the war, there was a shortage of farmers. Men between the ages of 21 and 45 had to register for the military. Men went off to war, while women went to work in plants and factories. Since America needed farmers, Congress instituted draft deferments for them.

Leland Mitchell had always wanted his employees to appreciate anyone who served in the military. Sometimes Leland wished he too had served in the military during the Big War, but his wife had always pointed out that he served by helping to feed America's families. He knew it wasn't the same type of service. Leland had heard so many men tell their war stories, and all he had to boast about was how much corn he grew or how big the pigs had gotten. Leland also understood the deep fear of people with loved ones in the military. His grandson had just received his draft notice last week for Vietnam. He was afraid for him and all the young men who traveled thousands of miles from home to fight.

"Mr. Fletcher will start tomorrow morning. I know under his guidance, this department will turn out the fine work it always has. Now let's get back to work."

Leland returned to his office. Some of the employees were surprised that a man was being brought in from another office, especially those who were in a position to be promoted for the job. But that was life at the Arsenal. You never knew who was transferring in or out.

Mary Faye went to her desk and began her work. It made no difference to her who was in charge. She knew her job, did it well, and never had any complaints from any of the previous supervisors. Her job pleased her parents because it was a steady government position. Mary Faye had earned a four-year degree with a major in music, but it was just a few business courses that gave her the job at Redstone Arsenal.

"That job will give you all the financial security you will ever need," her daddy had told her. Mary Faye's brother, Jimmy, was a doctor and she worked for the government. Webb and Etolia Hunter were proud of their two children.

Being a shipping clerk and typist wasn't the job Mary Faye had visualized for herself. Music was her calling, but Mary Faye knew her parents were right. The government offered security that music could not provide.

"Mary Faye." Andrea Brown placed a file on her desk. "Can you double check this list with the master list?"

"Sure." She flipped through the file. "Is there a problem with it?"

"I know you're good at catching errors. I'm just worried I might have overlooked something."

Andrea rolled her eyes and sighed. "I'm worried to death about our new boss. There's already talk that he's a slave driver type."

Mary Faye giggled. "How do you know that?"

"Because he was in the military."

"So?"

"Well, he was in Korea for over five years because he kept volunteering to stay in the heat of the action. Now he drills his employees like they are soldiers."

Mary Faye pored over the numbers and names.

"Just who told you such foolishness?" chided Mary Faye. "And why do you believe that anyway?"

"Louella told me a bunch of stuff. It makes sense."

Mary Faye's eyes traveled over each page. "This looks fine to me."

"What do you think he will be like?" asked Andrea.

"I don't know. Can't be as good and nice as Mr. Mitchell. He was an excellent office manager."

"I know. Guess that's why I'm worried. Mr. Mitchell has been in our office for almost ten years, and I've never heard a bad word against him."

"I think it'll be okay. Just don't listen to Louella." Mary Faye smiled.

Lunchtime brought the women to their regular table, and it was Louella who eagerly turned the conversation to the new boss.

"I bet Mr. Fletcher will be gorgeous."

The other three women stared at Louella.

"Last night I was watching *Twelve O'clock High* on television. Joe Gallagher is so handsome, so brave—"

"Just who is Joe Gallagher?" asked Peggy.

Louella was astonished. "You don't know who Joe Gallagher is?"

Peggy shook her head.

"He's Colonel Joe Gallagher. His father is General Maxwell Gallagher..."

Mary Faye listened to the women talk as she ate her sandwich, but did not contribute.

"And this TV show is about the war, and Joe Gallagher is so handsome. He's got that lean, rugged, manly look about him."

"Wait a minute. What does this have to do with our new supervisor?"

"Well, nothing, but he was in Korea. Just imagine how much action he saw. Since he was a soldier, he must be handsome, just like Joe Gallagher. Think about all that training they go through to keep in shape."

"So, you believe that just because a guy was in the military, he's good looking?" Andrea joked.

"Why not? My Jeb was. He was strong. So handsome. He was just plain beautiful in his uniform. Did I ever tell y'all his eyes were so black that in the sunlight they actually had a purple hue?"

For a moment, Louella's eyes clouded with the remembrance of a lost love. Quickly, she smiled and shook her head slightly. She reached up to make sure her honey blonde, flipped bob was still in place.

"Of course, this new guy could never measure up to my Jeb. Not even Colonel Joe Gallagher could measure up to my soldier."

* * *

The next morning when Adam Fletcher entered the room, Louella decided her words were true. He was no Jeb Ramirez. Despite being very tall at well over six feet, he was mostly average looking.

"Everyone," Leland began, "I want to introduce your new supervisor. Mr. Adam Fletcher."

Mr. Fletcher towered over Leland Mitchell. His dark brown hair was parted neatly to the side. The black, horn-rimmed glasses magnified his intense blue eyes. After a brief introduction, Mr. Fletcher shook hands with each employee in the department. When he took Mary Faye's hand, she dropped her eyes, and meekly said, "Hello." He nodded, then moved on to the next person.

Mary Faye hated meeting strangers. She never knew what to say, and even if she did, her nasally pitched voice made her uncomfortable. This guy already made her nervous. A new boss was the worst kind of stranger. The first thing he would notice was her speech, then the limp because of her bad hip. He would see all of that before he saw her work.

She pushed the idea of a new boss from her mind. After Mr. Fletcher made his way to each desk in the clerical office, Leland Mitchell took him to the warehouse to meet the rest of the staff. Mary Faye concentrated on her work.

* * *

Several hours later, Mr. Fletcher and Leland Mitchell went into the office. Mary Faye saw them walk by, but kept her eyes on the paperwork. After the door closed, Leland pointed to a chair in front of his desk. "Have a seat, Adam. What do you think of your new surroundings so far?"

"I'm sure everything will be fine. Your staff seems to be a good group."

"Overall, they are. Sometimes, you run into a few, well, you know, that have issues. I can assure you of one thing. There's a little lady, Miss Hunter, who will work her fingers to the bone and never complain about anything. She's a trooper."

Adam nodded. He didn't recall meeting Miss Hunter, but he didn't ask which one she was. He was nervous enough about the new position without trying to remember names.

* * *

The carpool traveled south on Interstate 65 toward Decatur. Mary Faye sat between Rick Overton and Paul Hurst. Stephen Harkins was riding shotgun while Almon Hensley was at the wheel.

"What did y'all think about our new bossman?" Rick asked.

"He seemed like a nice guy," replied Paul. "He was in the warehouse most of the day."

"Yeah, he was okay," added Stephen. "Someone said he was married and had a couple of kids."

"Wonder what branch of the military he was in?" asked Rick.

"Most likely the Army," Paul replied.

Rick turned to Mary Faye. "What did y'all think about

him in the clerical department?"

"I don't really know...okay, I guess."

She was scared to death of him.

Mary Faye dropped her eyes. The subject moved away from her.

-2-

"You're going to tell me you don't know how to balance a simple checkbook when you work with numbers all day!" yelled Martha at her husband with clenched fists.

They stood in the living room of their small house on Cecil Street in Southwest Decatur. Martha had the checkbook in one hand and a letter in the other.

"Those three dollar fishing lures you bought from the Bait Shop on Sixth Avenue will now cost you twenty-five dollars—and no telling what other checks would have bounced if I hadn't taken forty dollars to the bank this afternoon."

"I told you I'm sorry," Adam pleaded. I haven't been home five minutes, and you're hounding me about an overdraft!"

He sank into his armchair.

"You ever think I might have had a hard day at work?" he asked. "It was my first day in a new department, you know. So you're not the only one who had an exhausting day. All you had to do was take a little money to the bank."

"A little money to the bank? That twenty-five dollars would have bought groceries this week or paid the light bill! There are plenty of useful things that we could have done with that money instead of paying an overdraft. That was uncalled for."

"I'm sorry, okay? I'm sorry! How many times do you want me to say it?"

"Fine!" Martha stormed out of the room, but immediately returned. The veins in her neck throbbed.

"It's crazy when a grown man can't keep track of a checkbook. We're still fairly new to this town, and here you are bouncing checks."

"What do you want me to do? I said I was sorry." His voice cracked on the last syllable. He placed his hands over his face. Martha left the room again, but this time she slammed the back door as she exited the house.

Martha had six tomato plants in the back yard. To ease her anger, she hoed around the plants and checked for worms on the leaves. Each plant was like a lovely flower to her. In a few months, there would be juicy red tomatoes on the vine. Tending to the plants and watching them grow normally gave her a sense of peace and satisfaction, but not today. Martha was so furious at Adam that she could pinch his head off.

Martha threw the hoe down and marched back inside.

"Adam!"

"Yeah?" he answered from the living room.

Martha was standing next to the refrigerator with her hand out as soon as Adam entered the kitchen.

"What?" he asked.

"Gimme."

"What do you want?"

"The checkbook. From now on, I will write all the checks. You can have a cash allowance every week for gas and whatever, but we're not going to have two checkbooks floating around with both of us writing checks."

"Hey! I make the money—"

"The money is just as much mine as it is yours. I work just as hard as you if not harder, so gimme."

He pulled out the checkbook from his back pocket.

"Here. Have fun." He bolted out of the kitchen. The front door slammed.

Adam had not been the same since he came home from the war. Martha placed the checkbook on the top shelf of the kitchen cabinet. Now it was out of sight and out of mind. She didn't know what to do with him. Sometimes, Adam would sit alone and stare off into space. He could be reading a newspaper then suddenly as if some supernatural power pulled him from his body, would vanish into a world that no one else could see.

Martha knew the car was gone before she saw the empty space near the side of the house. Where did he go? She hated it when he left like that.

* * *

The cool breeze felt soothing. April weather was so unpredictable in Alabama. It could be very warm or cold, but today it was nice. Adam Fletcher didn't know where he was going, but he had to get away from the house and away from Martha. He loved his wife, but it seemed as if they argued more times than not. Adam had been back from Korea for ten years, yet sometimes it seemed like yesterday when he was in those frozen trenches fighting enemies in the rain and snow, trying to kill men that he had never met. All he had known was that death seemed inevitable. Adam remembered the ear-piercing explosions vividly. Body parts had blown completely off. So much blood. Those memories haunted him daily and often manifested into nightmares.

Not once had Adam ever been shot or hit with shrapnel, but his buddy and bunkmate from New Jersey had lost his leg while standing right beside him. Then there was Max Appleton. A great little guy from Georgia. His whole body had been blown to shreds when he stepped on a mine during a patrol assignment. Adam had fought beside those men, yet he survived.

Why him?

Adam turned right onto the main highway out of town. He searched for a secluded side road. The wind whipped through the driver's side window. It made him feel free.

Exhilaration coursed through his veins as the car sped down the asphalt. He turned left on Old Moulton Road, went a few miles then turned onto a dark, narrow road.

Here you are old boy, sailing down the road while so many of your fellow soldiers are sailing through eternity.

Why was his life spared? There was nothing special about him. He wasn't a priest, doctor, philanthropist, or humanitarian. So why did he live, while others had perished? That's the one question that kept haunting him. He still saw their faces, heard their cries, and remembered all the fighting; all the blood, and all the young men fighting just to stay alive.

Adam turned on the radio. The music relaxed him somewhat, but then he thought about Martha and that stupid checkbook. She ruled that house just like a drill sergeant. When and how she became the ruling force in their marriage, he wasn't sure, but it happened. The Army had discharged Adam in September of 1953. They were married the following spring. Martha had wanted to be a June bride. Twelve years later, she had him on an allowance like he was her teenage son.

In the distance, the sun slipped away behind a small mountain. Adam turned into a church driveway, drove around the circle, and came back out on the highway. There was no place to go, but home. The anger in him had subsided. Maybe Martha's had too. After all, she did have the checkbook now.

Later that night, Adam and Martha stayed on opposite sides of the bed. Neither said anything else about finances. Sometimes the unspoken was louder than the spoken.

Chapter 5

May 2, 1966

Rick Overton watched Mary Faye limp down the steps from her front porch. She was such a nice woman. It made no sense that she had never married. Rick had two failed marriages. If Mary Faye had married, then divorced, it would make sense why marriage would be the last thing on her mind. She wasn't a bad looking woman. Maybe it was because she was so shy. He probably would have never noticed her if not for the carpool.

"Rick, you gonna go fishing this weekend?" Stephen Harkins asked. He was sitting at the wheel of his stark blue, 1962 Rambler.

"Might. Depending on the weather."

"My understanding, it's going to be a nice weekend," Paul Hurst said from the backseat.

Almon Hensley got out of the car. He hated riding in the middle. Mary Faye was so much smaller and wouldn't miss the room he needed. Besides, he liked to look out the window.

"Good morning, Mary Faye." He tipped his hat as the young woman reached the car.

"Good morning, Mr. Hensley," Mary Faye said as she eased into the Rambler.

"Happy Birthday, Mary Faye," Rick said as he turned to face her.

"Why thank you! How did you know it was my birthday?"

He snickered. "Oh, I have my ways."

"Oh, he's like Double-O-Seven," said Paul. "He has his ways of knowing everything."

The men laughed, and Mary Faye smiled. She had not seen the James Bond films, but knew Ian Fleming's spy novels. She had read all fourteen books since the first one. *Casino Royale* had come out in 1953. She continued to wonder how Rick Overton knew today was her birthday.

Rick didn't tell Mary Faye that it was his girlfriend, Nancy, who had told him about her birthday. Nancy attended the same church as Mary Faye. The subject came up because Nancy had explained to Rick that the church pianist was having a birthday, and the choir planned to give her a small gift. When he had asked Nancy for the name of the pianist, she confirmed that it was Mary Faye Hunter.

"You got big plans for your birthday, Mary Faye?" Almon asked.

"Yesterday, momma cooked a nice dinner for us with all my favorites. Chicken and dumplings, mashed potatoes, and green beans. A big coconut cake for dessert. My brother Jimmy and his family were there too."

"Didn't your brother become a doctor?" Paul asked.

"Yes, he's working in Birmingham."

The conversation moved on to fishing and sports.

I watched the Yankees game too, Mary Faye almost mentioned that, but didn't. She willingly faded into the background as she did so many times before.

* * *

"Mary Faye?"

Clark Jeremiah Cantrell, known to everyone as CJ, stood by Mary Faye's desk.

"You mind giving these to Mr. Fletcher?"

He held a stack of envelopes.

"These came over from Building Four. Someone left them in the warehouse, and I don't know why. Guess they think just because we ship 'em out, we get all the mail too." CJ laughed.

"Sure. I don't mind." Mary Faye accepted the envelopes.

"And a belated Happy Birthday to you!"

She laughed. "Thank you. How was your boys' birthday?"

"We had a party with all the family on Saturday. It worked better than having it on Sunday, which was fine with me. The twins turned one you know, but I won't ask how old you turned."

He grinned and winked.

Mary Faye tilted her head. "And, you better not. Hey, did you watch the ballgame yesterday?"

"I sure did," CJ replied enthusiastically.

CJ was 31-years-old, had been married for nine years. He was the proud father of twin boys. His wife, Joan, was a school teacher. CJ was going to college for an engineering degree. In Mary Faye, he found the perfect person to share his love for the New York Yankees and also music.

CJ had been at the Arsenal for four years. His friendship with Mary Faye had grown slowly over the last two years. His blue eyes sparkled as he talked.

"I yelled so much, Joan was afraid I'd wake the boys. She said if I didn't quiet down, I was going to have to go outside and listen to the car radio. Lucky for me, the twins didn't wake up while the game was on." He laughed. "I probably would have moved the TV to the front porch."

Mary Faye giggled and nodded in agreement.

There weren't many people at Redstone that Mary Faye was comfortable enough with to be friends, but CJ was different. Not only did he love baseball, but he also played the piano and the guitar. CJ was the music minister where he went to church and sometimes filled in for the pianist. He also had a love for the classics as well as country music. He was tall, friendly, nice looking, with dark hair that curled around the nape of his neck. CJ always kept his hair combed straight back, but sometimes a loose curl would fall across his forehead. He didn't smoke or drink.

CJ glanced over his shoulder and scanned the office. He grinned when he met Mary Faye's eyes again.

"Here," he said, and handed her a small brown bag.

"Does this go to Mr. Fletcher too?"

CJ chuckled.

"No, but I'd love to see the look on his face. It's for you. Just a little something. I'm still trying to convert you to country music. I know you love your Beethoven, but give this a try."

"And what country artist are you trying to convert me to?"

"Not the artist, just the music."

Mary Faye peeked into the bag. Inside was a 45 vinyl record of Bill Anderson's album, *Still* along with the sheet music to the song. Mary Faye didn't know what to say. She was flattered.

"Thank you," she said tenderly. No man outside her own family had ever given her a gift before.

"It's a beautiful song," he said. "I love the arrangement. I think you'll enjoy it. My little band played that song last Friday night at the Moulton Armory. It was a hit."

"I really appreciate it. I'll listen to it as soon as I get home."

CJ tapped his fingers to his head as if to tip his hat. He turned around and went back to the warehouse. Mary Faye put the record in her desk with her purse and took the envelopes to the office. She tapped on the door before she entered.

"Yes?" said Mr. Fletcher. He stopped writing but kept his head down.

"These letters were left on the warehouse side by mistake."

"Okay. Just put it in that basket." He pointed to the flat wooden tray on his desk.

Mary Faye placed the envelopes on top. Without looking up, he said, "Thank you for bringing them in. By the way, happy birthday."

Surprised, Mary Faye stammered, "Oh, well…thank you." She left the room and silently closed the door.

Chapter 6

May 11, 1966

"Wreck on Highway 31 North," the voice came over the phone. "Need assistance."

"Pete!" Rusty Cole yelled as he came out of the office holding a notepad, "Let's take number three!" He wedged the pencil between his left ear and the dark, shiny pomade styled hair.

Pete Foster maneuvered his massive frame into the passenger seat as Rusty jerked open the driver's side door and turned the ignition key. They left Fourth Avenue with the siren blaring in route to the river bridge. They arrived at the scene right behind the Decatur Police.

"Looks like you beat all the others, boss."

Rusty smiled. "And that's how you make the money."

Pete unloaded the gurney as Rusty approached the wreckage.

"Whatcha got, Daryl?" Rusty asked the man in

uniform. Another police officer was speaking to the couple inside a late model Chevy. A 1950's model Ford was stopped a few yards away. Rusty surmised that the old beater had seen better days even before the accident.

"Best we can tell," began the officer, "the driver hit his head on the steering wheel, and the passenger said her head hit the side window then popped back."

The officer opened the car door. "Sir, can you move? Let me help you out."

The driver extended his arms so the officer could ease him from the car.

Pete brought in the gurney and carefully rolled the man to the rear of the ambulance then placed him inside. Pete returned to the car with another gurney. Rusty and the officer had already removed the passenger.

"I don't need to go to no hospital!" she rebuked. "If that dang fool had been paying attention, this wouldn't have happened!"

"You ready to give a statement as to what did happen?" the officer asked her.

The woman stopped in her tracks, grabbed Rusty's shoulder. "I...I...um...where am I?"

The two men exchanged glances.

"Take it easy, ma'am," the officer said.

"Here," Rusty offered as he guided her to the ambulance.

She took a couple of steps then collapsed into Rusty's arms. With Pete's help, they placed her on the gurney and lifted her into the ambulance. The earsplitting siren sounded as they made their way to Decatur General Hospital on Somerville Road.

* * *

"Hello, Rusty," greeted Vicki Shipley from the front desk of the emergency room. "Whatcha got for us?"

"Wreck... might be bad. I'm not for sure. The woman was talking, and then couldn't stand up."

"Jennifer will check them out and get the doctor on call to examine them."

Vicki had known Rusty Cole since they were in school at Decatur High. Back then, he had been one of the most handsome boys in class, but the years had not been too kind to Rusty. He was beginning to develop deep wrinkles on his forehead, and a few around his mouth from holding cigarettes. But it wasn't just his appearance. Rusty had a cynical attitude that he always carried with him.

"Yeah, they plastered themselves up against a utility pole over on Sixth Avenue, but hey, everyone I pick up, it's like picking up money." He leaned against the nurse's desk. "How you been doing Vicki?"

"Fine. Just working."

"I hear ya there. Between this job and my other job—"

"Your other job?"

"Oh, yeah, the service station I got." He produced a pack of Camels from his shirt pocket.

Vicki shook her head. "Rusty, you know you can't light that thing in here. Something might blow up."

"You ain't got nothing in here that's gonna blow up." He lit a match, but Vicki leaned over and blew it out.

"Hey!" he protested.

"I told ya. Something might blow up."

"What would that be?" Rusty demanded. His hand folded around the matchbox as he jerked the cigarette from his mouth, fingers curled around the cigarette.

"Me!" she exclaimed.

"Whatcha mean, girl?"

"I'm going to blow up if you light that cigarette and get me in trouble for letting you. My boss would have my rear end if he came in here with you standing there smoking."

Rusty laughed. "Well, sugar," his southern accent

heavy, "I wouldn't want to git yo rear end in trouble." He looked her up and down and grinned. Rusty turned to leave when Officer Beckett entered the emergency room.

"Good morning, Vicki. Is Rusty telling you how he saved those people's lives?"

"No, he didn't say anything about that."

"What are you talkin' about, Bobby Beckett?" said Rusty.

The officer laughed. "The way that woman grabbed you…if not, she might have hit the ground and messed up her head even worse."

Rusty chuckled. "I got my own thoughts on that."

"Yeah, me too. The other driver said they pulled out in front of him then swiveled to keep from being hit broadsided. Now, I need to know their side of the story. You hear anything in the ambulance?"

"You know I'm not supposed to repeat anything like that. Goes against my ethics."

"Uh, huh. Sure. What'd you hear?"

"Nothing except he told her not to say a word till they talked to a lawyer…maybe he said agent…something like that."

"Can I see them, Vicki?" asked Beckett.

"I'll check," she said.

Vicki left the room.

"How's it going at the police department?" asked Rusty.

"Nothing new," said Beckett. "Just everyone on their toes."

Vicki appeared around the corner.

"Yeah, go on back to room three on the left. Doc said it'd be fine."

Rusty checked the clock behind the desk on the wall. "10:45. Morning is flying by, and I'm not making any money standing here."

"Be seeing you, Rusty," Beckett said as he swaggered

out of the room.

"Well, girl, I'll see you later," Rusty said as he waved a hand at Vicki.

"See you around, Rusty."

"Oh, I'm sure you will."

Vicki watched Rusty and Pete leave the emergency room. No, Rusty Cole was no longer that kid from high school. There were many rumors about him. Bad rumors. Just how many were true, she didn't know, nor did she want to.

-2-

May 13, 1966

Rusty sat behind his desk. He had three men and one woman working for him. There was decent money to be made in the ambulance service, but also a lot of rules and regulations. Nevertheless, it was Rusty's other job that turned over the quick bucks. If there were enough of those jobs, the ambulance business could be his secondary job. The problem with that job, however, was that he never knew when a payment was coming. It might be two in one week, maybe even three, but then nothing for three months. In the beginning, six months went by before the word got around about his new business. Now, jobs were coming in from all over the place. Athens, Huntsville, Florence, Birmingham, and even the Gulf Coast. There was one that even came in from across the state line. Three hundred dollars for a fifteen, maybe twenty-minute job wasn't bad.

The phone rang, breaking his thoughts.

"Hello."

"Is this Rusty Cole?" asked a male voice.

"Speaking."

"I was told, uh, that you could help—you could help a person."

"I don't know what you mean exactly. We run an ambulance service. Do you need an ambulance?"

"Ambulance? No...I don't need an ambulance. I need an abortion." The voice became stronger.

"Well sir, you'd be the first man I ever heard of that needed one."

"Listen, I don't have time for jokes! My girlfriend needs the abortion."

"This here is an ambulance service, sir. You do know abortions are illegal, don't you?"

"Yes, I know it's illegal!"

"Hey now, you best chime down. You the one saying you want to break the law here, not me."

The man's voice changed, once again anxious. "I just heard you were the man to call."

"Who told you such foolishness?"

"Dr. Carter. He told my girl that you were to the man to see."

This might be the real deal.

Carter had taught him the service of helping out women—that was how he relayed it to him. They had a password. Rusty waited to see if the man would use it.

"I am if you need an ambulance."

"No!" The man's voice was breaking. "He said you had a service of you know, helping women."

Bingo.

"That's a high dollar service there. It'll set you back three hundred."

"Not a problem. When can we do it?"

"Tomorrow night. Meet me at the Traveler's Rest Motel on Highway 31 at seven sharp."

"Great." The man sounded relieved.

"Room 303."

* * *

By 7:00, Rusty Cole had sat on a lumpy motel bed for almost 30 minutes. He scanned the parking lot. The last thing he needed was a bust. The motel was quiet. No one came in or out until a few minutes before seven when a gray car pulled into a parking space one door down. A young couple was in the car. Rusty waited for them to get out, but they just sat there. He moved away from the window.

Were they my customers or what?

He waited. Nothing. He tapped his foot on the floor. A nervous habit from way back. He checked his watch. 7:05.

Slowly, he eased back to the window and peeked out from behind the curtain. They were gone.

I'm getting out of here. Something ain't adding up.

Quickly he started for his bag. A light timid knock from the door stopped him. He turned, stared at the door for a moment, and then hurried to the window again. It was the same couple.

Where did the car go?

Rusty jerked the door open. The couple rushed by him as they entered the room.

They didn't want to be seen. That's good.

"Where did you go?" Rusty asked.

"What?"

"You moved your car."

"Oh, that. We didn't want it known which room we were in."

"You bring the money?"

"Yeah."

The man pulled out three, one hundred dollar bills from his wallet. His hand was shaking.

Rusty snatched the money. "You," he said to the young woman. "Take off your bottoms and lay down."

She removed her jeans and panties. From his black duffle bag, Rusty produced a tube, suction cup, and a long wire hooked on one end.

"How far along are you?" Rusty asked.

"I don't know for sure, but I didn't have my period last month."

"I see."

Was she really pregnant or just scared? There's only one way to find out for sure.

"Do you do this often?" asked the man.

"Just relax. I've got it under control."

Twenty minutes later, the young man and his girlfriend were gone. Rusty Cole didn't know them or their names, but he knew they were from somewhere on the other side of Decatur. He didn't want to know anything else about them.

Rusty watched the bloody water swirl around in the commode—then gone. Just like that, he thought. The bloody stained towels were on the bathroom floor, but it didn't matter.

Could have been a bad nosebleed.

Besides, this room was Rusty's reserved room. Management knew not to ask questions.

Rusty strolled out into the warm southern night. The sky was alive with billions of bright glittery stars. He got into his tuxedo black, 1964 Chevelle Malibu SS with a 327 V8 motor.

My pride and joy.

Rusty had ordered this baby back in October of 1963 when they first came out. Little jobs like tonight helped pay for it. Usually, he didn't drive this one to the motel. Rusty didn't want anyone to see it here, but since it was dark outside, he made an exception.

Tonight was the third one this month and only the sixteenth of this year. Rusty had given the doc his cut, ten percent off every dollar. Rusty's reputation was growing, and who knows, maybe one day he wouldn't have to depend on the doc's referrals anymore.

The Chevelle left the parking lot unnoticed. The little black bag sat on the back seat, ready for the next time.

Chapter 7

May 17, 1966

"Joan," CJ said as he got out of the car.

His wife was bent down near a flowerbed.

"What are you doing?"

"Pulling those weeds that you should have pulled before the birthday party. Remember? You said you would do it."

"Oh yeah. I forgot."

"Yes, and I know why," Joan said as she jerked a long-rooted weed from the ground. "Do you remember what I said when we agreed to put in this bed?"

"I thought we agreed that you would take care of the flowers and I would mow the grass."

"Yeah, but it seems like these weeds are everywhere."

CJ trotted over to his wife and helped her to her feet.

"Just like this dang grass… it grows everywhere. What's for supper?"

"Your favorite. Fried catfish."

"Yes, it is." He caught her hand. "C'mon. Let's get supper started. Where are the boys?"

"At my mother's. She wanted to watch them this afternoon a little longer after I got out of school. Those boys can wear me out faster than the first graders at school."

"We'll be playing this Friday night at the Fort. Are you coming?"

"If my mother will watch the boys. I might need to be there to make sure some pretty girl doesn't try to steal away the leader of the band."

He laughed. "Only you, baby, only you."

The young couple went into the house to prepare supper. A couple of hours later, Joan's mother dropped off the twins.

CJ and Joan had been married for five years before she got pregnant. They planned to wait five years before starting a family. Just like it was part of the plan to finish their education before marriage, but CJ decided he wanted more than just a business degree. Going to school at age thirty was unexpected, but CJ convinced Joan that it was for the best in the long run. Right now, however, it was just an added stress to the already stressful household with both of them working and raising twins. It wouldn't be long until school would be out for the summer and Joan was counting down the days. She needed the long summer days where she could sleep late, or as long as the boys would allow, and be able to spend more time with her children.

There were times that Joan resented CJ's band. It allowed him time to get out of the house and have fun with his friends while she was at home babysitting. Feeding and changing the diapers of crying babies; that seemed to be her world these days. She should have told him no when he came up with the crazy idea of having some of the boys from the church choir to form a band when he discovered they not only could sing but could also play different instruments. Joan was surprised when he asked if she wanted to go Friday night. Most of the time, she was too tired to even think about going, let alone want to go. Come to think of it, here lately she had been too tired to do a lot of things. That wasn't good.

Joan had a good looking young husband. He was three years younger than her. They had met in college. CJ was a freshman and Joan a junior. He would have married her the year she graduated, but she had told him no, that he had to finish his degree first. They were not married that year, either. Got to have a job she had told him when he graduated in 1960. Then he foolishly joined the Army, throwing their plan further off balance. When he had come home from basic training, Joan decided it was best they get married. Fear had driven her to proceed with the marriage plans. What if he had found someone else while he was away from her?

They were married the following September. CJ had gone back to finish his training in heavy equipment. The plan was for Joan to join him wherever he was stationed once the training was over, but Vietnam was a hot spot, and the military decided they needed him. He was sent there for two years. When he came back, he went to work at Redstone Arsenal. They had been thrilled when he got on at the Arsenal. It was a government job that he could work his way into a leadership position. The engineering training would be the completion of their plans.

"Yes," Joan said, as she handed CJ the plate of catfish. "I will go with you on Friday night." She'd invested a lot of her life and time into this marriage and was not going to take the chance of some other woman making eyes at her young, good looking husband.

"Good," he replied as he accepted the fish.

Wonder what changed her mind?

Chapter 8

May 26, 1966

Adam Fletcher had built a reputation for being a nice, quiet, polite man unless orders were not finished on time or any other detail that did not pass his approval. His employees mostly liked and respected him, but at other times longed for their old boss, Leland Mitchell. At least Mr. Mitchell had no problem with turning a two day weekend into a three day when the holiday fell on a Friday or a Monday. The first holiday had come in January, and the Arsenal took that Friday off, but some of the department also took Thursday for a long weekend to travel or be with their children before school resumed after the Christmas break.

"No one and I mean, no one, had better call in to work tomorrow. Is that understood? Just because Monday is Memorial Day, doesn't mean you get to take Friday off as well."

Adam stood before the room of workers in the

conference room down the hall from the clerical office. "I know how tempting it may be to want to stay home tomorrow, but Friday is not a holiday. So unless you are deathly ill or dead, you have better be here."

Silence fell over the room as he waited for his words to sink into each employee. A lone hand rose from the back of the room.

"Yes?" said Adam Fletcher.

"What if we take a vacation day?"

"Are you planning on being dead?"

"No."

"Then you best be planning on being at work."

"But Mr. Fletcher, when a holiday falls on a Monday or Friday, that, of course, gives us a three day weekend, and it's not uncommon for the day before to be taken off as well," Louella said.

"Common or uncommon, we will not continue with such a practice. We will be at work tomorrow." He hesitated. "If there are no other questions—"

"I have one other question."

"Yes, Mrs.—" For the life of him, he would not remember the woman's name.

"Ketchum. Louella Ketchum. And what if we're sick tomorrow if you get my meaning?"

"Let me make this clear. Unless you want to suffer the consequences, you will be at work if you get my meaning." Adam Fletcher surveyed the room. "Okay people, if there are no more questions, let's get back to work."

* * *

The Hunters were seated at the supper table. Mary Faye was animated as she passed a bowl of peas to her father.

"Can you believe this man is being so strict?" said Mary Faye with narrowed eyes.

"Well, he's right," Webb said. "The last thing a company wants is for workers to lay out during the holidays."

"But daddy, it's how he went about it like he was still in the military barking at his soldiers. And, as long as I've been at Redstone, people have always taken off an extra day."

Webb Hunter shook his head.

"But, daddy—" she pleaded.

"No buts to it," he said. "A place of employment expects its employees to be at work unless there is an emergency. Etolia, pass me some cabbage."

Etolia handed the bowl of boiled cabbage to her husband.

"And another thing," he added. "A lot of people fail to realize how fortunate they are to have a good-paying job." He took a piece of cornbread from the bread plate. "Too many people want the job, but not the work."

"But daddy, it's not like these people lay out of work. It's always been one of the privileges workers get."

"No, it's one that the workers take. There is a difference there."

"Mary Faye, stop arguing with your daddy," said Etolia.

"I'm not. I just want Mr. Fletcher to understand that we are hardworking people and he's not being fair."

"Didn't you say he fought in the Korean War?" Etolia asked.

"Yes, ma'am."

"He's still got discipline leftover from those days. Everything straight and narrow." Etolia picked up the tea pitcher. "Webb, you need any more tea?"

He shook his head. "Best thing you can do, Mary Faye, is not to argue with the boss. He knows what he's doing. He may be trying to weed out some of the slackers."

"He can't fire someone over this."

"No, but he might make them wish they had a different job. Employers always have their ways, Mary Faye. Best you don't let anyone talk you into anything concerning this. Let them do whatever they want, but you stay clear. Go to work and do your job."

Webb pushed his plate back slightly. "That was a good supper, Etolia."

She smiled and nodded. "Thank you. Mary Faye, your daddy, is telling you the truth. Don't get involved with people who want to create trouble."

The tea glass was Mary Faye's escape. Without saying another word on the subject, she turned her glass up and swallowed the last of the sweet tea. She took the last bite of the pork chop.

"Thank you for supper, momma. It was delicious."

"Thank you, hon. Since Monday is Memorial Day, what do y'all want to do?"

"I guess cookout," Webb said. "Find out if Jimmy can come up and make some homemade ice cream. Should be fireworks at the boat harbor."

Webb pushed his chair away from the table and patted his full belly as he crept into the living room to read the newspaper. The holiday plans had been made, and Mary Faye would stay out of debates about off days.

When Mary Faye went to bed that night, she thought about her new boss.

Mr. Fletcher is the meanest man that I have ever met!

Mary Faye didn't agree with her daddy's opinion, which was strange because all her life she had idolized him. Daddy was her hero. She had always been a daddy's girl and still was. She couldn't allow that Mr. Fletcher was right. He wasn't right about anything because he was always ready to jump someone if they were wrong. From Mary Faye's perspective, that supported her view of him as mean and wrong.

Sleep carried her into a fog where she was on a

winding, dark, lonely road; trees hanging over each side as she searched for the end of the path. Mr. Fletcher yelled at her as she went around a sharp curve. The pathway grew narrower.

Mary Faye jolted awake. She took deep breaths to calm her nerves. Mr. Fletcher haunted her at work and now in her dreams.

No... her nightmares.

* * *

Friday morning, the carpool arrived a few minutes early. It was Rick Overton's turn to drive. When Mary Faye sat down in the backseat next to Paul Hurst, Rick explained. "Just wanted to make sure we ain't late today. Not after yesterday."

"Good thinking," she said.

From the passenger seat, Stephen Harkins shook his head. "Don't let that sour puss get to you."

Rick pulled his vehicle away from the curb. The clutch popped as he changed from first to second gear. A trail of black smoke plumed from the tailpipe. The exhaust drifted through the open windows.

Paul coughed and tried to clear his throat. "Rick, if you don't get this car fixed soon I'm gonna repair it myself."

Rick turned to the backseat and smiled at Paul. "I won't stop you."

"Instead of working on cars, I think we need to get together for another card game," Almon Hensley said. "Been a while since we've had a good card game." The other men quickly agreed. The men in the carpool played cards at each other's house sometimes on the weekends.

* * *

Adam Fletcher did not want enemies, especially at

work. That was the last thing he had wanted. Why should he care if people took off an extra day? It wasn't going to change his life. In fact, his life was so structured that nothing ever changed. At times, Adam felt like he had no control. Every day was the same. He got up, dressed, had breakfast, kissed his wife goodbye, and left for his tedious job.

Adam's life had become mundane and scripted, right down to the fifteen dollar allowance. It was absurd that his wife gave him, a grown man, an allowance. At least when he had been in the army, the money he earned stayed in his pocket.

With the river bridge behind him, Adam should have veered right at the fork. Instead, he absentmindedly remained in the left lane traveling north toward Athens. He rode several miles before taking a side road that wound back around to Highway 20. It was as if he was taking a casual Sunday drive through the countryside instead of going to work. The cotton fields were in full bloom. The corn was tall and green. Cattle dotted the pastureland. Crystal clear water ran through the creeks and streams.

That's what he wished he was doing today. Fishing under the blue skies. Hearing nothing but birds singing. That's how a summer day should be spent. Not pushing numbers.

* * *

The crew was beginning to wonder if their boss had decided to take the day off. When Mr. Fletcher finally arrived, the office was fully aware that he was over thirty minutes late. The reason why Mr. Fletcher was late, no one knew, and he offered no explanation. He went into his office without a word.

"Well, I do declare," Louella said at lunch after all four women were at their regular table. "I was beginning to think Mr. Fletcher flew the coop this morning."

Andrea looked around. Lowering her head, she replied, "I'd keep those snippy remarks to myself, Louella. He'll make you whine like a whipped dog if you keep popping off to him."

"Huh! I'm not afraid of him. You never know how he's going to behave. He can be friendly in the morning and then bite your head off in the afternoon. He barks orders, not to mention how everything better be perfect." She leered at Mary Faye. "And don't say it. I know you think it should be perfect anyway."

"Mary Faye hasn't said a word," Peggy said.

"I know, but that's what she's thinking."

Peggy and Andrea laughed.

"I'm not saying you're wrong, Mary Faye," said Louella. "I just get so mad at him sometimes. Mary Faye, you know exactly what I mean."

More than once, Mary Faye had been on the receiving end of Mr. Fletcher's short commands. She didn't say anything, though. Louella, however, would not let it go.

"I'm telling you, he's been here—what, six or seven weeks? And makes life miserable for us." Louella took several gulps from her RC Cola before she continued. "I think we ought to try to get him relieved of his duties."

"Oh no, that wouldn't be right," said Mary Faye.

"Maybe he will settle down. He's probably just trying to make sure he does a good job," Peggy said. "Give him time."

Louella ate her sandwich and drank her RC without another word, but she wasn't too pleased.

How funny, thought Mary Faye, just last night she tried to convince her daddy how horrible Adam Fletcher was and today she was standing up for him.

Who would have thought?

Chapter 9

CJ Cantrell watched Mary Faye leave the cafeteria. He quickly finished his drink, grabbed his brown paper lunch bag, and dropped off his trash as he went out the door. His long gait promptly caught up with Mary Faye.

"Hi," said CJ. "I was hoping I would see you."

Mary Faye looked up at him and smiled. His tall stature towered over her small frame.

"You were?"

"Yes. I wanted to have a quick word with you before you made it back to the office."

"Okay."

"You free next Friday night?"

Mary Faye paused and wrinkled her forehead. Was there a wedding? A rehearsal? There were no concerts. "I think so."

"Good. Can you meet me at the Fort?"

"Huh?"

"I'm playing at the Fort. Not too far from your house. You could come down, and I'll take you home."

"Okay." She smiled at him again. "You need a critic?"
He laughed. "Always. Thought it might be fun."
"Sounds like it. What time?"
"Be there at seven."
"Okay, I will."
"You can tell me how good I am."
"I already know you are."
They both laughed.

From the other end of the hallway, Louella and a small group of women watched CJ and Mary Faye part ways near the clerical office.

"Wonder what they were talking about?" Louella asked.

The other women shrugged.

Chapter 10

May 31, 1966

"I told you how I wanted those order forms typed up!" Adam Fletcher barked at Mary Faye. "But you still typed them all wrong! Every one of them!"

Everyone in the office could hear him. Mr. Fletcher was in one of his moods. Mary Faye bit her lower lip. The pain was to keep the tears at bay. Never in the ten years that she had worked at the arsenal had she ever been spoken to like that. When Mr. Fletcher was assigned to the department, who knew he would be such a brute? The first day, he had been polite to everyone. Today, like several days in the last few weeks, his outbursts were cruel.

Mr. Fletcher slapped the file down on her desk.

"I want these order forms, every one of them, retyped. Then I want you to go to the warehouse and personally place them on each box." He put both hands on her desk and leaned closer. "Do I make myself clear?"

She took a deep breath, let go of her bottom lip, and in

a soft voice, replied, "Yes, sir, I understand perfectly."

Mr. Fletcher straightened. "Good. Thank you."

He went into his office, but Mary Faye did not lift her eyes to his back or the people in the office. She felt like sticking her tongue out at him. Instead, she took each file and retyped them just like she had previously.

Because he was wrong.

There was no way she was going to break protocol deliberately. The paperwork would be returned, and she would get the blame.

Crazy man.

It took Mary Faye two hours to retype all the documents. She then gathered them up, put the papers on a cart, and brought them into the warehouse. She placed each label on a box of missile parts. When finished, Mary Faye clapped her hands to remove the dust. She turned around and bumped into Mr. Fletcher.

"So, you got it done?"

"Yes, sir. Done and right."

Mr. Fletcher picked up one of the boxes and inspected it carefully. Then another. His face turned crimson. "You call this... right?"

"Yes, sir. I do."

"This is the same way you had them to begin with!"

Mary Faye met his eyes with contempt.

"The right way."

"I told you how I wanted it done," his voice quivered with rage.

"And that way was wrong."

"You think you know this job better than me?"

Mary Faye's eyelids drew to a squint.

"You listen to me, Mr. Fletcher. You may want to do your job wrong, but I'm not. Yeah, I do know this job better than you. I've been here ten years so why wouldn't I? You've been at Redstone, what, four years? And in this department for six months?"

Mary Faye patted her foot and folded her arms defiantly.

"Yes. I do know your job better than you, and I will not change those forms. Those are the proper forms, typed correctly, and ready to go."

She whirled around. "And if you want them changed again, do it yourself!"

Mary Faye grabbed the cart and pushed it from the warehouse back into the office.

Adam Fletcher watched her march down the hallway.

Who would have thought that little mousey woman had that much fire?

At 3:45, Mr. Fletcher stepped out of his office. Mary Faye's desk was only about five feet away, but it seemed longer than that.

"Look," he said to her. "I guess—" His voice was low.

Mary Faye smiled. "Are you trying to say something to me?"

"Yes, I am," he replied. Mr. Fletcher cleared his throat. "Miss Hunter, I would like to offer an apology for my outburst earlier. I hope you will accept it."

Mary Faye tried to conceal her shock.

"I am a Christian woman, and it is my duty to forgive whoever asks."

"Thank you."

Without another word, he went back into his office.

Well, I'll be, thought Mary Faye. Never would she have expected an apology from him. The way Mr. Fletcher could get into moods, yelling at people over nothing sometimes and in his mind, he was never wrong. Mr. Mitchell said he had fought in the Korean War, which was how he was able to move up so fast at Redstone. Maybe the war had done something to him. Her parents had talked about cousins who went off to fight in the big war, but they weren't the same when they returned. Nice, gentle boys returned as hard, rugged men. In some cases, men were irreparably damaged.

"Mary Faye, time to go," Peggy Wallace said. "Want to walk out together?"

"Sure." Mary Faye covered her typewriter. Peggy didn't usually walk her out, but then again, she and everyone else had heard the argument. Before they left the building the subject was brought up.

"I know you wanted to slap his face this afternoon when he pulled that stunt. No sense in a grown man yelling that way."

Mary Faye shrugged her shoulders.

"You know he was in Korea," said Peggy. "Sometimes, war makes a person nutty. I have this uncle who fought in Korea, and momma said he was the best thing on earth until the army corrupted him. For about five years, he got drunk every weekend. When people would ask him about the war, he wouldn't say a thing. His wife said sometimes he would wake up in the middle of the night screaming."

"That's sad." Mary Faye said.

"Yeah. I'm not saying that Mr. Fletcher is just like that. I don't know enough about him. Most people don't. I mean, he's friendly, but still, those explosions…"

* * *

A week later, Mr. Fletcher's office door was cracked open. If Mary Faye's desk had not been so close to his door, she wouldn't be able to see him. Mr. Fletcher was at his desk, staring blankly into space. He seemed so sad. The sight tugged at her heart.

Slowly she rose from her desk and gave a light knock on the door.

"Yes," Mr. Fletcher said.

She eased the door opened. "May I come in?"

"Yes. Have a seat." He rose from his chair. Mary Faye

stepped into the room. With the door open, she took a seat in front of his desk.

"I, too, would like to offer an apology."

A slight smile parted his lips. "You would?"

"Yes. You are my supervisor, and I shouldn't have talked to you in that tone. You do know more about your job than I do." She smiled. "Your job and my job are two different positions, and I shouldn't have behaved in such a manner."

His smile grew. "Well, I think we can both forget about it. But you were right. Thank you for not letting that order go out incorrectly. I appreciate that."

"Thank you."

Mary Faye left the room.

Just who was Mr. Adam Fletcher?

* * *

On Friday night, Mary Faye forgot all about work and Mr. Fletcher. Instead, she enjoyed her evening listening to CJ and his band at the Fort. After the concert, however, Mary Faye's thoughts shifted back to work. She told CJ about the incident with Mr. Fletcher and questioned whether or not he could handle being a supervisor in her department. CJ assured Mary Faye that everything would work out in due time.

When Mary Faye arrived home at almost eleven, her parents were in bed. They knew she had gone to the Fort to meet with a co-worker, but she did not mention that the co-worker was a man. There was no need to worry them over nothing. Sure, there was music and dancing, but that was all. Mary Faye knew there were rules that a decent Christian woman lived by, and she didn't want those rules to keep her at home.

-2-

June 23, 1966

Employees from the shipping department were in the conference room again for one of Mr. Fletcher's bi-weekly meetings. Sometimes the meetings were canceled and were getting farther and farther apart. The department seemed to be operating rather smoothly.

"I know at times that I may seem to be harsh," began Mr. Fletcher, "but the one thing I want all of you to know is that I am also capable of changing my mind if I feel like I was in the wrong. With that said, I would like to remind everyone that we are approaching another holiday in a couple of weeks. The 4th of July falls on a Monday this year. I realize that summer is in full force and will quickly be gone. If anyone wants to take Friday off, you won't be punished for it. Any questions?"

There were surprised gasps and whispers, but no questions. Mr. Fletcher was about to dismiss the group when a lone hand rose in the back of the room.

"Yes?" he asked.

"I don't guess this is really a question. It's more like a comment. I won't be here on Friday. I'm going to Lake Guntersville. Just thought I'd go ahead and put my cards on the table, my name in the pot, or whatever you want to call it."

"And your name?"

Mr. Fletcher knew her name, and everyone in the room knew that he knew. In the last few months, he had learned all their names, and Louella was the type of person you could not miss. She always had something to say or an opinion to voice.

"Louella Ketchum. I work as a typist in the clerical office."

"Very well. It has been noted that Louella Ketchum will not be at work Friday, July 1. Are you willing to work over on Thursday to make up for any time lost on Friday?"

"Now wait a minute. I didn't say that."
Faint laughter spread across the room. Mr. Fletcher joined them with a chuckle of his own.

"Any more questions?" he asked.

No one else said anything. "Okay, let's get back to work." Oh, one other thing. I will be here that Friday. Please, don't feel that I am discouraging anyone to take off. Remember, there won't be any consequences if you choose to do so."

Everyone nodded as Mr. Fletcher spoke. Some of them approached him with warm smiles and expressed their appreciation.

* * *

Mary Faye's brother, Jimmy, his wife, and two daughters came up on Sunday and spent the day with the family. They celebrated the 4th of July with a cookout and homemade vanilla ice cream. Everyone sat in the front yard and watched the fireworks from the boat harbor as did many other neighbors. It was a peaceful night of family time; talking, laughing, just being together. They enjoyed the warm southern night air, sipping on sweet tea, or maybe a cold beer. Jimmy and his family left around 9:00, and Mary Faye was in her bed by 10:00. The next day, her life would change forever.

Chapter 11

July 5, 1966

The supply and maintenance department sectioned into hallways, bathrooms, offices, conference rooms, as well as the clerical room, which was situated next to Mr. Fletcher's office. His staff was a varied group from all walks of life. Relationships developed; very few of them were private. Most valued their jobs and dared not risk the chance of being fired over an illicit love affair, yet the whispers of gossip remained. Most employees, however, kept quiet over what they had seen or heard. No one wanted to jeopardize a co-worker's job security.

Everyone in the department was gathered in the conference room waiting on Mr. Fletcher. Peggy, Andrea, and Louella stood at the back of the room. A few feet away, CJ was leaning against the wall, whistling a tune. Others had gathered around a long table. Secretaries and warehouse workers were chattering about the purpose of the meeting. CJ's eyes scanned the room, but Mary Faye was nowhere in sight. She was usually one of the first to arrive.

Then he saw her.

Mary Faye entered the room and stood in a far corner. She didn't speak, nor did she look around. Her attention was on her own hands as if something was interesting about them. In truth, she didn't know what to do or say to people in such a setting.

"Well, I was wondering where you were."

Mary Faye glanced up. CJ stood beside her, smiling. His smile caused her to smile in return. "I was finishing some forms. I knew Mr. Fletcher was still in his office, so I figured I had time to finish them."

"I figured if anyone knew the purpose of the meeting, it would be you."

She grinned. "Afraid not. I haven't heard one word from anyone. You're gonna have to wait like everyone else."

"Speaking of Fletcher." CJ tilted his head toward Mr. Fletcher as he stepped through the doorway.

The meeting was quick, informing them that in the next couple of days they would be expecting a dignitary to their department.

"No, we won't be doing anything special," Mr. Fletcher had begun, "because they want to see what kind of process is used to ensure all missile parts are shipped in an efficient manner, free from error." He examined the group. "Which I'm sure that none of you people would ever make a mistake." A few of them chuckled.

Mr. Fletcher's gaze swept the room and came to rest on Mary Faye.

Was he referring to her?

No cross words had passed between them since that horrible blowup, so why look at her now? Why did she always feel like someone was watching her in crowds? Why did it make her so uncomfortable?

"So I'm just giving you a heads up," Mr. Fletcher continued, "if you see a stranger snooping around it's because they are."

Laughter filled the room.

"I just want you to do your job and not feel that you are under any pressure. It would not make any difference even if you were. They will be here, regardless of how you feel. I know from the way everyone handles themselves, it wouldn't be any different if it was your mother coming for a visit. For some of you, though, it might be more like your mother-in-law, so be on your toes."

He scanned the room.

"Any questions?"

No one answered.

"Okay then, let's get back to work."

Mr. Fletcher stopped Mary Faye as she was leaving the room.

"I have some files," he said, "if you would please take these over to Office Three."

"Yes, sir." She held the files close to her as she shuffled out of the room.

Mary Faye took the short corridor that led back to the clerical office. She didn't notice him until he bumped into her, causing the files to scatter across the floor.

"Oh!" she exclaimed. "I'm so sorry!"

He knelt next to Mary Faye and retrieved some of the scattered papers. His hand touched hers, and she peeked into his eyes. He didn't smile, but his eyes were warm. She dropped her head and moved her hand away.

Mary Faye collected the papers and walked away, feeling a little embarrassed, confused, but unusually energetic.

Chapter 12

September 22, 1966

"I love talking to you."
"Oh, you do, do you?" Mary Faye smiled. No one had ever said that to her before.
"Yes, you are very interesting."
"You really think I am?"
"Of course."
Mary Faye's eyes watered. She turned away and rubbed them.
"Thank you. That's so sweet." She blushed.
"And I love how you are always blushing."
She giggled.
"It's your fault. You should stop making me blush."
I don't want you to stop.
They were standing in the hallway that led toward the conference room. It was 2:15. The department was on its last break. They could walk to the cafeteria for a snack and visit with one another. The first break was always at 9:15, and lunch was at noon. The 15-minute breaks were usually spent laughing, talking, and sometimes flirting.
Mary Faye never thought of herself as being a flirt, but

with him, it came very naturally. The smiles, the lifting of her eyes, the laughing. It was all natural because Mary Faye didn't know how to flirt. The fact that she didn't know how, made her actions and remarks even more appealing. She was fresh and innocent, unlike so many other women who seemed to understand how a woman got a man's attention. Mary Faye had read in a magazine that women should always appear to be interested in a man's work or whatever he enjoyed doing. When she asked him about work, however, he did not seem to care for it.

"I don't want to talk about work."

"What do you want to talk about?"

"You. I want to know all about you."

"Oh, there's not much to tell."

"Tell me how you got to be so sweet and so kind."

Her laugh was soft. "I'm not really. You should see me when I get mad. There's nothing sweet about me then."

"Oh, I know you have a temper."

He grinned at her as he gazed deeply into her eyes.

Something stirred in her when his eyes locked onto hers, almost as if they were pulling her into his bold, blue eyes. She felt like the man on the parched creek bed that had found a fountain of water. Life seemed to bubble up within Mary Faye every time he looked at her. New feelings surged through her body. She laughed and giggled like a teenage girl's first crush. When his hand brushed hers, it was electric.

"I want to see you," he said softly. He glanced over his shoulder. Everyone was busy talking, paying them no attention.

"You are seeing me. See, I'm standing right here."

"No. I mean, *really* see you. Alone. We could meet tonight."

Mary Faye looked down at her feet. What could she say? She wanted to, but how could she do that?

What would I tell my parents?

"I don't know..."
"Please."
"Maybe."
"We could meet in the park. Sit and talk. Just us."
She looked up. The pupils of his eyes enlarged. In a magazine article she had read that when a person liked someone, the pupils enlarged. How exciting.
Mary Faye smiled and nodded.
"When?" she whispered.
"Tonight. Meet me at 8:00."
Her parents would still be awake. What excuse could she give for leaving the house?
"Could you make it nine? Delano Park is not far from my house. We could meet there."
"Perfect. Meet me at the Rose Garden."

* * *

Mary Faye slipped out of the house from her bedroom door directly to the porch. She glanced over her shoulder and stood very still. Listening. The night was quiet except for crickets. No dogs barked, no cats fought, but most importantly, she heard no movement from her parents' bedroom. Nervously, she glanced at her watch.

8:50. The park was only five minutes away.

Mary Faye's legs were weak, and her mouth was dry, but the excitement rushed through her body as she descended the porch steps. She turned left onto the sidewalk. Hopefully, there would be no nosey neighbors wondering where she was going this time of night. If anyone mentioned to her mother that they saw her tonight, Mary Faye would say that she couldn't sleep and took a walk.

The night was warm and soothing. Mary Faye took a deep breath. Never in her whole life had she ever done anything like this. Her parents always knew where she was and what she was doing. She came home from school, ate a snack, practiced the piano, read a book, and listened to music. Mary Faye's mother never had to worry about her being out with some boy on a date. All the girls at school dated, but Mary Faye had never even been asked out. No one had ever shown a romantic interest in her. She had a few friends, but they were not close. They did not invite her to the movies, ballgames, or anything.

Tonight, her moment had finally arrived.

Mary Faye was 33-years-old and meeting a man for the first time.

A nice, handsome man.

Lampposts lit the park in a warm, yellow glow. Mary Faye saw someone as she approached the garden. Shadows prevented a clear view of the person ahead of her.

It had to be him. It had to be.

"I'm here." The voice was deep but soft. Mary Faye rushed to him. He grabbed her hand, pulled her over to the bench. "I'm so glad you're here."

"I'm glad I am too," she stammered. "I mean... I'm glad we're here." She laughed. "You know what I mean."

"Yes, I do." He slipped his arm around her shoulder. "Did you have any trouble getting out of the house?"

"No, my parents went to bed. They think I did too. I went out the door in my bedroom."

"Door in your bedroom?"

"Yes. You see, there are two front doors. One of them is my bedroom door."

"Oh, does that mean I can sneak into your room?" He laughed.

"I, um," she said nervously.

"I know. Your parents would shoot me."

He laughed again.

"Yeah, right after they finish with me."

She laughed with him.

They talked for over thirty minutes. Mary Faye told

him about her music and how she began playing the piano as a child. He told her about being in the military, and the course he had taken. They joked. They laughed. He hugged her, but he did not kiss her or make any gesture toward her. He knew Mary Faye Hunter was a lady. He also knew that he was a married man.

"I've got to go," he said.

"Yeah," she said sadly. "So do I."

They stood. His smile was bright despite the shadows. Mary Faye instinctively covered her mouth as she returned the smile.

BANG!

He grabbed Mary Faye and shoved her toward the bushes. She lost her balance, as they started to fall. He cradled her back and head before they hit the ground.

"What's wrong?" she said between labored breaths.

"Shhh," he hissed. His head turned, and eyes darted around, searching for the source of the sound. Then he whispered, "You okay?"

"Yes," Mary Faye said softly. She regarded him tenderly. His eyes were wild with panic. She stood up and scanned the park.

"It's okay," she said. "Look over there. See that truck?"

He pushed himself up and stood next to her. An old, 1952 Chevrolet rattled down the street toward the high school.

"It backfired," she said. "That's all."

She put her arms around him and hugged tightly. "It's okay."

He frowned. "I'm sorry. Sometimes—"

Mary Faye stepped forward and kissed him on the cheek. "It's okay."

He smiled against his trembling lips.

"I'll see you tomorrow at work."

She nodded. "Yes."

He pulled her up to him and squeezed her tightly. He wanted to kiss her. She felt it. He released her. "Goodnight."
Mary Faye could feel her eyes welling with emotion. "Night."
Mary Faye hurried down the path toward Eighth Avenue. She didn't glance back.
Romance was nascent like an early spring rosebud.

-2-

October 10, 1966

On their second date, they decided not to meet in the Rose Garden. It was a warm October day. Fall was always pleasant in the south, with warm days and cool nights. Apples, cotton, corn, and soybean fields lined with workers as the last days of harvest came to a close. The blistering summer was gone, and so was the hot, sticky humidity that the burdened the south from spring until fall. It was also a season for romance and weddings.

Mary Faye did not hesitate when he asked her to meet him. "I'll pick you up on the sidewalk near the park," he said.

"Okay," she said. "6:30."

Mary Faye was excited when she skipped through the front door after work. The more she was around him, the more she wanted to be with him.

"Momma?" Mary Faye entered the kitchen. Her mother was taking something out of the oven.

"What?" asked Etolia without turning around. She placed the cast iron skillet of hot cornbread on the stove. "Hello, honey. Did you have a good day at work?"

It was the same greeting she had used when Mary Faye was in high school.

"Yes, ma'am. What can I do to help?"

"Oh, nothing. Your daddy will be home soon. Got beans cooking with the ham." She lifted the lid and inspected the beans. Taking a large wooden spoon, Etolia stirred the beans. "Get me those pork chops out of the refrigerator please."

Mary Faye retrieved the meat and handed it to her mother. The cat clock read 5:15. In just a little over an hour, she would be with him. She didn't want any food, just wanted 6:30 to hurry up and get there.

After supper, the hands on the cat clock had moved to 6:30. Webb and Etolia were sitting at the kitchen table when Mary Faye went to the front door. Her hand was on the doorknob when her mother noticed her.

"Mary Faye, where are you going? It's dark out there."

"I thought I would go for a walk."

"In the dark?" Webb said. "I don't think you should do that."

"Why not just sit on the front porch?" her mother suggested.

"But I'd rather walk."

"I know, dear, but it's going to get chilly out there."

"You ain't got no business walking down that sidewalk in the dark," Webb said.

He pushed back his chair and went into the living room. He retrieved his pipe and reentered the kitchen.

As he put in the tobacco, he continued, "No sense in that at all. Like your mother said, if you want some fresh air you can go out to the porch. Besides, what are the neighbors going to think with you out walking up and down the sidewalk."

"Yes, sir," said Mary Faye. Her hand released the doorknob. "Guess I'll get my sweater and sit on the porch for a while."

"Okay, baby." Her mother came into the living room. She sat down on the sofa and picked up her knitting.

Mary Faye went into her bedroom, pulled on a sweater,

and went out to the front porch. He would be looking for her.

What am I going to do?

Mary Faye checked her watch. She was already fifteen minutes late.

A white car drove by her house slowly. She glanced over her shoulder.

Will Momma and Daddy see me if I go over to talk to him?

The car stopped two houses down. Mary Faye rushed down the steps and labored up to the vehicle. He reached over to open the door, but she put her hand on it.

"I can't go," she said, fighting back tears.

"Why not?"

She could not say that it was because of her parents.

"I'll explain later. I gotta go."

She rushed back to the porch and sat on the swing. Just as she sat down, her mother stepped on to the porch.

That was close.

"It's such a nice night that I thought I would join you."

Mary Faye smiled. "Yes, ma'am, it is." She watched the white car pull away from the curb. What would she tell him tomorrow?

I hope he's not mad.

* * *

The next day, Mary Faye told him the truth. He was disappointed, but not angry. She explained that it wasn't easy for her to get out of the house at night without a good excuse. He admitted that it wasn't easy for him either. They decided perhaps it would be better to meet later at night, while her parents were asleep and when he had a meeting at the Veterans of Foreign Wars. He had a meeting on Thursday night they planned to meet two blocks from her home.

At 9:15, he pulled up next to Mary Faye and stopped long enough for her to get into the car. They cruised along Highway 20 for several minutes, making casual conversation. Mary Faye sat next to him in the middle with her hands rested in her lap. Suddenly, he picked up her hand and held it lovingly. A few seconds later, he brought Mary Faye's hand to his lips and kissed her knuckles. She trembled slightly. The windows were down, and the radio played softly. He flipped on the heater. Currents of warm and cool air circled them. Mary Faye snuggled against him. The conversation soon turned into laughter.

I should kiss her on the lips he thought, but he didn't. Mary Faye was a lady. As long as they were just friends, guilt should have no part of their relationship, and that's what they were building. A relationship built on friendship, yet no one would understand this kind of friendship. A married man doesn't just talk, but that's what he really wanted. She was such a soothing person with her soft, gentle approach to things, yet she was also strong. Gentle and strong.

What more could a man ask for in a woman?

Nearly an hour later, he dropped off Mary Faye close to her home.

I should have kissed her he told himself as he drove away. Any other man would have kissed her and made wild passionate love to her. But he couldn't. Not yet. Right now, they were just friends, but he wanted to take her, know her completely, touch every line of her body, and make her cry out his name.

Next time?

He knew there would be a next time.

Chapter 13

Mary Faye Hunter fascinated him. She was such an innocent creature. Delicate. Soft-spoken. A sweet woman with a quiet disposition. That's what drew her to him. In the beginning, she was easy to talk to, but also intriguing. At first, he didn't feel guilty about their relationship, but now it nagged at him because he desired her in a way that he had not felt for a woman in a long time. It wasn't fair to his wife. It was wrong, but it seemed as if he could not walk away. The gravitation to Mary Faye overpowered his judgment and chased away the guilt.

He parked the car under the carport and sat there for a few moments, thinking about the evening, the ride with her. If someone asked what drew him to Mary Faye Hunter, he would not say it was her eyes, her smile, or her laughter. No, it was simply... Her. The entire package. She was a nice, gentle southern lady with class. She walked with a limp but had beautiful legs. He had noticed them, but it wasn't just her lovely figure. It was her personality. The more he yearned for her, the less noticeable the limp became. Mary Faye was as delicate as butterfly wings but as strong as the blowing wind. She lifted his spirit and calmed his temperament like no other. Yes, she drew him to her. Mary Faye's strength made him stronger.

Yes, that's what I'll say if someone asks me.

But no one would ask him that because no one knew about his feelings for Mary Faye Hunter.

He rolled the car window up, got out of the car, and went inside. The house was dark. He wished he was still with Mary Faye. He sat in the living room next to the fireplace. Stillness surrounded him. A deep breath left his body.

"Mary Faye," he whispered, "Mary Faye, I..."

-2-

She found him in the living room, slumped over in his chair. He never came to bed last night.

What time did he get home?

It was a little after nine when she had gone to bed, but it seemed as if sleep carried her away as soon as her head touched the pillow. It had been a busy, exhausting day. She hated to wake him up. He seemed to be resting so well.

Kinda odd. Many nights he had been restless.

She thought about her friends' remarks from last night. One friend had said that on nights she was most tired, her husband wanted sex. The other women who were sitting around their small table agreed, saying it always seemed as if they all had horrible timing. She had laughed but didn't say anything. That was something she had not thought about in a long time. Her husband seldom wanted sex, regardless of the situation. Most times, she was the one to make the first move, and that was getting old. She was too embarrassed to share that information with her friends.

He grunted in his sleep then stirred in the chair. He drew his arms over his head to stretch. He opened his eyes then spotted her standing in the doorway.

"Oh, hi," he said. "Good morning."

"Good morning to you too. What are you doing out here?"

"I sat down for a moment, and I guess just fell asleep." He stood. "Oh. I think every muscle I've got is out of whack. Maybe a hot shower will help."

She nodded, then headed toward the kitchen.

Chapter 14

November 17, 1966

"Mary Faye, can you come with me for a moment?"

He was at her desk before she even realized it. Pushing back her chair, she got up and followed him down the hallway between the warehouse and the clerical office. On one side there were bathrooms and a water fountain. The supply room was on the opposite side. It contained order forms, white standard typing paper, copy machine, drink machine, and an old desk.

He held the supply room door as Mary Faye entered.

"I want you to take these boxes back to your desk so you can finish typing up the order forms. Several packages are being shipped out today..." He picked up two boxes, laid them on the old desk, turned to Mary Faye, and pulled her into his arms. He kissed her on the cheek. "You are the loveliest woman I have ever met." Then he planted short, tender kisses on her lips. One-Two-Three.

Oh, my!
Never had she felt this way. His kisses were as light as angel wings. She closed her eyes, her mouth reaching up for more.

"Mary Faye, Mary Faye!"

The sound was so distant. Invading.

"Mary Faye..."

A knock on the door. "Mary Faye, you better get up. It's almost 10:00. You have that hair appointment at 10:30." The voice stampeded into her brain.

It was her mother.

Mary Faye opened her eyes. It had been a dream. She felt warm and happy, even if it was just a dream. It had seemed so real. She blushed.

The very idea of kissing a man!

"Mary Faye?"

"Yes, momma, I'm getting up." She touched her lips.

What would it really be like to kiss his lips?

"Mary Faye, you better hurry."

"Yes, ma'am."

Mary Faye pushed the thoughts from her mind. Her day fell into its routine, but the dream still lingered.

* * *

The following Wednesday, Mary Faye stepped out of the bathroom as Mr. Fletcher was coming down the hallway.

"Oh, Mary Faye, glad I caught you. Would you please come with me for a moment? I need you to take these boxes back to the office."

Mary Faye followed him into the supply room.

Was she dreaming again?

"These need to go out today, and you might want to get one of the other girls to help you type it all up."

"Okay," she said, feeling a little disoriented.

Mr. Fletcher picked up one of the boxes, but before he gave it to her, he said, "I shouldn't say this because we are at work, but, Mary Faye..."

He stepped closer to her. "I can't stop thinking about you."

Mr. Fletcher slipped his arm around her waist. His lips briefly touched hers.

"Oh no," she said, "not like that."

"Okay. How about like this?"

Then he kissed her—quick, tender kisses.

One-Two-Three. Soft as angel wings.

Electrifying emotions washed over her body. The feeling radiated from her lips to her toes. Never in Mary Faye's life had she experienced such a sensation. A rush of warmth bathed her body. Her mouth watered as she hungered for more.

Adam embraced her tightly. When he pulled away, his eyes locked onto hers.

He smiled. "You are the sweetest woman that I have ever met."

Mary Faye blushed.

"Here, don't forget to take these."

Adam motioned toward the boxes. She nodded. Mary Faye's head was swimming, and her heart had just drowned.

Adam opened the door and went on his way, but Mary Faye returned to the bathroom before going to her desk.

I have to see my face.

Were there signs on her face to what had just happened? Could anyone see the evidence of what her body was experiencing? Oh, how she wished there was someone she could talk to about this magical moment.

Mary Faye examined her reflection in the mirror. She looked the same. No one would know that she had just experienced the first kiss of her life. She, Mary Faye Hunter, a grown woman, had just been kissed for the first time. Something that most girls experienced before they were even teenagers. No one could have been more excited than she was.

She stared at her face.

Was this what love felt like? Was she in love?

Whatever it was, it felt wonderful.

"Just like the dream," she said aloud. Her dream from last week had come true.

Oh, dear!

He was a married man. She had sinned.

Oh, dear Lord, please forgive me.

Had she sinned? It was just a kiss, but it wasn't because of the kiss. It was her response to the kiss. She had thoroughly enjoyed his kisses. A Christian wasn't supposed to enjoy sin.

But it was just a kiss.

The last thing she wanted was guilt to rob her of this beautiful moment.

She picked up the small boxes, wrapped them in her arms as if they were boxes of love. Mary Faye felt as if she was walking on a cloud high above everything, even sin. The kiss had been so tender and sweet.

How could that be sinful?

Never in her life had she experienced such a beautiful moment.

In the office, Mary Faye stopped by Joyce's desk.

"Would you please help me type all these up?" asked Mary Faye. "They need to go out today."

"Who are they going to?"

"All of the information is there. I'll do page one, and you can take page two."

"Okay."

Mary Faye pushed her earlier encounter from her mind as she concentrated on her work. On her ride home from work, however, she replayed the images over and over in her mind. For weeks they had been laughing and talking with each other, but today was unexpected. Even when they were a long way from work, he had never made any attempt to kiss her.

"You're awful quiet, Mary Faye," Paul said. He was sitting beside her in the backseat. "Long day at work, huh?"

"Long day as always. Paperwork can be very tiring at times."

"Yes, it can. Taxes the brain."

"Yes, sir."

When the conversation shifted, Mary Faye gazed out her window over the Tennessee River as they drove across the Keller Memorial Bridge into Decatur. The river reflected gold below the setting sun as lavender twilight brushed the western sky. It was a majestic fresco fit for the Heart of Dixie.

"Glad that bridge didn't get caught up today," Stephen Harkins said.

The drawbridge often delayed traffic 20 to 30 minutes as barges traveled underneath. Soon, Mary Faye was at her home on Eighth Avenue. She got out of the car, went into the house, and left her daydreams behind.

Chapter 15

December 3, 1966 - 4:30am

Winter days were long and cold, even in the South. Mary Faye rolled out of bed and began her morning routine. Sunrise was at least two hours away. Adam was picking her up at the corner. Hopefully, her parents would still be asleep when she returned. It would be the first time they had seen each other since he kissed her in the supply room.

Saturdays were her day to sleep late. No one banged on her door or attempted to disturb her. It was the one day that Mary Faye had complete control of her life. The only other appointment she had today was a 10:30 hair appointment at the House of Beauty.

* * *

Adam and Mary Faye traveled to the end of Mussle

Camp Road and parked close to the river. No one else was around. Only the darkness of a winter morning with bright stars against the backdrop of a black sky, and a three-quarter moon. Through the trees, they could see the faint moonlight reflecting off the water. It was quiet, peaceful. Mary Faye sat beside Adam, shy, and timid. He slid closer to her and stretched his arm across the back of the seat.

"It's nice here, isn't it?" he said.

Mary Faye nodded.

"See right over there—" He pointed to her right. She followed his finger. "That's the spot where I reeled in the biggest Largemouth bass I ever caught."

"Oh, really?"

"Sure did. And right over there—"

He pointed toward his left, and Mary Faye turned her head to follow, "was where—"

Adam gently kissed her on the mouth. Mary Faye's hands glided up his chest. He pulled her closer and kissed her deeply. He then kissed her eyes, nose, and neck before he kissed her lips again. His hand brushed across her breast. Adam moved it away quickly as he continued to kiss her. Her body felt as if it was on fire.

Mary Faye gasped. Adam pulled away.

Gazing into his eyes, she whispered, "I've never—"

"Never?"

"No. Never."

Adam took a deep breath and leaned back. He stared at the dark river.

"Does that make you want me less?" Mary Faye finally asked.

"Less? Oh no, no, no, my sweet lady." He clasped her hand. "It makes me want you more, but I want it to be something that we think about before we go that far."

"And if I was experienced, would you want to think about it?"

"You're all I do think about."

Mary Faye's eyes filled with tears. She touched his cheek then ran her finger slowly down his face. She leaned close and kissed the hollow of his neck. She moved her lips upward until she met his mouth. Mary Faye brushed away a lock of hair hanging over his forehead. She placed her head on Adam's shoulder and watched his chest rise and fall.

For a while, they listened to the waters slap against the bank. Adam's arm rested against Mary Faye's waist and the other around her shoulder. She nestled into his arms. He kissed the top of her head and inhaled the fragrance of her hair. Mary Faye tilted her head and looked into Adam's eyes. His lips came down on her in a powerful, passionate kiss.

Adam slowly pulled back.

"You are something else, you know that?" he said.

"No, I guess I don't." She explored his eyes, her hand on his chest, and with the expression of innocence, she asked, "What do you mean?"

"I mean, you are a wonderful, desirable woman, and I want to make love to you." He kissed her quickly on the lips. "But not today."

Relief showered over her. Mary Faye wanted to make love, but she wasn't sure that she could go through with it. He was married. It was so wrong for her to be here with him, yet she was in love with this man.

The moon shined boldly on the water, glimmering across the small waves.

Adam turned the knob on the radio. Soft music came across the airwaves. Music was always so soothing to him.

"That's so nice," Mary Faye said.

"Yes, it is. That's nice dancing music, don't you think?"

Mary Faye dropped her eyes. She'd never thought about dancing. "I don't know. I've never danced before."

"Never?"

"No."

He opened the car door. Catching her hand, he pulled her as he stepped out into the crisp air. "C'mon. We're goin' to dance. Can't have my girl never dancin'."

"But my hip…"

"Don't worry. Let the music carry you. Come with me." He put his arms around her waist. Gently, he guided her against him. She wanted to peek at her feet as she followed him.

"No," he said. "Look into my eyes. Focus on dancing, not your feet."

She giggled. "But I thought I had to focus on my feet."

"No. Your feet are moving, but it's your soul, your spirit, your heart, that is dancing and moving your body. Just relax. Enjoy the music and let your mind carry you away." He laughed. "See? You're dancing."

Mary Faye put her head on his shoulder. Her limp was no longer prevalent.

I'm dancing in the moonlight on a cold winter morning! Oh, how wonderful!

The music ended. He winked at Mary Faye and pulled her closer to him.

"See, I told you. I knew you could dance."

She smiled. He kissed her tenderly.

"One of these days I'm going to take you fishing," he said.

"And I will play the piano for you."

He smiled. "I was hoping that you would." He picked up her hand, turned it over, and inspected each finger. "You have the perfect fingers for the piano."

She laughed. "You sound like my instructors. 'Oh, Mary Faye, you are so gifted, and God gave you the perfect fingers to play the piano.'"

"Are you telling me the truth?"

"Yes!"

Adam grabbed Mary Faye's arm and tickled her ribs. She laughed uncontrollably and wrestled away from him.

"Okay, okay," she said, trying to catch her breath. "They may not have used those exact words."

"Have any other men noticed your hands?"

"Men?" She laughed. "No, there weren't any men who noticed my hands."

Men hadn't noticed her at all.

"Older women are the ones who had always said that, even when I was a child."

Mary Faye wanted the subject to change. She didn't want to talk about her life.

"You're taking me fishing, huh?" she asked.

"Yes, I am."

"What about today?"

"Maybe next time. It's probably too cold."

Mary Faye moved closer to him. She wanted to tell him that he could keep her warm, but he might think that she's pushing herself on him. That was the last thing she would ever want to do.

Mary Faye smiled at him. "Well, if you come down to the church this afternoon, I'll play the piano for you."

"Great! What time are you gonna be there?"

"I'll probably get there at noon. I usually stay there for a couple of hours."

"It's a date." He smiled. "I best get you home."

They returned to the car and drove back toward Decatur. Before they reached town, he pulled into a small country store for gas. Mary Faye waited in the car. When Adam returned, he had something in his hand.

"Here." He handed her a small red ball. She examined it closely.

"A gumball?"

She laughed.

"Yes, and don't get choked on it."

"I won't. I think I'll save it."

Adam smiled. He never thought about a woman saving something as trivial as a gumball, but then again, he'd never met a woman like Mary Faye before.

By 6:00 am, Mary Faye was in her bed again. She was buried deep under the covers, daydreaming about the last hour she had spent with Adam. She looked forward to seeing him again at noon. The red gumball lay in a small dish on her dresser.

* * *

The house was dark when Adam pulled into the driveway. That was good. Martha was still in bed and maybe never realized he had left. He put away the fishing gear, eased into the bedroom, and quietly undressed. He pulled the covers back on his side of the bed and lay down gently.

Martha felt the mattress move when Adam got into the bed.

Where had he gone? Probably fishing again.

It seemed like he'd rather be out there or anywhere else as long as he wasn't with her.

Adam lay on his side, his arm resting under his pillow. The arm that went around his waist surprised him.

He turned to her. "Thought you were asleep," he said.

"I was. Where have you been?"

"At the river, fishing."

"Fishing? It's too cold to fish."

"I know."

Martha inched closer. She nuzzled his neck.

Adam patted her hand but made no effort to turn to her. Martha pulled her hand back.

It had been a long time since making love was an integral part of their lives. Martha wasn't some old woman whose desires had dried up like a dead fig tree. She was still young, and her body was in good working order. Adam behaved like an elderly man trapped between two worlds. Sometimes he with her, but a lot of times he was still in

Korea fighting in a war that no was no longer applicable to him. There was so much that Martha wanted to convey to Adam, but she did not know how to express it. Instead, her heart grew colder and harder.

What bothered Martha the most was Adam's depression, anger, and mood swings. One moment Adam seemed happy, and the next, he was sad. When Adam had come home from Korea, he brought back more than just himself. He brought back the war. Awake or asleep, he continued to fight the enemy. His moods had pushed her and their sons farther away until it seemed like they too were his enemies.

If it weren't for their sons...

They kept her going. Martha was determined to hold the family together. She held out hope that Adam could someday conquer his demons, but her optimism had nearly reached its limit.

Martha returned to her side of the bed. Adam's toes touched her foot. She moved it away.

Adam fell asleep thinking about Mary Faye, but his dreams transported him into a battlefield in a strange land.

"No! NO!" he shouted.

"Adam," said Martha, ripping away the covers. "Adam!"

"NO!" he bellowed, arms flailing. His left hand swung toward his wife, but she ducked. Adam's voice softened, turning into low mumbles.

Then silence. The nightmare had passed.

Martha laid back down. She put out her hand to pat his shoulder but decided against it. He appeared to be okay now. If she disturbed Adam, it might set him off again.

* * *

Adam awoke in good spirits. He entered the kitchen, poured a cup of coffee, and sat down with the latest edition of The Decatur Daily. He read it as he sipped coffee.

"Good morning," he greeted as she sat down with her cup of coffee.

"You seem to be in a good mood."

Better than when you almost knocked my head off. It wasn't the first time his arms had swung at Martha. A few times, he had hit her during those nightmares and left bruises.

"I feel on top of the world," he said.

"You want eggs?" asked Martha.

"Yeah, sure."

She fixed breakfast, and they talked for a while.

"I'm going downtown for a haircut this afternoon."

She nodded. "You're beginning to look a little shaggy around the ears."

They ate the rest of the meal in silence. At 11:15, Adam left the house and drove downtown to get a haircut on First Avenue.

-2-

Mary Faye put the key into the back door. The lock turned, and she entered a downstairs hallway inside the church. She went up the stairs to the sanctuary. Taking sheet music from her bag, she placed it on the piano. Slowly her hands touched the keys as she played. Soft music filled the room as her fingers brought forth the music of *The Old Rugged Cross*.

She didn't know Adam was there until she suddenly felt his presence behind her and heard the low voice.

"On a hill far away, stood an old rugged cross, the emblem of suffering and shame, and I love that old Cross where the dearest and best for a world of lost sinners was slain, and I'll cherish the old rugged Cross till my trophies, at last, I lay down I will cling to the old rugged Cross, and exchange it some day for a crown..." he sang.

When the song ended, she turned and applauded him. "Very well done!"

He smiled. "I'm not a very good singer, but your music would make anyone want to sing."

Mary Faye smiled. She was used to compliments about how she played, but his comments warmed her heart.

"When you said you could play the piano, I didn't realize you were this amazing. Play some more."

Beethoven's *Moonlight Sonata #14* began softly. Again her fingers owned the keys, demanding their perfection as they brought forth pleasure as if it would carry the spirit to the height of peace. The music was soothing at first, and then it penetrated the walls, pounding, like a raging storm of emotions.

Adam pulled back. The sound stirred negative emotions, reeling his mind to the past, and reminding him of the roar of troops trekking across the hills and valleys. Planes and bombs. Helicopters. And blood. Oh, so much blood. His hands rose to his head.

Soft notes changed the mood of the music again. His hands relaxed. His body calmed. Mary Faye didn't notice there had been a change in him because the music absorbed her completely as she played.

The song ended. Adam sat down on the piano bench beside Mary Faye. She dropped her hands into her lap. He drew them to him. Long, delicate fingers; gentle, yet demanding. He kissed them.

"I'm going to be honest with you. I've never heard anything that beautiful."

Mary Faye blushed and chewed on her bottom lip.

"I didn't realize how truly gifted you are." He released her hands. "Play again."

She beamed at him. For the first time, she didn't try to cover her smile.

Johann Sebastian Bach's *Prelude in C Major* surrounded them. The music was soothing, relaxing

Adam's mind, body, and soul. It had been years since he had felt entirely at peace.

Chapter 16

December 17, 1966

December was busy with church practices, decorations, and preparation for the Christmas programs at church. The workload increased as people took off for the upcoming holidays. It was also a busy time in the Hunter household.

"We've got to get our shopping finished," Etolia said when Mary Faye walked into the kitchen. "I know you have practice at church with the choir and all, but it's just one week till Christmas Eve."

"I know," said Mary Faye. "I'm so excited. We must decorate the tree today. Bake and make candies and—"

Her mother laughed. "Mary Faye, we can't do it all in one day. How about we bake next week? We need to go shopping this afternoon after your hair appointment."

"Okay. Meet me at the beauty shop, and we can walk over to Second Avenue. If we buy too much, we can leave some with daddy at the store, and he can bring it home later."

Etolia laughed again. "Or take a taxi home."

"Oh yeah, we could." They laughed.

Mary Faye ate her breakfast and hurried to get dressed for her hair appointment. She would love to get Adam a Christmas gift, but she probably couldn't do that.

What could I buy him?

What would be something that no one would be suspicious about?

Handkerchiefs? No. Candy?

She had never brought men's gifts before except for family members. She dismissed the idea.

You can't buy a married man a Christmas gift.

* * *

Later that afternoon, Mary Faye and Etolia entered David Lee's Department Store on Second Avenue. Her mother bought daddy a new hat. Mary Faye picked out little purses and a small tea set for her nieces. For her brother, she bought a crimson sweater.

"Have you not seen anything to get your daddy, Mary Faye? He can always use some socks and handkerchiefs."

No, that wasn't what she had in mind.

Something else.

"Not yet, momma." She wandered away, searching through items in the men's department. Maybe a new tie, but no, that wasn't any better than handkerchiefs. Her eyes scanned the area. Nothing jumped out at her.

Then she saw it.

In a small black case lined with dark gray velvet. A silver keyring with a little silver bar dangling from it.

"How much is that?" she asked one of the salesclerks.

"$8.98," said the salesclerk.

"I want that."

"Okay, do you want it engraved?"

"Engraved?"

"Yes, we can engrave it at no additional charge, and you can pick it up one day next week."

What would she put on it? No, nothing. It's better this way. Simple. Elegant.

"No, thank you." Mary Faye paid for the keyring and moved on.

When they returned home, Mary Faye put the gifts on her parents' bed. House shoes, toys, sweaters, shirts, pants, hat, pipe, little purses, leather gloves, and a bag that Mary Faye told her mother she could not open because it held her gifts.

"Can I not have a peek?" her mother teased.

"No ma'am, you may not."

In the bag were jewelry, gloves, headscarves, and a one-pound box of Whitman's Candy.

"Tomorrow after church, we'll decorate the tree," Etolia said.

-2-

On Wednesday, Mary Faye waited for Adam in the hallway after lunch. She stood next to the bathroom and fiddled with her billfold as if she was either going in or coming out of the restroom. People that passed by Mary Faye did not appear to be interested in what she was doing. They were socializing or hastily returning to their workstations.

When Mary Faye saw him, her pulse raced. Adam greeted her with a smile and continued to walk. Mary Faye fell into step beside him.

"Here," she said abruptly. From the fold of her skirt, her hand withdrew a small black box.

"What's this?" Adam tilted his head. A light smile touched his lips when he opened the gift. "Oh, this is nice."

The smile faded.

"But I feel awful. I didn't get you anything." His shoulders slumped.

"Oh, no, no. Don't think that."

He slipped the box into his pocket.

"I just wanted to get you something," she said.

"Thank you. I will cherish it always."

She blushed.

They stopped at the end of the hallway before going into the office.

"I wish we could see each other this week," he said.

"I do too, but it's Christmas. There just isn't a lot of time."

"We'll get together right after the first of the year. Promise."

"Yes. It's a promise."

They both laughed.

Paul Hurst watched them, but he didn't say anything to anyone. He just watched and pondered.

Chapter 17

January 21, 1967

A northwest wind whipped across Mary Faye's face as she left the beauty salon. She tightened the headscarf and adjusted her coat. The church was just a short distance away. She might call a cab after practice if the wind kept up. Mary Faye hurried down to the corner of Grant Street and Fourth Avenue until she reached the massive confines of Central Baptist Church.

Once Mary Faye was inside, she waited and listened for any sounds.

Silence.

She waited a few more seconds.

Still nothing. There was no indication that anyone was in the building. Mary Faye continued up the stairs.

Mary Faye sat on the bench in front of the piano. She studied the hymnal and practiced each song. The notes flowed smoothly, almost as if the piano anticipated which keys her fingers would stroke. To Mary Faye, the piano held the prettiest sound of all instruments, but it produced more than just the pleasant sounds of vibrating strings. The music from the piano stirred something deep within her soul. It was her passion. If she had it her way, Mary Faye would earn all of her money performing at weddings and teaching piano lessons. But Mary Faye's parents had said that if she wanted a secure job, she needed to work for the government. So she did.

After all of those years, Mary Faye was now glad her plans had not worked out. If not for Redstone Arsenal, she would not have crossed paths with Adam Fletcher. She smiled thoughtfully. Oh, she was so glad they had met. Adam was kind and so sweet. His presence excited her so much that her heart seemed to—what? Beat faster? Skip a beat?

She felt warmth. Excitement.

Love.

"That's what it is," she said to herself. "You're in love."

Mary Faye did not know if Adam was coming to visit her, but she had left the door downstairs unlocked just in case. So far, their promise to meet after the first of the year had not materialized due to the weather and schedule conflicts.

It was around 2:30 when Adam tried the door. It was unlocked. He stepped into the hallway but didn't hear any music. Before going any farther, Adam locked the door behind him just as Mary Faye had instructed him. He climbed the steps two at a time. At the top of the staircase, the door in front of the sanctuary was open.

Adam stepped into the hall. A few feet away, another door swung open. Adam staggered and placed a hand on the doorframe to steady himself.

Then he saw her.

"You scared me," he said.

Mary Faye gasped and placed her hand on her heart. She drew a deep breath and smiled. "You scared me half to death!"

He laughed. "What have you got?" he asked, moving toward her.

"Some old hymnals and Sunday School books that I was moving out of my youth classroom. They'll be given away to a start-up church that can use them."

"Here." He grabbed the books from her. "Let me help you. Where were you going with them?"

"This way." Mary Faye led Adam farther down the hallway to a door at the end of the hall. She pushed through the door and switched on a light that revealed a set of stairs. She descended the steps slowly. At the bottom, there was another hall, doors on each side. Mary Faye continued to advance until she reached the last room.

"In here." Mary Faye opened the door and flipped on the light. There were boxes of clothes, books, magazines, shoes, and closed boxes layered with dust.

"What's all this?" he asked.

"Leftovers from the rummage sale a few months ago. The Deacons have decided to give the rest of this stuff away to ministry groups."

"Where should I put this?"

"Over on those shelves, please. That way, they can decide what they want to do with them."

"Where are we?" he asked, monitoring the room.

"The basement."

"Oh..." He glanced around. He caught her hands and pulled her closer. "So...all alone in a faraway room."

"Sorta."

"Hmmm."

He kissed her.

Not softly like before, but passionately. "Mmm...I...want...you..." his voice grew husky and low, "so much."

Mary Faye wrapped her arms around him. She pulled Adam closer and caressed his neck. She wanted him.

I love him.

Adam eased Mary Faye against the door. His hands stroked her back. He then reached behind her, locked the door, and gazed into her eyes. Mary Faye nodded. They continued to kiss as he guided her to a soft mound of blankets on the floor.

The kisses were light now. Adam's hands gently traveled over Mary Faye's body. Touching. Exploring. Her body responded and came alive under his touch. His lips moved from her mouth to her neck. His hand swept over her breast, across her waist, caressing her hips. Adam pushed her skirt aside and parted her firm, shapely legs. Mary Faye adjusted her legs so he could lie between them. Their bodies moved in rhythm. She fiercely pulled his face closer and kissed him hard.

Adam removed Mary Faye's blouse, and then her bra. His hand cupped her soft breast and kissed it lovingly. His mouth drew on it ferociously, demanding, stirring her body, her breast rising to his mouth. Her hands stroked his head. Their bodies pleaded for more, rising to heights mere kisses could not satisfy.

They tossed the clothes aside. Adam eased inside her. Each movement a little more…a little more…until they were completely one. Passion and desire burned between them in an ecstasy of bliss.

"Ohhhhhh," she moaned. "Oh…my love."

They lay on the blankets with one of them tossed over their naked bodies. Light kisses passed between them.

"I never dreamed it would be so wonderful," she said.

He draped his arm around her. "I knew making love with you would be special. I just didn't know how special."

"I love you," she whispered. Her eyes brimmed with tears.

Adam smiled. "And I you," he said.

He pulled Mary Faye closer. She lay swaddled in his arms. Her head rested on his chest. They spoke softly until their tired, satisfied bodies fell into a light sleep.

Several minutes passed. "Look out!" he shouted. "Here they come! Duck your heads!"

Mary Faye jumped upright. She looked down at Adam. He was asleep.

His head tossed. She leaned over him and called his name softly. "It's okay. They..."

Who were *they?*

"They went the other way. Everything is fine now. Adam?"

Adam opened his eyes and smiled at her.

"You okay?" she asked.

"Yeah." He rose up on his elbows. "What did I do?"

"I think someone was coming after you," said Mary Faye.

"Yeah, they always do." He looked away. "I hope—"

"I love you. It doesn't change anything."

He pulled her down to him. They made love again. Slow and gentle at first. Moments later, their cravings intensified until they climaxed.

Adam rolled off her. "You don't know what you do to me."

"Yes, I do." She pulled Adam's face closer, her breath in his face. "Because I know what you do to me."

They rested for a few minutes. Mary Faye checked Adam's watch.

"Oh, shoot! I've got to go. It's 4:00."

He kissed her. "When can I see you again?"

"I don't know, but it's got to be soon." She laughed.

"Definitely."

They dressed quickly, but before they left the room, they hid the top blanket on the bottom of the mound. There was a small spot of blood on it.

She would deal with that later.

Together they hurried up the stairs. Adam exited through the backdoor. A few minutes later, Mary Faye followed. All the way home, she thought about the fact that she, Mary Faye Hunter, wasn't a virgin anymore. She now knew what it was like to lie in the arms of a man she loved. And it felt wonderful!

-2-

Saturday, January 21 – 8:00 pm

Adam sat on the dark porch in the cold night. Martha saw him through the kitchen window. His coat pulled close, head tucked down into the upturned collar. A cap on his head.

"Why don't you come inside?" Martha said as she opened the backdoor.

"Go away."

"It's freezing out here."

"Go...away."

"You are going to catch a death of cold."

Adam pursed his lips. "GO AWAY!"

"Fine! Sit there and freeze your rear end off!"

Martha slammed the backdoor. From the kitchen window, she waited to see what Adam would do.

Was it another flashback?

* * *

It was cold. Bitter cold. Adam could see them. They were like ants crawling down the hillside. Thousands of them marched toward his platoon. There were too many. Closer and closer they came. They didn't look like ants anymore. They rushed towards him. Closer. Closer! Closer! He raised his rifle to fire.

Planes moved in overhead. One...two...three...bombs

dropped, killing thousands of North Korean soldiers.

He jumped and waved his arms. "Hoo-ah! Get'em, boys!"

Adam fell back into his chair and scanned his surroundings. He wasn't in Korea. He was at home on his back porch.

Adam shivered.

He opened the back door and saw Martha a few feet away. She stared at him as he stepped into the kitchen.

Martha threw her arms around Adam.

"I love you," she said. "Don't ever forget that. You hear me?"

He nodded. "Yeah."

And I cheated on you.

She rubbed his arms. "You're cold. Come on."

Martha led him to the gas heater that hung on the wall in the kitchen.

"You need to warm up."

He offered his hands to the heat, rubbed them together, and offered them again. The warmth of the flame felt good. Martha removed his coat and hung it on a hook in the utility room.

"I'll get you some coffee if you want."

"Thanks."

Martha placed the coffee in front of Adam as he sat down at the kitchen table. The hot caramel colored coffee warmed him. Just the right amount of cream and sugar. She sat down across from him. What had just happened on the back porch was not mentioned.

Chapter 18

Darkness enveloped Mary Faye's room. She lay in bed with her chin rested on her grandma's quilt. Was it the darkness? Being alone? Or just time to think? Whatever joy she had felt walking home was now gone. Guilt slammed against her like a tidal wave and washed away any happiness that she had felt.

Mary Faye pulled the quilt over her head.

Oh, dear Lord, what have I done?

But the guilt would not relent.

"Please, please, forgive me," she whispered. "I promise I won't ever do anything like that again." Tears streaked down her cheeks.

Mary Faye bit her knuckles and sobbed into her hands.

Words can be said, promises made, but once there has

been a fire ignited, it was hard to quench. Mary Faye had meant her words when she said "never again," but the love inside her grew each time she saw Adam. His smile, laughter, and his teasing tone while they stood in the hallway fueled her desire to be with him again.

And they were.

Again…again…and again.

Chapter 19

March 18, 1967 – 2:30 pm

"Momma, I'm gonna go to the church for a while," said Mary Faye.

Etolia was sitting at the table snapping green beans. She glanced up at her daughter. "You going to practice?"

"Yes, ma'am. It won't be long till that wedding. I want everything to be perfect for the bride. Music is the main part of a wedding—other than the bride and groom." She laughed.

Mary Faye was in a good mood and couldn't hide it. She kissed her mother's cheek. "I won't be late."

"Call if you are."

It didn't matter that she was 34-years-old, had a job at Redstone Arsenal, or was an accomplished pianist. None of those things applied to the way her parents saw her. She would always be their baby girl.

Mary Faye left the kitchen, grabbed her sheet music,

and went out the door. Her step was light, and if not for people thinking she had gone mad, Mary Faye would have skipped down the sidewalk to the church. Excitement surged through her body like electricity.

In the sanctuary, Mary Faye was seated at the piano, and the sheet music was placed delicately on the music desk. Her fingers swept over the keys as if it were her lover's body. Gentle. Strong. Demanding. The music of Johann Sebastian Bach filled the sanctuary.

Hands squeezed Mary Faye's shoulders, but she kept playing. Lips kissed the top of her brown hair. Mary Faye's fingers stopped. Her body fell back against him. Adam leaned over her and grinned. She gazed into his dark blue eyes and smiled.

"I didn't hear you come in."

"I know," he replied, pulling her closer. "So you just let anyone kiss you?"

"No...just you." She stood and wrapped her arms around his neck. "Only you."

"Not here, someone might come in." He grasped her hand. "Come on."

The vestibule was dim. Mary Faye and Adam tip-toed down the corridor behind the sanctuary to a door at the end of the hall. He opened it and flipped on the light switch. A winding stairway led to the basement. Hand in hand, they followed the steps to another hallway. To the left, they entered a room stocked with tables and chairs. Long forgotten in a far corner, the soft nest of blankets that the lovers had stumbled upon was still there. Until that day, Mary Faye and Adam had only embraced and kissed. They had never planned to make love, but it happened. Now, every chance they got, Mary Faye and Adam indulged themselves. Their desires were fueled by a passion that could not be satisfied until they were one again.

Afterward, as she lay in his arms, Mary Faye rested her head on his shoulder. Her fingers stroked his chest.

"Do you remember the first time we made love here?" she asked.

"How could I forget?" He kissed her softly on her shoulder. "It was truly amazing."

Mary Faye took his hand and kissed his fingers, one at a time. "I was so scared, but I wanted to make love with you." Her voice, soft and low. "I never thought when we came down here that we would do that."

"I know, but sometimes things just happen."

She thought about the blood left on one of the blankets hidden on the bottom of the pile.

"January 21," said Mary Faye.

"Hmmm?"

"That was the first time we made love. Two months ago."

"Oh."

Mary Faye giggled. "I know. Men don't keep up with dates."

She passionately kissed him.

"I don't want to ever forget that date," she whispered to him. "Making love with you that day was the most exciting thing that's ever happened to me."

Adam grabbed her playfully by the shoulders. "More exciting than playing the piano in front of a large audience?"

He kissed her neck.

"Um," she said, "let me think about it."

He lightly slapped her naked hip.

She laughed. "Hey!"

"What?" He snickered.

"I love you," she whispered.

"I know. And I you."

The word love did not escape Adam's lips as easy as it did for Mary Faye, and she knew why. Her guilt was with God. Adam's guilt was with God, his wife, and two children. Mary Faye still wanted to hear the words.

* * *

Mary Faye propped herself up with her elbow and leaned close to Adam's face.

"There has never been any man but you," she said. My mother had always told me never to allow a man to lie between my legs without marriage. Tell me you love me."

"Mary Faye—"

"Say it."

"You know I do."

Mary Faye sat up. Her arms wrapped around herself as if she could hide her nakedness.

"Never would I do this with a man if I didn't believe he loved me. Wouldn't matter how much I loved him." Without regard, she whispered almost inaudible. "I was a virgin."

He stroked her back. "I know."

There had been so much blood that first time.

Mary Faye was Adam's second virgin. His wife had been his first. She wouldn't let him touch her until the next day after their wedding. Martha had been scared to death that first night, telling him to stay away from her and making him sleep on the other side of the bed. Mary Faye had been timid the first time he saw her, but the first time they made love, she allowed him to enter her with a passion he'd never experienced before. No amount of guilt could extinguish their blazing fire.

"You know how I feel," said Adam, watching her closely.

"I guess I need to go." She reached for her bra. He snatched it from her hand.

"I love you," he whispered.

Mary Faye fell back onto the soft blankets. Adam pulled her body close and stroked her back. His mouth gently kissed her lips.

He loved her.

Mary Faye moved atop him. She kissed his face, eyes, and lost herself once again in the love she felt for him.

-2-

The screen door slammed behind Mary Faye upon her arrival home.

"Mary Faye," her mother called from the living room.

"Yes, ma'am."

"Honey, will you come here and try on this dress? I've almost got it finished. It's going to look real nice on you next Saturday for the wedding."

Mary Faye stopped. The last thing she wanted was to be near her mother right now. The scent of her lover was on her. His aftershave. Maybe even their lovemaking. No, she could not go near anyone.

Oh, the lies, the secrets I had to hide!

"Not, now, momma, I need to lie down for a while. My head is killing me."

Her mother put the dress aside. Mary Faye could see her from the small hallway off the living room. She was coming her way.

No. No. No.

Quickly Mary Faye hurried toward her bedroom.

"I'll be ok. Just need to lie down for a moment."

Before her mother could reply or reach her, Mary Faye closed the door. She dropped her dress to the floor, put on a housecoat, and sprayed her body with perfume just before a light knock came from the door.

"Yes?"

"Mary Faye? Are you okay, baby?" Etolia stepped into the room.

"Yes, momma. Just need to rest for a while to get rid of a headache. We'll do the dress this evening."

Her mother gave her a questioning glare.

"I'm fine, momma."

"Well, I'm concerned you might be coming down with something. Sinuses flaring up again?"

"No, just a headache."

Etolia came on into the room. She touched her daughter's cheeks. "You do seem a little flushed, but not feverish." Leaning over, she gave Mary Faye a light kiss on her cheek. "Okay, you rest. We can do the dress later."

Etolia left the room, and a sigh of relief washed over Mary Faye. Normally when she returned home after being with Adam, she could sneak into the bathroom and remove any evidence she had been with him. They had only made love a few times, and each time they did, she loved it even more. Mary Faye's mother would die of shame if she knew. Her father would never speak to her again. And worst of all…

They would be deeply hurt.

Mary Faye didn't want that, but she didn't want…no, she couldn't give up Adam, regardless of everyone else. They would have to be careful, keep their love a secret from everyone. She had her parents to contend with and Adam's wife.

-3-

Adam didn't think about his wife being in the kitchen when he came through the backdoor. He chose the back entrance thinking Martha would be in the living room or the boys' room. He had not expected her to be shopping at 3:45 in the afternoon. He was lucky she was at a store and not in some movie theater on Second Avenue. It never entered his mind to check what was playing at the Princess. Martha could have seen him when he was in the church parking lot. Adam had to be more careful and not so anxious to get to Mary Faye.

"Hi, honey." Martha greeted him. "I'm making some stew for supper. Where've you been?"

"Went downtown for some shoes."

She peered at his feet. "Shoes? What's wrong with those?"

"Nothing." He got a glass, ran some water, turned it up, and emptied the glass. "Nothing. They just squeak sometimes when I walk. I hate shoes that squeak." He slipped off the shoes.

"I never noticed."

"Of course not. You aren't the one wearing them."

"Well, you don't have to be so snippy."

Careful. Don't give her any reason to think anything.

"I'm sorry." He kissed the back of her neck. She turned.

"Want to go into the bedroom?" she asked, smiling up at him.

"Bedroom? Where are the boys?"

"Sleeping." Again, she smiled up at him. "Can I proposition you?"

He kissed her deeply and then pulled away.

"Not right now. The boys might wake up."

Martha's smile faded.

"Maybe later tonight when the boys are in bed."

She nodded and turned back to the stew.

* * *

Later that evening, while Adam was in the shower, Martha took one of his brown loafers that were next to the bed. She plodded up and down the wooden hallway that ran between the bedrooms. The shoes didn't squeak.

Martha returned the shoes to Adam's side of the bed, but in her haste, not in the same spot.

Chapter 20

By 6:30, supper had ended, and the kitchen cleaned. Mary Faye had taken a bath before supper. She seemed relaxed, no signs of being ill, and in an overall happy mood. She talked and shared laughter.

"You look so pretty, Mary Faye." Etolia Hunter straightened the back of the formal dress. "You're going to be prettier than the bride. You will look so beautiful at the piano."

Etolia pinned up the hem of the dress. "Turn again for me, baby." She talked as she worked. "You seem to be feeling better."

"Yes, ma'am."

Webb Hunter sat in his chair by the fireplace and propped his feet on the ottoman. He was the picture of a southern gentleman relaxing after an evening meal. He put down the newspaper and slid the pipe from his mouth.

"You been sick, Mary Faye?" he asked.

"No, daddy, just a headache earlier. I'm fine."

"Turn, please," said Etolia.

Mary Faye complied. Her mother pushed down more pins in the dress hem.

"I think it's the weather."

"Weather?" Webb was puzzled. "What did the weather have to do with headaches?"

"You know how the weather changes...messes with a person's sinuses."

It was fascinating to hear her parents talk about her headache like she was still a child. They checked for fevers and analyzed her coughs. Mary Faye was surprised her mother didn't ask if her nose was running.

In two months, she would turn 34. But this time it was different. There was a man in Mary Faye's life who loved her. She knew he was married, but what if he left his wife? Or she left him? They must not have a good marriage, or he would have never turned to her. Wasn't that what they said about married people? Maybe Adam's wife has someone too and will leave him for her new lover.

"I said turn, Mary Faye," Etolia snapped.

"What? Oh." She turned again.

"Guess you got your mind on next Saturday's wedding?"

"Yes, ma'am."

How easily the lies rolled off her tongue now.

Lies had never been part of Mary Faye's vocabulary, but they were now.

Momma, I'm going shopping. Momma, I'm going to the church to practice. Momma, I'm going to the movies. Momma, momma, momma...always attached to a lie to explain why she needed to leave the house.

"We're going out to eat for your birthday in May, but would you like to take maybe a short trip as well?"

Etolia put the last pin in the hem.

"There, that's done. Would you want to go somewhere for your birthday?" She looked up at her daughter, who was standing on the coffee table.

"Well, I don't know. That's two months away. I'd have to check to see if I could get off from work."

"Shouldn't be a problem, should it?"

"A trip?" Webb folded his newspaper and laid it on the table by his chair. "I doubt if I can get off work myself. Springtime is when people like to buy furniture, wanting a new look, and such. Warm weather makes people spend money. Don't matter if it's a couch or a new car. Warm weather gets into people's pockets."

Etolia leaned back on her heels as she observed her daughter wearing the pastel blue sleeveless dress.

"Yes, perfect. I'm telling you, Mary Faye, that dress looks so nice on you. People are going to be staring at the beautiful Mary Faye Hunter instead of the bride."

Etolia laughed. "The bride is gonna wish you'd stayed home."

"Oh, momma." Mary Faye blushed. "The Lord is gonna get you for lying."

Both women laughed.

"Well, I know you're going to perform the most beautiful music that people have ever heard. That much, I know."

Mary Faye smiled at her mother. Everyone knew how much she loved the piano. Many times, as a child, even as a young woman, Mary Faye had made the comment she would rather have a new Steinway piano instead of a new car. They all knew of her love for the piano, but no one knew how she longed to be a bride. Mary Faye could not be the bride if men never asked her out. The man who loved her had a wife. He couldn't ask her to marry him or even take her out to dinner. To love a married man cuts not only into the heart, but into the soul. Nothing had made Mary Faye happier than being with Adam, but the guilt was the heaviest burden she had ever carried.

Quickly the thoughts were brushed away. A young

bride needed her music next week. Music was the one thing Mary Faye would always have and not have to feel guilty about it.

"Mary Faye?"

"Ma'am?"

"I said you could step down and take off the dress."

Mary Faye stepped from the table.

"You going to stay for the reception?" Her mother gave one more flip to the dress tail.

"Yes, ma'am."

"I think you should too."

It was always good when Mary Faye had stayed, giving her a chance to socialize with people at church. She didn't have much of a social life, but she wasn't like most young women. Etolia didn't want her to be like so many of them. Boy crazy or whatever you called it. Her daughter was a good woman. Pure. Innocent. Not too many like her anymore. God, family, church, and her job. That was her life, a Christian life close to God. Etolia was proud of her daughter.

"You want your daddy to pick you up when it's over?"

"No, ma'am. I'll just take a cab. Not sure what time I'll leave."

It would be a perfect time to meet Adam, but the wedding was at the church. Mary Faye didn't like meeting at the church anyway. They had only met there twice, but she always felt overwhelmed with guilt afterward. Mary Faye justified her feelings by thinking they didn't make love in the sanctuary, just in the basement of the church building. Not the house of God, but a basement. If she repeatedly said that in her mind, maybe the guilt would subside. When Mary Faye was with Adam, it never felt wrong. Guilt settled over her as soon as they were apart. When she was alone to think about her sin. But each time they were together only made her long for him more. Guilt became dimmer as desire grew stronger.

Mary Faye wondered if Adam could pick her up after the wedding. Maybe they could go for a ride. Probably not, but she would mention it to him.

"I guess I could just walk home," suggested Mary Faye.

"You know I don't like the idea of you walking at night," said Etolia.

"Neither do I," added Webb.

Mary Faye laughed. "What could go wrong?"

Chapter 21

March 19, 1967

"Next Sunday is Easter."

"What?" Adam flipped over in bed. His wife stood by his side, dressed in a housecoat with rollers in her hair. "Next Sunday? I thought it was in April."

"No, silly. It changes every year. You know that."

"Oh, right."

Martha leaned down to kiss him, but he turned his cheek.

"What's the matter?" she asked.

"You know I don't like to kiss first thing in the morning. I need to brush my teeth."

Yeah, and you didn't want to make love last night either.

She patted his cheek. "Well, I'll save you one."

She stepped out of the bedroom and then returned a moment later.

"Will it be okay if you eat cereal for breakfast?" she said. I need to get the boys ready for church."

"Yeah, that's fine." He threw back the blanket. "I've got to get a shower myself."

Adam pulled out a pair of slacks and a dress shirt from the closet. From a bureau, he withdrew socks, shorts, and a tie. He side-stepped around the bed.

Where are my shoes?

They were laying right there last night. Adam returned to the closet. Had they been put away last night? One thing he could say about his wife, she was always tidying up. If any of his belongings were out of place for a second, Martha would move it out of the way.

Adam scanned the bottom of the closet. He moved some other shoes, sneakers, rain boots, pushed aside a suitcase that should be up in the attic, but no loafers.

What on earth did she do with my shoes?

Adam turned and saw the loafers by his side of the bed next to the nightstand. Had she moved the shoes just to get them away from her bedside?

Adam shook his head and went into the kitchen. He dumped Frosted Flakes into a bowl and poured milk over it, but his mind wasn't on food. Adam's mind was on Mary Faye. She was one of a kind. A good woman. Mary Faye was the sweetest, kindest person he had ever met. Never said an unkind word about anyone. She was timid, but once she got to know you, was talkative in a soft, friendly manner, unlike other women in the office. Mary Faye never told off colored jokes or flirted with anyone.

There were women in his office that cheated—it was easy to spot, the way they behaved around men. Some took extended lunch breaks or shopping trips. They always returned, laughing with the others, making excuses why they were gone so long, if they returned at all. Office gossip was rampant with affairs between co-workers, then in a few weeks, they moved on to someone else. Some didn't even bother to hide it, even though they were married. It didn't matter to him what they did. He wasn't interested.

Adam had never been the ladies' man type. He had

only been with two girls in high school. One was known for pleasing the boys. Adam had been nervous about sex, but Estelle Bailey had taken care of that. He would never forget the little five-foot blonde. He had forgotten the other girl's name. Funny, because they had dated for a few months.

But no one was like his Mary Faye. No one.

He finished his cereal, turned the bowl up, and drank the milk.

The water was nice and hot when Adam stepped into the shower. It felt good on his tired body. Sleep didn't come easily last night. Mary Faye was on his mind. He loved making love to her. Each time filled him with excitement that went to every part of his body. It wasn't just the sex—it was her, the way she moved, and the way she kissed him. When Adam was with Mary Faye, there was no other world. He had finally gone to sleep, thinking about how it felt to enter her.

Adam shook his head as water ran down his face and body. He would love to take a shower with Mary Faye. His body stirred.

"You need to hurry, hon."

The knock on the bathroom door startled him. Martha's voice immediately brought him back to the present.

"Okay, okay," he called through the door. Thank goodness she had not opened the door. Could she have seen him through the shower door? He looked down. Would have been okay even if she had. Her knock had chased Mary Faye from his mind and body.

It wasn't that Adam didn't love his wife, he did, he told himself as he toweled off. He loved her and Mary Faye, just not the same way. But no man could keep two women for long. One gets suspicious, the other impatient. Mary Faye knew he was married, but she had never asked about his wife. Not yet, anyway.

-2-

It was hard to believe that just yesterday Mary Faye had been in Adam's arms downstairs. Guilt had to be kept at bay, or she could not perform the music for today's service. The piano music filled the sanctuary. Music had been a part of Mary Faye's life for as long as she could remember. It gave her a purpose in life. She had played at talent shows in her youth, concerts, weddings, churches, and a long list of other events. Mary Faye had always had music, but now she had Adam too.

He loves me.

Her fingers fluttered over the keys like butterfly wings over a flower, as she played How Great Thou Art.

Emotions swept over her.

Oh, Lord, my God. Please forgive me. I love him. I really love him.

A small tear formed in the corner of her right eye.

Stop it! She scolded herself. Mary Faye's fingers continued with the music, but guilt gripped her heart. Oh, how could she ever let him go? The first time in her life, she had experienced a man's love, to know what it felt like to be kissed, to make love.

The music grew louder as the keys proclaimed God's love at the song's climax, then slowly her fingers gently touched the keys as the song came to an end with a quiet low tone.

Pastor Van Arsdale regarded her as he stood behind the pulpit.

"Thank you, Mary Faye. That was beautiful."

He made announcements and then returned to his seat. The choir stood. Mary Faye touched the keys as they began to sing, Amazing Grace. The choir sang two more songs. As the ushers passed around the offering plate, Mary Faye always played a soft old hymn, but today was different. Today the song, Strange Things Happening Every Day roared into the sanctuary. Mary Faye had not planned it. It was not something everyone would appreciate, but it was a beautiful song with a powerful message. Perhaps it was Mary Faye's own way of expressing rebellion. Everyone expected her to be perfect, to never make a mistake. She was placed high on a pedestal.

The higher the pedestal, the higher the fall.

As the plates passed around the congregation, glances also passed among the parish. Never had Mary Faye Hunter played such lively offertory music.

Clois Redding leaned over to Linda Blackburn. "What is she doing? I don't know that song."

"Just showing off that piano, I guess. Kinda snappy, isn't it?"

"I guess." Then she poked Linda, tilting her head. "See Emma Wallace, tapping her foot?"

Both women looked across the aisle to where the elderly lady sat. Emma tapped her foot and nodded in rhythm with the music.

"Is that a Christian song?" Clois asked.

"Has to be. She wouldn't play it otherwise. Mary Faye is about as Christian as a woman can be."

"True."

"The music is different, kinda pretty though." Linda Blackburn began to tap her foot as the music came to an end.

"Well, Mary Faye, that was mighty powerful music there," the pastor said. He smiled at the congregation. "I recognized that song. Very old."

Pastor Van Arsdale didn't want them to think that some new version of worldly music had made its way into the church.

"Yes, Jesus is the holy light turning darkness to light." He began to sing. "There are strange things happening every day. Jesus is the holy light. Turning darkness to light."

Mary Faye began to play the song again, not as loud this time, allowing the people to hear the pastor's soft voice.

"There are strange things happening every day. He gave the blind man sight. When he praised Him with all his might. There are strange things happening every day."

He stopped singing, and Mary Faye stopped playing.

"Thank you, Mary Faye. Yes, a beautiful song, beautiful. The Bible tells us that we are a peculiar people. As peculiar people, we should be looking for those strange things every day because God is at work all around us."

The ushers were still standing in front of the pulpit looking up at the pastor, waiting for him to pray over the offering. As if their eyes made contact, the preacher said, "Let us pray."

Sunday afternoon was spent quietly by Mary Faye and her parents. Her mother had prepared meatloaf and green peas for lunch. Mary Faye fluffed the instant mashed potatoes and buttered the rolls. After dinner, Webb read the Sunday paper, Etolia worked on a baby blanket she was crocheting for one of the young mothers-to-be at church. She had known Lily since she had been a little girl in Etolia's Sunday School class.

Etolia glanced at Mary Faye, who was reading a magazine. Lily was much younger than Mary Faye but was already starting a new family. Etolia sighed.

"Something wrong, momma?"

"No, honey. Just thinking."

"About the blanket?"

"Oh, nothing in particular."

It wasn't that Etolia didn't want Mary Faye to have her own family. It just seemed there was never anyone for her. Most men were probably intimidated by her mind. Mary Faye was highly intelligent and very talented. Yeah, she could see that. Of course, Mary Faye was also shy. That didn't help. She was a meek soul with a gentle spirit.

Blessed are the meek, for they shall inherit the earth. That was Mary Faye all right.

"I think I'm going to take a nap," Mary Faye said as she stood, the magazine still in her hand.

"Okay, just make sure you're up in plenty of time for church tonight. Are you going over to practice before the service?"

"No, ma'am. The youth aren't singing tonight, so there aren't any new songs to go over."

"Speaking of new songs...Where did you get that one this morning?" Webb asked. He leered at her over the top of his glasses. "I don't know if I liked that or not."

"It's an old Christian song, daddy, even the preacher said so."

"Yeah, but I don't think all Christian songs belong in the church. Depends on how they sound."

She laughed. "Oh, daddy. It just had a little get up to it."

"Well, I don't think you need any more of those get and go songs at church. You need to keep that kind of music at home."

She smiled and kissed the top of his head. "Yes, sir." She smiled and left the room.

Laying across the bed, she thought about Adam. That song was more than just a song with get up and go as she had said. Sister Rosetta Tharp wrote the song in 1944. Some people didn't like the way Rosetta had turned Christian songs into rhythm and blues. This song had a double meaning, calling out the church people about how they were.

If you fall, you will be crucified.

If the church knew Mary Faye's secret, they would never forgive her. Never. But there was no way she was going to give up Adam.

As long as she walked that narrow path, she was everyone's perfect Christian lady, but they never acknowledged their own sins. No one in that church was perfect, yet that's what they expected of Mary Faye. Even if Adam left his wife to be with Mary Faye, the church would look down on her. What would her parents do? People would whisper behind her back, just like they did all her life because of her speech, but now because she was an adulteress.

There was no way out now. Mary Faye loved Adam more than anything in the world. But he would never be hers entirely. No one can ever know about them. Sometimes the price is just too high to pay. But yesterday in his arms, they were one.

The magazine lay across Mary Faye's stomach as she daydreamed about yesterday. The feeling of his breath on her face as he gently kissed her. Oh, how she wished they could make love today, every day.

Mary Faye rolled over onto her stomach and flipped through the magazine. A man with a broad smile stared at her from the page. He was selling aftershave, but with his bold smile, you'd think it was toothpaste. Probably most people didn't notice a man's smile. She did.

Chapter 22

March 20, 1967

Mary Faye Hunter stood in her bedroom, whirling a lock of chestnut brown hair around her finger as she gazed at her reflection in the mirror. It was 6:15 and her ride to work would be there soon. Normally, she would be ready for another day at Redstone, but today for some reason that she couldn't pinpoint, she didn't feel like her usual self.

"Get with it, girl," she said aloud.

"Did you say something, Mary Faye?" her mother asked as she walked past the bedroom door. Her mother had an armful of towels that she was taking to the bathroom.

Mary Faye turned. "What? Oh, no, momma. Just talking to myself."

"Well, you better hurry. Almost time for your ride."

"Yeah, I know." She picked up her lipstick, colored her lips, pressed them together, and then ran the lipstick across her lips once more.

"Mary Faye, be careful with that lipstick. You don't

need to put so much on. It will give you that...that—"

"That what, momma? Trashy look?" Mary Faye laughed.

"No," her mother replied softly, yet with a mischievous tone. "You know better than that. I was thinking more in line of not lady like, or an artificial look."

Mary Faye laughed. When she came out of the bedroom, she leaned over and kissed her mother's cheek. "There," she said with a grin, "I'll leave some of it with you."

Her mother laughed as she moved down the hallway with the towels. "Make sure you take a sweater. You know how chilly March can be."

Mary Faye stepped out of the small house on Eighth Avenue and sat down in the swing. In her hand was a white sweater, which she put on quickly. Her mother was right. It was a chilly morning.

A few minutes later, Paul Hurst's car pulled up in front of the house.

"Bye, momma," she called as she went down the steps to the waiting car.

"Well, Mary Faye," Almon said as she got into the backseat. "You ready for another week? It seems like Saturday and Sunday pass faster than any other days of the week. Monday rolls around mighty fast."

"I'm fine, Mr. Hensley. Mondays don't bother me. Got to look at Mondays as a new beginning. First day of the week to accomplish something good."

Almon smiled. Of course, Mary Faye didn't mind Mondays. She didn't seem to mind anything. She was the most stable, gentle, polite person he had ever met. It always amazed him that some fellow hadn't snatched her up and married her.

"Mary Faye, did you have a good weekend?" Paul asked. He pulled the car away from the curb.

"Yes, sir. A very nice weekend. I had a piano concert

on Friday night. Of course, on Sunday we went to church. Momma made the best dinner for us afterward."

Paul Hurst nodded, his eyes on the highway as they made their way toward Highway 31 North. Soon they were on the Steamboat Bill Memorial Bridge headed northeast toward Huntsville. Redstone Arsenal was about five miles southwest of Huntsville. Redstone had opened in 1941, but Paul didn't start working there until after he had sold his machinist store in Decatur. After he had passed the civil service exam, he was cleared to begin his position in the Supply and Maintenance warehouse within the U.S. Army Missile Command Building. That's where everyone in their carpool worked. Paul Hurst, Almon Hensley, Mary Faye Hunter, Rick Overton, and Stephen Harkins.

"Did your momma make you some fried chicken for Sunday dinner?" Rick Overton asked.

"No, sir. But she did make a wonderful meatloaf. It was delicious. I guess I just love meatloaf."

"Oh, I do too," Almon said. "My mother-in-law makes the perfect meatloaf. Not too dry, but firm and easy to cut. Some just fall all to pieces, but not hers." Then he laughed. "I don't know how she does it, and neither does my wife."

They all laughed, even Mary Faye, but her laugh was small, not bold. Her hand sheltered her mouth.

Paul knew Mary Faye was self-conscious of her speech even among friends. Everyone at work knew that she rarely spoke or laughed. He had, however, noticed something unusual about her lately. Paul felt ridiculous for even entertaining the idea. Mary Faye was a good Christian woman, worked hard in the church, played the piano, worked with the youth. No, Mary Faye wouldn't do anything like that.

Paul did not know another woman who had built a finer reputation than Mary Faye Hunter. A perfect Christian lady. Everyone that knew her was aware of that.

In the rearview mirror, Paul glanced back at the riders

in the backseat. They were fixated on the river. The morning sunshine flickered across the water.

Would be a nice day to fish for crappies.

Mary Faye was peering at the sparkling river, but her mind wasn't on what she was seeing. Instead, Saturday occupied her mind. It was a wonderful time.

"Mary Faye, you and your family decided where y'all going on vacation this year?" Mr. Harkins asked.

"No, not really. I wish we would go to Hawaii. We thought about Mexico."

"Oh, that would be nice," Mr. Harkins replied.

"Yes, it would."

Mary Faye turned back to the window. She would love to go to Hawaii, but not on a family vacation. Hawaii would be a perfect honeymoon trip. The idea carried her off into a daydream as the humming of the car and the passing scenery lolled her mind into a perfect world with Adam Fletcher.

-2-

Not seeing Adam when Mary Faye first entered the building did not surprise her, yet her eyes still scanned the hallway as people made their way into the building, going to different departments. Mary Faye scrambled down the hall to the clerical department where a room full of women worked at desks typing and filing papers for the U.S. Government. Her eleven years inside that office had passed uneventfully until Adam walked into her life. He had introduced himself to her earlier, but she hadn't remembered his name, but she noticed his smile. He had the prettiest smile of any man she had ever seen.

It had been less than a year ago before they truly talked. Just small talk. Then a few laughs. As the months passed, their friendship grew, and there was no day to pinpoint when things changed. There was the day that he gave her paperwork and his hand accidentally brushed against hers. A sensation ran through her body like touching an electric short wire. The feeling ran over her so fast. She looked away, not wanting him to see her face. Mary Faye Hunter never allowed any man's hands to brush hers, and it happened so fast, it made her wonder if perhaps she had done it on purpose. That was a horrible thought. That would be lustful. That was a sin. Today though, she wasn't thinking about sin or lust.

Love wasn't lust.

Mary Faye's desk was in the right back corner from the main entrance of the office. The large room housed clerks and secretaries from her division of the missile program. She had been there for over ten years. Her workstation was in a perfect location, free from intrusion. No one sat to her right, and the desk to her left was several feet away. There was no one directly in front of her as it was with many of the others because she was right next to the supervisor's office. She had always loved the position of her desk. Especially now.

Sometimes when Mr. Mitchell had come out of his office, he would stop to speak, give her paperwork he needed typed or filed. She stayed busy all day long. Typing up order forms, receiving orders for parts and for the supplies coming into the warehouse.

Mary Faye sat down in her chair. This morning though, she really didn't want to see anyone or even be there. She just didn't feel well. Mostly weak and a little tired.

She shuffled papers, typed, and filled out forms. The work on her desk quickly disappeared and so did the morning. When lunch came, she ate in the cafeteria. She bought a drink and with her lunch bag, sat down at a table alone. Other women, one by one, joined her. Their conversations turned to their weekend, but Mary Faye said very little. She mostly listened.

"Mary Faye, did Mr. Fletcher give you copies of those

forms to fill out for those parts to be sent to building three?" Andrea Brown said.

Her meatloaf sandwich seemed stuck in her mouth, Mary Faye quickly shook her head. Finally, she gave a weak, "No." She took a sip of her drink. "He hasn't given me anything this morning."

"He probably will after lunch."

"He's probably got something else to occupy his mind," Louella Ketchum said. "He's been mighty busy." She smiled, cutting her eyes toward the other two women with a half wink as if she knew something. "I think he's got a lot on his mind—if you get my drift."

The other two women snickered. Mary Faye continued to eat her sandwich, preoccupied with her drink and chips.

"Louella," Andrea said. "Watch what you're saying. He's a nice, quiet man and married with children."

"Um..." Louella giggled and then took a sip of RC Cola. "You know what they say about those quiet ones."

Peggy Wallace bumped Louella's knee under the table.

"What?" Louella asked as she bit into a potato chip.

"You want one of these cookies?" Peggy asked, but Louella knew that wasn't why Peggy bumped her knee.

"I'm just saying..."

Mary Faye never knew what to say when women talked about men. It made her uncomfortable. Daddy always said to say nice things about people or say nothing at all. But sometimes the way women spoke about men was crazy. Some of the language they used was just plain disgusting. Mary Faye wanted to leave, but if she did the reason would be obvious, which would just make Louella laugh at her.

"I mean, after all, you never know what men are up to."

"Well, before you decide that your boss is some womanizing man, you might want to keep in mind he is the supervisor, and you wouldn't want your name tied to office gossip." Peggy gave her friend a cautionary glance.

Louella thought for a moment. "But what if it's not gossip?"

"Could still get you in trouble." Andrea looked closely at her friend. "Okay, come on Louella, what have you heard?"

Mary Faye stood. Her sandwich wrapper was in her brown paper bag, as were the half-eaten chips. Three cookies were also inside the bag untouched.

"Well, I guess I'll stop by the bathroom. See y'all in the office."

Mary Faye picked up her bag, tossed it and her drink can in a trash can by the door as she left the cafeteria.

"I hope you're satisfied," said Peggy.

"What?" Louella asked. She continued eating her sandwich.

Andrea and Peggy shook their heads. "That remark about the quiet ones," Peggy said.

"Oh, I didn't mean her. Mary Faye? Little Miss Perfect?" She wrinkled her nose and mouth. "Mary Faye wouldn't know what to do with a man if she had one—married or not."

"I don't know about that," Andrea said.

"I do." Louella took her last swig of her RC. "She's so prim and proper. She is sitting so high on her pedestal." Her voice raised slightly.

"Would you please not be so loud?" Peggy asked.

Louella lowered her voice and her head. "Everyone in this office knows how she is. All she cares about is piano and church. She never does anything without her parents. I saw some of those pictures—always her parents, never anyone else." Louella crushed her lunch bag in her hands. "She doesn't even drive a car. Can you imagine in this day and time? Living at home, no car—no life."

The other two women were silent as if they were thinking over what their friend had just said. Then Peggy replied, "I think Mary Faye has the life she wants."

Louella started to stand, but Andrea grabbed her arm. "Wait! Tell us what you were talking about a while ago."

Louella shrugged her shoulders. "When?"

"Office gossip."

Louella laughed. "Oh, you want to know, huh?"

"Well, yeah. What do you know?"

"Sorry, Charlie," Louella laughed, a reference to the *Charlie the Tuna* advertisement. "I have no good office gossip." She laughed again as she stood, then leaned down to her friends. "I'm telling you now—right now." She tapped her long red fingernail on the table. "What Mary Faye needs is a man!" Louella turned around and strutted across the cafeteria, her hips swinging in her tight skirt.

Louella had been married three times. Her first husband, Jeb Ramirez, was killed in 1960 in Vietnam when his helicopter crashed under enemy fire. Four men were killed. Her second husband, Watson Brooks, had left her after he found out that being married without children would not keep him out of the military. Once Brooks had discovered this, he joined the Air Force and never returned home. Brooks decided that he liked the military (and the women he had met all over the world) more than marriage. Louella never heard from him again.

Her present husband, Melvin Ketchum, had asked her to marry him two weeks after their first date. Three years later, they had an 18-month-old baby boy. Louella tamed Melvin, but deep down in her heart, she trusted no man. It wasn't Jeb's fault that he had gotten killed, but it was rotten of Brooks to abandon her. She didn't trust men, but she loved them. She could never see herself without a man. Never could she live like Mary Faye Hunter. Nothing to caress but piano keys.

"Your friend needs to watch her mouth," Peggy said.

"My friend?" said Andrea. "I figure she's just as much your friend as mine. And you are the one who sits beside her in the office."

"Okay, *our* friend. No need for her to say those things around Mary Faye. You know how quiet and shy she is." Peggy grabbed up her trash. "Although I will admit, Mary Faye is a strange character."

"Strange? I wouldn't go that far. Different, maybe. That's the word. Different. Quiet. Reserved. There's plenty of words besides strange."

"How about pitiful?" Andrea threw her trash in the can.

"That's probably the best word. Pitiful." She grinned. "C'mon, let's get back to work," Peggy said.

As they left the cafeteria, the women noticed Mary Faye and CJ ambling up the hallway toward the office. Whatever they were discussing made Mary Faye laugh.

Chapter 23

"Rusty," Marty Tyler said. He was sitting on the edge of Rusty's desk at Decatur Ambulance Service. Rusty had been in the ambulance business for the last two years. Marty had been working for him for about 11 months. "I'd think with all your money, you could afford to give your driver's a raise."

Rusty laughed. "Yeah, I'm rich, all right. Rich with debts. Do you realize how expensive it is to run an ambulance service?"

"If anyone knows how to turn a dollar, it's you, Rusty."

Marty pulled a pack of Kools from his shirt pocket. He struck a match to light the cigarette. "How about all those side jobs?"

Again Rusty laughed. He rebuilt cars, sold cars, ran the ambulance service, and had a service station, yet there was never enough money. That's how he got mixed up with his other side job. A person could never make enough money.

Those doctor friends of his proved that. They were doctors, but they wanted their ten percent cut for every person they sent his way. Rusty took all the risk, but they got their cut. Every woman they sent his way, they got thirty dollars out of the three hundred he charged.

Abortions were illegal in the state of Alabama, but it was a misdemeanor with a fine of fifteen hundred dollars and up to a year in prison for the first offense. He wasn't the only one in the area who was willing to take the risk though. There was competition in Huntsville, Florence, and especially Birmingham if a woman was willing to travel over a hundred miles to keep her secret. Most weren't though.

He was convenient, reasonable, and he was good at his work. Dr. Carter taught him very well.

"C'mon, Rusty. How about it?"

"No raises. That's final. Don't have enough money coming in here for raises."

Marty leaned closer and glanced over his shoulder. "Rusty, how about giving a friend a helping hand?"

Rusty tilted his head slightly as if he didn't understand.

"Come on, Rusty. You know what I mean."

Yes, he knew. His reputation loomed like a shadow, but he wanted Marty to say what he actually wanted and not make him guess.

"And what do you mean?"

"I got this girl...she's...ah...well, she's a friend of mine...we're close. Real close."

"How close?"

"You know, Rusty."

"No. You tell me. I don't know what you're trying to tell me."

"Abortion. That's what I mean. This girl needs an abortion."

"You tellin' me you got some girl pregnant, and you think I would know where she could get an abortion?"

Rusty Cole trusted no one.

No one.

Rusty made no promises to anyone. He was his own best friend. Right now, he glared at Marty Tyler as if he didn't even know his name, let alone what he was talking about.

The two men stared at one another for several seconds.

"Fine," Marty said. "Guess I'm wrong." He stood up from the desk.

"Hope your friend can find help. Maybe she could just keep the baby."

"Yeah, yeah, sure." Marty walked toward the office door. "You hear of anyone, let me know." He stopped and looked back at Rusty. "You know, Rusty, you need to try to do something about those rumors going around about you."

"Rumors?"

"Yeah. That you know how to get rid of an unwanted pregnancy. But like I said if you hear of someone that can do it, just let me know."

Rusty nodded.

Once the door was closed, Rusty picked up the phone, dialed a number and waited for an answer on the other end.

"Hello."

"Thanks for that tip. The rat offered his cheese."

"Yeah, I figured. That's why I notified you. You better be careful who you deal with, my friend."

"Always," Rusty said. He replaced the receiver. It was good to have friends at the sheriff's office. There were plenty of others out there those cops could be after instead of him. People came to him, not the other way around. Those women didn't want their babies, or they would never have come to him. It's not his job to talk them out of it. They have their own conscience for that.

* * *

Marty Tyler slammed the ambulance door.

Rusty did abortions.

Marty knew he did. The word was out all over Decatur.

Need an abortion? Rusty Cole is your man.

The sheriff had offered Marty fifty dollars to get Rusty to confess to performing abortions, and he got nothing out of him.

Marty Tyler removed three candy wrappers and several coke cans from the ambulance and discarded it in the trash. He took the keys and drove the ambulance behind the building to wash it. Before he started, the next call came in. A woman at the nursing home needed to be transferred to Decatur General Hospital.

Chapter 24

Supper was on the stove when Mary Faye got home. Etolia was setting the table.

"Mary Faye, you want a glass of tea?"

"Yes, ma'am. That'd be nice,"

Mary Faye removed her white sweater and placed it on the arm of the platform rocker. Etolia handed Mary Faye a glass of tea as she entered the kitchen. The cold sweet tea refreshed her mouth and her spirit. Today had been a long, hard day.

"Did you have a good day at work?" asked Etolia.

"Yes, ma'am." She went back toward the living room and grabbed the sweater from the rocker.

"Supper's ready. Just waiting on your daddy."

"Is there anything you need me to do?"

"No, hon. Just relax for a while. Your daddy should be here any minute."

Mary Faye entered her bedroom. The room had its own door that led outside onto the front porch. Sometimes at night after her parents were in bed, Mary Faye sat on the porch in the warm summer evenings alone, thinking, looking at the stars.

She opened the door to the front porch, and sat down in the swing. The women at work were just another reminder that she was different. It wasn't them. It was her.

Your voice is horrible. I'm surprised that anyone can understand a word you say, or even talk to you.

Mary Faye never had any real friends. Just the ones at church. But no girlfriends to share secrets, have lunch, go to the movies, anything. Her friends were at church, doing things in a group. Most women her age were married and had children, at least the ones she knew.

There was no point in telling her mother how uncomfortable those women made her feel today. It wasn't the first time. Ever since Mary Faye had been a child, she cried on her mother's shoulder because some kid had made fun of her.

You talk funny, Mary Faye. You got a weird smile, Mary Faye. Your nose is too big, Mary Faye.

But the one that hurt the most was what one girl said when they were 14 years old.

You probably won't ever have a boyfriend, Mary Faye. You're too plain, and you talk funny. You even laugh funny.

Mary Faye never forgot those words or that girl. Annie Jo Matthews. Today was no different. She knew why Peggy had bumped Louella.

Her mother had always told her they were jealous because she could play the piano so brilliantly. As a child, that was what she wanted to believe, even told herself that Annie Jo was just jealous, especially after she beat her in the talent show two years later.

Things were no different now. She was a grown woman, and people still ridiculed her. Just not to her face. Always some little remarks or whispers they'd think she didn't hear when her back was turned. Adults could be just as bad as children with their cruel words.

"Mary Faye."

She jumped. "Huh—ma'am?"

"Would you please bring in the newspaper?"

"Yes, ma'am." Mary Faye set her tea glass on a small metal table next to the swing. After getting the newspaper from the box on the street, she came back up the steps of the porch. Grabbing the screen door with one hand, she picked up the tea glass with the other. Mary Faye put the newspaper on a small table beside her father's chair.

"Honey, please pour out those peas for me."

"Yes, ma'am."

Mary Faye removed a bright red potholder from the second cabinet drawer beside the stove. She poured the peas into a green flowered Pyrex bowl, which she sat on the table.

"You know, I actually like these things better raw," said Mary Faye.

"Good way to eat a bug."

"Oh, momma." Mary Faye laughed. "They're so good when fresh and tender and uncooked."

"Well, those came out of a can."

"No bugs?"

"Oh, Mary Faye. Hush. Your daddy will think something is wrong with the peas."

"What's wrong with the peas?" Webb stepped into the kitchen.

"Well, ain't you one to sneak in?" Etolia teased.

"Sounds like I need to know what's wrong with the peas," he said.

"There's nothing wrong with the peas. Mary Faye was just saying she likes them raw."

"Might eat a worm that way," Webb said. He washed his hands under the warm water at the kitchen sink.

The two women laughed.

"We're not eating any bugs or worms tonight. You two

sit down." Etolia took the meatloaf from the oven. "Thought we could finish this off. If not, y'all can take it for lunch."

Mary Faye didn't want meatloaf three days in a row, but she nodded anyway.

They sat down to a supper of peas, mashed potatoes, meatloaf, and hot buttered rolls. Mary Faye liked her sweet tea, but Webb and Etolia enjoyed their hot coffee. At the end of the meal, Webb went into the living room. On the table, by his chair, a pipe lay in an ashtray. He took the pipe, filled it with Captain Black tobacco, then went back to the kitchen and once again sat down at the head of the table. Mary Faye removed the dishes and placed them in a sink of warm, sudsy water. Her hands were busy as her parents talked.

"I heard the craziest story today," Webb said.

"You did?" Etolia picked up her coffee cup, drank the last drops, then set it aside where Mary Faye could easily pick it up to wash. "What was it?"

"You remember Rusty Cole that worked over at Cooper-Wells Hosiery?"

"I never knew him, but I heard you mention him."

"I heard that his boy, Rusty Cole Jr...this is awful to say...but that boy of his performs abortions."

Etolia gasped. "How on earth! He's no doctor. Is he?"

"They don't have to be. Backroom or backstreet abortions is what I'm hearing. Done by people for money."

Webb drew on the pipe. Mary Faye picked up her mother's coffee cup and put it in the water.

"Mary Faye," Webb continued, "do you remember Rusty Jr? Were y'all in school together?"

"I remember seeing him, but I didn't really know him. He was in a grade above me."

"He's going to get himself in trouble, might end up in prison if he keeps doing abortions."

Etolia dropped her voice. "That's dangerous. There

was an article in the paper where a young woman died when she got an abortion. It wasn't around here…somewhere out west I believe. Don't see how on earth a woman could do that. Sinful. Just sinful."

The coffee cup fell from Mary Faye's hands and shattered on the linoleum.

Etolia jumped. Mary Faye muttered weakly, "I'm sorry." She bent down to pick up the pieces. "Ouch!"

"Are you okay, honey?" Etolia asked.

"Yes, ma'am. Just cut my finger."

"Be careful. Get the broom and sweep it up, so you don't hurt yourself."

Mary Faye got the broom, removed the broken cup, and then finished the dishes. Her parents continued to talk at the table. The conversation moved away from abortions and Rusty Cole. Mary Faye thought about her parents' words and her mother's reaction to anyone having an abortion. Momma would die if she knew her own daughter had laid in the arms of a married man.

-2-

All day long, Mary Faye never got the opportunity to talk to Adam. Maybe tomorrow. She rolled over on her stomach. The cool sheets felt good on her weary body. Today had been so frustrating. Those women at lunch were irritating, throwing around their remarks.

But were they even talking about her? Or did she just imagine it? Perhaps her own conscience fed her guilt? Maybe they were just talking. Women make crazy statements all the time. A guilty conscience can make your imagination run wild.

She sighed.

The first time Mary Faye had seen Adam, she was afraid of him. But it was his smile that had disarmed her. When he smiled, a tingle ran through her stomach. Her body started feeling things she didn't understand, and it had scared her...at first.

Sure, as a teenager, Mary Faye had her share of crushes, but never a boyfriend. Even in college, there had been no boyfriends. She might not be a beautiful woman, but not all women are pretty. Some women who are lacking in the looks department end up with handsome husbands. Some just knew how to attract men, get husbands, boyfriends, or even just friends. Yet, there was never anyone for Mary Faye. Never. Long ago, her piano and job had replaced the idea of a husband. Love can be in many forms, as her love for music, but it wasn't the same. The music of a piano can take you places, enable you to see the world as the pianist travels the world in concerts. Yes, music can open many doors, but a piano cannot hold you on winter nights, cannot kiss you, or smile gently into your own eyes.

Perhaps that's why Mary Faye had noticed Adam. It was as if being around him opened up an entirely new world for her. She had been as nervous as a sore-tailed cat in a roomful of rocking chairs. That old saying had never held any meaning to her until she met him.

When Adam had introduced himself, and Mary Faye said her name, he smiled. It was the prettiest smile she'd ever seen on a man. No words had ever passed between them to indicate that Adam was interested in Mary Faye until the day he deliberately touched her hand. Not one word was said, but their eyes locked. He saw it in her eyes. Quickly her gaze had dropped. A weakness spread throughout her body.

Oh, my.

From that day forward, a relationship began to blossom. They had so many things in common. Adam was always trying to introduce Mary Faye to new things. Simple things. Exciting things. Now everything had changed. No longer were they just friends. She was in love

for the first time in her life.
Yet...
Tears silently formed and ran down her cheeks. There were no sobs—just slow tears dropping on the rose flowered bedspread.

Chapter 25

March 21, 1967

The house was quiet when Mary Faye got home at 4:30. The day at work held a pleasant surprise when Adam told her he was going fishing later.
"Can you get away this evening?"
"I should be able to."
"Change your clothes, and walk toward the church, and I'll pick you up."
The idea excited her, unable to keep from smiling.
"Okay, what time?"
"5:15. Sun won't go down until about 6:30 or so."
Mary Faye nodded. She thought about it all afternoon.

What could she tell her mother? Piano practice again? Nothing else came to mind. She did have a wedding on Saturday. Yeah, that will work. She could practice for hours.

"Momma?" she called as soon as she hurried through the door. There was no answer. Mary Faye hurried to her bedroom. She put on a pair of navy pedal pushers, a pink blouse, white sneakers, and tied a ribbon in her hair.

Mary Faye took a deep breath. She was nervous and excited. This was the first time she had ever went anywhere with Adam in the daytime.

"Mary Faye?" her mother called from the kitchen. The back screen door slammed shut. "You home?"

Mary Faye gave herself one more glance in the mirror. She thought about putting on lipstick but decided against it. She might get it on his shirt.

"I'm here, momma." She hurried into the kitchen. "I called for you when I got home but didn't see you."

"I was out back." In her hand was a small bouquet of buttercups. They came from a large flowerbed near the white fence that separated the two yards. "Aren't these beautiful?"

Etolia removed a white milk glass vase from beneath the sink. She filled the vase with water and placed the flowers in it. "I guess I should have been cooking supper instead of picking flowers, but I was at the sink when I saw them and thought they'd look pretty on the table. Whatcha think?" Etolia fiddled with the flowers.

"I think they're pretty, and don't hurry with supper." She leaned down to one of them and sniffed the sweet scent.

Mary Faye straightened. "I think I better go to church and practice for the wedding."

Etolia peered at her daughter and noticed how she was dressed.

"You're going to change, aren't you? You think that's

going to be okay for church?"

"Momma, I'm not going to a church service. Just to practice."

"I know, but you're wearing shorts into the sanctuary."

"But momma…"

"I don't think you should wear shorts in the church."

"But, momma, they're not shorts. They are pedal pushers."

Etolia stared at her daughter a little longer. Finally, she responded. "All right, I guess it's okay."

"Sure, it is. No one else will be there."

"Okay, sweetie." Etolia sat the bouquet on the kitchen table. "Don't be too late."

"I won't. Got to practice a lot, though."

"Okay, but what about supper?"

Mary Faye checked the black cat clock on the kitchen wall. 4:50. Its long black tail counted off the minutes. She had to hurry.

"Don't worry. I'll eat when I get home."

Mary Faye hurried out of the room before Etolia could ask any more questions. She went out the front door and bounced down the front steps. She felt like a teenager going off on a date. Her path down Eighth Avenue was brisk. Mary Faye wasn't sure what time Adam would get there. He'd said 5:15. What if he couldn't get away? What if he had gotten there early before she could get there?

What if…

Mary Faye scanned the street. Where was he? She didn't want to leave Eighth Avenue or walk all the way to the church.

Then she saw him. Adam pulled up close to her and stopped. She opened the passenger door and got in. They turned and worked their way across town on side streets until they reached Somerville Road, following it past the country club. Soon they were out of the city limits heading to Upper River Road, then onto Mussle Camp Road.

Their conversation was light, simple, in the way that people are when they're comfortable with each other.

"This is my favorite fishing spot," he said moments before they pulled into the gravel clearing. As he parked the car, he continued, "You can't tell anyone about this place." His voice was teasing.

"Oh, I would never reveal your favorite fishing spot to anyone." It was as if they were serious in their conversation, sharing a secret place, but in truth they were, for no one could ever know they were there.

"C'mon." Mary Faye scooted across the seat, and followed him out of the car. Two fishing rods were removed from the trunk as well as a tackle box and minnow bucket.

"What kind of fishing are we doing?"

"Crappies. Best time of year to catch them."

She nodded as if she knew what he meant. To her, fish were fish.

They sat on the bank for hours, after which one largemouth bass and five crappies lay in the fish basket. It had been a very productive afternoon. The sun slipped downward across the river, creating a golden hue on the water and sky.

"Pretty, isn't it?" he said.

"Yes. I love your fishing spot. It is so quiet and peaceful here."

"I know—guess that's why I love it here."

They sat side by side holding hands, watching the sun and the rippling water. They didn't talk about the future but enjoyed one another's company now. Twilight enveloped them as they put the fishing gear and the fish into the trunk. Once they were inside the car, he pulled her into his arms. They made love in the front seat with the sound of the waves slapping the riverbanks and the crickets singing into the night.

Two and half hours later, he dropped her off at her

door. They figured that made more sense. Her parents would not be able to recognize his car in the dark. It was just a cab for all they knew.

Mary Faye ate a leftover meatloaf sandwich at the kitchen table. As she ate, her mind drifted away, reliving her first fishing trip.

-2-

"Don't mention this to anyone," said Paul.

Madolyn sat up in bed and peered at her husband through the gray darkness. She could easily see him as the light from a full moon filtered into the bedroom.

"What's wrong, dear?"

"Well...nothing."

"You're swearing me to secrecy over nothing?"

"No...it's because I don't know what to make of this."

Madolyn laid back down. "What?"

"I've been noticing Mary Faye at work..."

"And?"

"I hesitate to say this...but she's...well, she's been talking to this man at work."

"Man? Well, it's about time."

"You don't understand...well, it probably doesn't mean anything."

"Paul Hurst! What are you trying to say?"

"He's married."

"What?"

"Married. The man's married."

"Mary Faye and a married man? I can't believe that."

"I know—I know."

"Not a sweeter, better reputation than Mary Faye Hunter." Madolyn looked toward the window to the bright moon. Its brilliant glory was beautiful as if it had something magical about it, pulling you to it. Many lovers had fallen under the magic of a moonlit night. But Mary

Faye? A married man?

"Paul, are you sure?"

"No." He stared up at the ceiling. "Sometimes we notice her talking to this guy—kinda off to themselves. Sometimes laughing."

"That's it?"

"Yeah."

"Doesn't mean anything."

"I know. I've just never seen her act like that before, and that girl has been working there for over ten years."

"I'm sure it means nothing."

"I sure hope you're right."

The couple lay in silence for several minutes.

"Don't you think if there was anything to it, you'd see them leaving together or something?" Madolyn asked.

"Probably." Paul put his arm under his head. He didn't call any names, no point in that.

The full moon moved on across the sky as they fell into a peaceful sleep.

-3-

Never in their marriage had there been any real reason to think Adam had cheated on Martha. There was that one girl years ago who seemed to want to cling to him. He had at one time taught Sunday School to a group of high school seniors. There had been one girl that had puppy dog eyes for him. It was so bad that her mother came to their house. She wanted to know if Adam was aware that her daughter had a crush on him and that he needed to make sure he never encouraged her in any way.

"I don't believe you're that kind of man, but Dora can be kinda dippy when she thinks she's in love. You know how teenagers are when it comes to emotions. They get funny ideas in their heads."

"Of course, I would never encourage any young

woman. I am a happily married man."

"Oh yes, I believe you. You just never know what kind of silliness they will do."

Martha had never thought Adam cheated then or now, but sometimes there were things which didn't make sense. Squeaky shoes that really didn't squeak. Trips downtown on Saturdays. A haircut, but Adam had just gotten one two weeks prior. When he shopped for shirts or pants. Car parts.

Always alone. Gone for hours.

Even when she wanted to go with him to buy groceries at the A&P, he gave some strange excuse to go alone. When Adam had gotten home, he'd babysit while she went to the grocery store. It wasn't any one excuse, but all of them together.

Now today. Fishing in the middle of the week in March.

Could there be another woman?

She rolled over and slipped her arm around his stomach and snuggled up to his back. No woman was getting her husband.

* * *

In his sleep, Adam put his palm over Martha's hand and moved closer to her. He was dreaming. Some woman, he couldn't see her face, held out her hand toward him as she traversed a foggy path that was showered in golden lights. She drew closer and closer, her hand out, reaching for him. Adam's hand reached for hers and caught the small, delicate hand. Before he could see her face, she faded away.

Adam loosened his hold on Martha's hand.

Chapter 26

March 22, 1967

Mary Faye's breasts were sore. She had just vomited, and she was a week late. When Mary Faye raised her head from the commode, fear coursed through her body.

Pregnant? Maybe she wasn't. Maybe it was a stomach bug. Maybe her period was close and that's why her breasts were so sore. Maybe it was the excitement of being in love or she was stressed about the possibility of getting caught. But it couldn't be—mustn't be…pregnancy.

That's the one thing it couldn't be.

It would kill her parents.

No. No! She wasn't pregnant. They hadn't been together that often.

Only takes one time. The words boomeranged in her brain.

Mary Faye ran cold water in the bathroom sink. The white washcloth felt good on her hot face. She examined herself in the mirror. Her face was red, eyes burry, even her hair was slightly disarrayed. Her stomach was settling, but her weak knees seemed frail.

Mary Faye's last period had been February 16. She had

never had a reason to keep up with it until now.

She thought for a moment.

Mary Faye figured that she was almost a week late. They had made love on March 14, when they went fishing, but would she be sick at one week pregnant? Surely not. It had to be something else.

Mary Faye thought about March 2. That was the night she sneaked out of the house and met him after his VA meeting. They had made love while her parents thought she was in her own bed asleep—made love while his wife thought he was at a meeting—made love while the city of Decatur slept. They had been buried in each other's arms in an alley behind a closed Winn-Dixie Grocery store. Dark. Alone. They were together for only about thirty minutes.

Your sins will find you out. The thought flashed through her mind. A quote from the Bible.

"I can't be. Oh I can't be!"

What would I do if...

"Please God," she whispered. "Don't let me be pregnant."

Would God answer such a prayer?

The Bible says we reap what we sow. Was this the end results of her sin? Her punishment?

Mary Faye went into her bedroom. She made her bed, and then removed a white blouse and a blue skirt from her closet. She slipped her feet into beige flats. The red face was gone, but she was a pasty white. Makeup covered the pale face, and lipstick put the right amount of color on her numb lips, but neither removed her fears. No blush was used. Her cheeks didn't need any artificial color this morning.

"Mary Faye?" Her mother was outside her bedroom door. "Breakfast is ready." Etolia moved away from the door and returned to the kitchen.

"She okay?" Webb asked. He set his coffee cup on the saucer. A plate of scrambled eggs and bacon was in front of him. He reached for a biscuit. Etolia had always sent her family off to work with a full stomach.

"Oh, I'm sure. Sometimes it just takes a woman longer to dress."

Mary Faye came into the kitchen, sat down, and sipped the coffee her mother placed before her.

"Here you go, hon." Etolia offered her a plate of bacon and eggs.

The sight and the smell sent deep waves of nausea through Mary Faye's stomach, but she managed to control the urge to run back to the bathroom.

"No, ma'am. I'm not that hungry this morning."

Mary Faye wanted to push the plate away from her, but instead took another sip of black coffee. If only it would settle her stomach.

When the carpool drove her across the bridge that didn't help her stomach, but as they drew close to Redstone, Mary Faye felt somewhat better.

It has to be a virus. It has to be.

Maybe one of those 24-hour bugs. If it didn't clear up, she would go to the doctor.

Chapter 27

March 24, 1967 – Good Friday

Mary Faye could not see Adam this weekend. She was sad when she left the office on Friday afternoon. May Faye had a wedding on Saturday, which meant she had a rehearsal on Friday night as well. The groom's family was taking the wedding party out to eat afterward, and she had been invited. If Adam had been able to get away, she would have skipped the dinner and met him somewhere, but he couldn't. Too big of a risk he had told her. People planning Easter events, her with a wedding, and too many people moving around town overall. She knew it was risky.

But still…

"You got big plans tonight, Mary Faye?" Rick Overton asked.

"Well, I don't know if you'd call them big," she chuckled, "but I'm playing at a wedding, and tonight is the rehearsal."

"Sounds like another busy weekend," Paul Hurst said.

"Yes, sir. Lots of planning goes into a wedding."

They drove away from Huntsville toward Decatur.

"Well, I'm going fishing, "Almon Hensley said.

Mary Faye turned to face him. "What kind? Crappie?"

The comment surprised the older man. He never knew Mary Faye had been interested in fishing. "Didn't know you fish, Mary Faye."

She had said too much.

"Oh no, sir. I…I don't." Her mind searched for an answer. "I heard some people talking about fishing last week or so, and that's what they were saying. My daddy used to fish a little when I was younger. I think…I think it was crappie, but for all I know I could be wrong."

Shut up, Mary Faye.

"Crappies a good fish," Almon said. "Paul, it's my week to drive next week, isn't it?"

Just like that, the subject of fishing was dropped, and the men discussed weather and work. Mary Faye was quiet until Rick's commented on baseball. It was a safe subject, one she knew and enjoyed.

-2-

March 25, 1967 11:25 am

Mary Faye left the House of Beauty on Grant Street and headed toward Dr. Carter's office. He saw patients until noon on Saturdays. Again that morning, Mary Faye had awoken feeling nauseous. She still had not started her period, but remained hopeful that the symptoms could be attributed to a lingering stomach virus.

"No, Mary Faye," Dr. Carter said, "You don't have a virus."

"What is it then?" She sat in an examining room at his office on Bank Street.

"Have you eaten any strange foods?"
Possible food poisoning?
"No."

"Mary Faye, I don't want to say this, not even suggest it, but..."

"What is it? Am I dying? Is it some horrible disease?"

"Well, it has been known to be contagious."

"What?"

"Mary Faye, I know you're not pregnant, but have you been around a lot of women who are pregnant? Women see pregnant friends, then they end up pregnant too."

Dr. Carter was trying to be light-hearted, but it didn't work. He had worded it all wrong.

"Are you saying I'm pregnant?"

"Oh, no. Of course, not. I'm saying you have all the symptoms."

Tears formed in her eyes. Fear clutched her heart. "I can't be."

Dr. Carter patted her hand.

"No, hon. I'm not saying that. Sometimes a woman will have symptoms but not be pregnant. It's called pseudocyesis. Missed period, swollen stomach, enlarged and tender breasts. Some women actually believe they feel the movement of a baby."

Mary Faye wanted to give a sigh of relief but feared the doctor might suspect that she had a good reason to think that she was.

"I could draw some blood. Probably just your hormones."

Would it reveal that she was sexually active?

"I don't really have time for blood work today. Just thought it might be a bug. Been feeling kinda tired, and all. She stepped down from the examining table.

"You sure?"

"Yes, sir. I'm sure."

"Okay, but if you don't get better, let me know. We'll

pull that blood and find out what's wrong."

"I will."

Mary Faye left the office and walked home. Should she have told him the truth?

No.

There was only one person Mary Faye wanted to discuss this with, but there was no way she could call him. She wouldn't see him until Monday, but couldn't tell him something like this at work.

Mary Faye followed the sidewalk down Grant Street toward Sixth Avenue and made her way back home. She thought about how to tell Adam and decide what she was going to do if she was pregnant.

But maybe, just maybe, I'm not pregnant.

What was that word the doctor had used? Pseudo...something. False pregnancy. Maybe that's what it is. She had been nervous about sneaking around with Adam, and the guilt. Yeah. That could be it — just symptoms of pregnancy.

I'm not going to worry about it anymore. Maybe then I'll have my period.

Mary Faye didn't realize it, but she had spoken the words out loud, so faint that even if there had been someone around her, they would not have heard her. But the sidewalk was empty, except for the young woman who walked alone from the doctor's office.

-3-

March 25, 1967 - 4:45 pm

When Mary Faye entered the church, a member of the bride's family called out to her.

"Mary Faye!"

She turned to the voice, but quickly shielded her face when she realized the person was photographing her. Mary

Faye had on a new dress, and her hair had been freshly set that morning, but it embarrassed her when someone pointed a camera at her. Pictures. That was not her strong point. Every time a camera came into play, so did her smile.

She hated her smile.

Mary Faye sat down at the piano in front of the church. People were buzzing around like butterflies as they came in, talking, laughing, and producing the sound of unrecognizable chatter. The music filled the sanctuary. Some of the voices settled, while others continued to buzz. Mary Faye's control over the notes dominated the room.

Then she struck the key that introduced the bride. Everyone immediately stood, as if the queen had entered the room. And on this day, the wedding day, the bride was the queen. She was the guest of honor.

For as long as she could remember, Mary Faye had dreamed about walking down the aisle as a bride. Mary Faye was known to be content with her job, church, and her music, but no one knew about her deepest desires.

The tears on my pillow. The longing for a husband.

Since no one had ever asked her out, the last thing she had wanted known was her heart's desire to be courted. But Mary Faye was considered middle age now. Or at least, close to it.

Mary Faye figured that most people probably thought she had never been lonely because she lived with her parents. When she observed her parents laughing, talking, and sharing tender moments, it reminded Mary Faye of how wonderful it would be to be married. It also reminded her of something else. She was alone.

Regardless of how Mary Faye felt with Adam in her life, at the end of the day, she was still alone. She loved him with all her being, but where could the relationship go? They had never discussed it.

Mary Faye's fingers swept over the keys effortlessly. Her whole life had been one long practice session to be able to perform with such grace. Mary Faye imagined that everyone thought of her as an old maid who preferred the piano over anything else. Those Christian friends would die of shock if they knew Mary Faye had lain in the arms of a married man just a few days ago.

She smiled. That gave her some satisfaction. Mary Faye wasn't a virgin anymore. She now knew the love of a man. The amusement pulled the smile bolder.

"You can tell Mary Faye loves her music," whispered a woman in the audience to her husband. "Look at that smile."

The smile disappeared as Mary Faye thought about the doctor visit. Adam's baby could be lying inside her.

The bride slowly moved down the aisle, coming to a stop in front of the groom, bridesmaids, groomsmen, and the preacher. The music softly faded.

"Who gives this woman?" asked the preacher.

Vows were said, songs sung, music played, candles lit, flowers given to the mothers, and just like that, the bride and groom were no longer single but married to each other till death do them part. Unless they later divorced. Either way, their lives were now changed forever.

Mary Faye struck the ivory keys, bringing everyone to their feet as the bride and groom, smiling as if they had won the golden ring of life, retreated up the aisle.

It would be fantastic, thought Mary Faye as she played the wedding march. To be married to the man you loved. Oh, if only she could.

The couple left the church, and the guests moved out into the bold sunlight. Everyone cheered as the couple ran along the sidewalk to the reception hall while the photographer snapped photos. Mary Faye stood on the church steps and watched the scene unfold.

"Mary Faye." The bride's mother approached her. "You did such a wonderful job." Mary Faye smiled. "Here's a little something for you."

She handed Mary Faye a check for two hundred dollars.

"I know it's more than we agreed on, but don't argue with me about it. You did such a great job." She gave Mary Faye a quick kiss on the cheek. "I love you, hon."

Before Mary Faye could respond, the woman quickly went down the steps to follow the couple to the back of the church. Next week the check would be cashed, and half of it placed into the offering plate the following Sunday. A routine that her parents had insisted was the right thing to do.

* * *

"How was the wedding?" Etolia asked as Mary Faye entered through the front door.

"It was beautiful, as always. I don't think I've ever seen that many flowers before. The wedding cake was huge, and the food was good." She laid her jacket on the back of the rocker.

"I should have gone with you," said Etolia. I love weddings. Beautiful day for one too. Can you believe tomorrow is Easter? Your brother called. He said they would be here in time to go to church with us tomorrow. I told him to meet us there and that your daddy would be out front waiting for them."

"Glad they're coming up."

Mary Faye thought about telling her brother about Adam but had never gotten up the nerve. What would Jimmy think of her? His sweet sister involved with a married man. No, she had to keep it a secret. Jimmy might be her best friend, worldlier than she, but what would he think of her if he knew?

Probably the same thing anyone else would.

Mary Faye feared that Jimmy would lecture about her reputation, their parents, and the church. But now she had another fear. Mary Faye needed to know if Jimmy would help her. Tell her if she was pregnant. And if she was, tell her that he would help her get rid of it. It sounded so cold.

Just get rid of it.

But Mary Faye had no choice. It wasn't just for her. Her parents would die from shame. The community regarded her as a fine Christian lady of the church — a role model. Her family, the church, and half of Decatur thought Mary Faye Hunter was above the sinful world...someone who could never succumb to worldly lust or greed like so many others. How often did she hear those words?

Mary Faye, you are such a wonderful God-fearing woman.

She was God-fearing all right, but she loved Adam more than she ever thought it was possible to love a man. She now understood how a woman could get herself in such a predicament.

"Mary Faye, I said, did you see any of her wedding gifts?"

"No, ma'am. I left before everything was over. The table was piled high, though. I heard someone say the bride wanted to open them after they came back from their honeymoon."

"That'll give them the chance to enjoy everything they got."

"Yes, ma'am."

Mary Faye went into the kitchen for a glass of tea. She returned to the living room and sat down on the sofa as her little dog, Mac, jumped up beside her. Mary Faye patted Mac's head and hugged her.

She needed a hug.

-3-

Never in his life would Adam have thought he would be one of those men. A wife and family at home. A lover at work. He had gone to church all of his life. Sometimes the guilt ate at him so much that he thought about confessing everything to his wife and telling Mary Faye it was over. But Adam couldn't do that to Mary Faye.

He loved her.

Adam also loved his wife. She was the mother of his children. He couldn't just abandon his family. But Mary Faye was so sweet, tender, and innocent. She had been a 33-year-old virgin. Both women were now in his life. He would have to learn to live with the guilt.

Adam sat on the back porch in the warm sun. Tomorrow was Easter. He would be with his family, and Mary Faye with hers. Monday they would once again see each other. Whenever they could, they would steal glances. A smile or wink. Anything.

Chapter 28

March 26, 1967 – Easter

"Just as I am, and waiting not to rid my soul of one dark blot, to thee whose blood can cleanse each spot, O Lamb of God, I come, I come," the congregation sang, as Mary Faye played Just As I am at the end of the service. Tears touched her eyes as she whispered to God.
I have sinned against You. Please forgive me.
Mary Faye did not want the tears, but her heart was so heavy with sorrow. What made it worse was the knowledge that she would continue to sin, for the sake of love.
I'm an adulteress.
Mary Faye knew the Bible. Christians knew that the word of God taught that whatsoever is sown will be reaped. Her sins were displayed in front of her, yet when Mary Faye was with Adam, nothing mattered but loving him, being with him, hearing his words of love for her. A lone tear fell from Mary Faye's left eye onto her hand as it swept across the piano.
When the song ended, Mary Faye glanced at the song leader as he turned the service back over to Pastor Van Arsdale, who closed with a prayer.

How could God forgive Mary Faye when He knew that on Tuesday night she would be with Adam again?

After church, the Hunters sat around the dining room table enjoying the meal Etolia had prepared. Later, the women cleared the table while the men and children were in the living room. Webb sat in his chair, Jimmy on the sofa, and the children were on the floor playing. Mary Faye tagged Jimmy's leg as she passed him. Jimmy followed her to the porch.

They sat on the swing. As kids, they had often sat on this same swing and played games together. They had always been close. As adults, they were still close even though Jimmy had his own family now and lived in Birmingham.

He was Mary Faye's best friend. There were no other friends to share secrets with or anything that was going on in her life.

Her brother was the opposite of her. Jimmy stood at over six feet, with a nice smile and handsome features. He had been the pretty baby. It seemed as if Jimmy grew more attractive with age. Mary Faye had never thought of herself as being pretty or having a lovely figure until Adam had complimented her. He told her that she had beautiful legs. Sometimes she would lay in bed at night and hold up her legs to inspect them. It surprised Mary Faye when she realized that Adam was right. Her legs were firm and well-sculpted from years of walking through downtown Decatur.

Jimmy gently pushed the swing with his foot. He knew something was wrong when Mary Faye led him to the porch. For a minute, they sat silently.

"What's wrong?" asked Jimmy.

She stared at his foot moving the swing. "Nothing really, it's just I know this woman, and she thinks she might be pregnant."

"Who is it?"

"Just some woman I know. She works at the Arsenal."

The swing stopped.

Mary Faye searched Jimmy's eyes for the friend she desperately needed.

His eyes narrowed. "Is she married?"

"Yes, she's married. The problem is her husband doesn't want any more children."

"Seems to me he should have thought about that before he got her pregnant."

"Well, she's not sure that she is pregnant."

"You say this is a friend of yours?"

"Yes, at work. Like I said, we were just talking, and she said that she might be pregnant and was having some of the symptoms and—"

"She should know the symptoms by now."

"Well, she isn't sure. She told me the symptoms aren't always the same. How would she know for sure?"

Do I sound suspicious?

"This is what's going on," said Mary Faye. "She told me she was about a week or so late, and she was afraid she might be pregnant."

"Just a week? That doesn't mean she's pregnant."

"She said she's been throwing up a lot, breasts tender, that kind of thing."

"Sounds like it to me. Or she could be having what is called false pregnancy. That does happen. If she is pregnant, her husband will just have to accept the responsibility. Why is she so worried?" Jimmy thought for a moment. "Unless she thinks that the baby isn't his."

"Oh, no, no. It's nothing like that."

Mary Faye thought for a moment. Actually, that angle might work — a reason for a woman to be upset about the pregnancy.

"Now that I think about it," said Mary Faye, "you might be on to something."

"Who is she?"

Mary Faye did not want to give Jimmy a name. There

was no need for that.

"It doesn't matter." She looked away. "Are there any ways to know for sure?"

He laughed. "Yeah, she'll know for sure in just a few more weeks. That's something you can't keep hidden."

That was the problem.

"Mary Faye, just who is this woman? If she's running around on her husband and having some other man's baby, I don't think momma would want you hanging around that kind of person."

"I'm not really hanging around with her. We just talk at work. You know how that is."

Jimmy nodded. He still didn't like what he was hearing. His sister was a good person, but she was also naive. She didn't need to be around this woman, whoever she was.

* * *

Etolia watched Jimmy and Mary Faye through the living room window. What were they talking about? They looked so serious. Etolia wanted to go out there, but when she looked toward Webb, he shook his head.

* * *

Mary Faye's foot pushed the swing. If she kept talking about the unknown woman, Jimmy might ask too many questions. But there was something that she had to ask him.

"If she decides not to have this baby, do you know of anyone who could help her?"

He didn't respond.

"Jimmy?"

"What are you asking, Mary Faye?"

"You know. Help her…get rid of it."

"You mean adoption?"

"No. I mean...abortion." Again she lifted her eyes to his. Searching.

He shook his head. "No, I don't, Mary Faye. I promised to protect lives, not end them."

"Do you know of anyone who would?"

"No." He shook his head again. The swing stopped.

"To be honest, I'm shocked you would ask me that. I know how strong your Christian beliefs are, and even to suggest for someone to have an abortion really surprises me."

"She just seemed desperate. Afraid, you know."

"Maybe her husband will get over it once he gets used to the idea."

Mary Faye didn't respond.

Jimmy stared across the front yard. He and Mary Faye had always gotten along and supported each other. Even when their parents got on to them for something, it was never because of fighting. Sure they had argued sometimes, but they hadn't fought like a lot of siblings.

Jimmy stood. He clutched Mary Faye's hand, and pulled her up from the swing. His strong arms embraced her.

"You may be two years older, but you're still my kid sister, and I love you. Just tell your friend that the best thing she can do is tell her husband. They can give the baby up for adoption if they decide they don't want it. Okay?"

Mary Faye nodded against his shoulder.

"You know," he said, "the Easter that stands out in my mind more than any other was when I was ten."

Mary Faye looked up at him and laughed.

"Oh, I remember that day too. It was on Good Friday. You chased me all the way home from school."

"Yes, I did." He laughed. "I was so mad. The night before, you asked momma if we could dye our own eggs, saying that you knew how."

"Well, I did."

"Yeah, but when momma said to boil them, she meant longer than just getting them soft boiled. I thought I was going to die when that boy...What was his name? I don't know, but to this day I remember him yelling, 'Hey! This egg ain't done!' I looked at him, and he had yolk spilling out of an egg he had peeled. It was all over his desk, and I recognized that dye job. It was one of ours. I looked away and didn't say a word. The teacher told everyone to put away their eggs. She had to wipe up the mess on that kid's desk. 'Put all the eggs away!' she kept saying. That is one egg hunt I will never forget."

Mary Faye was laughing as he retold the story.

"Yes, and by the time we got home," said Mary Faye, "we decided not to tell momma because she would never let us boil eggs again."

"I think today is a good day to confess," he chuckled.

Jimmy opened the screen door. "Momma," he said, "You know what Mary Faye did to me when we were kids..."

Jimmy repeated the story, and the Hunter family laughed hysterically. For the rest of the afternoon, Mary Faye forgot about her problems.

Chapter 29

April 6, 1967

Mary Faye went into her bedroom and put on a light sweater. Her parents had just gone to bed. They would never know that she left. They trusted her. It would never enter their minds that she would sneak out to meet someone.

Shortly after 9:00, Adam picked up Mary Faye two blocks from her house. They drove out to the Wheeler Wildlife Refuge. Established in 1938, five years after Mary Faye was born, the Refuge covered over 34,000 acres. It was a habitat for wintering and migrating birds, but it also had many dirt roads that led to the river. People came to see birds, fish, while others enjoyed the privacy of being with a lover.

Tonight, Mary Faye and Adam were not interested in fishing.

She didn't know how to tell him, so the words just came tumbling out of her mouth as soon as he parked. "I'm late, and I think I'm…pregnant."

Adam turned to face her. For a moment he didn't say anything. Then he stared through the windshield.

"Are you sure?" he asked without looking at her.

"I think I am. I went to the doctor because I thought I might have a virus. I was afraid to tell you."

Adam turned to Mary Faye. "No, baby, never be afraid to tell me anything." He touched her face gently. "What did the doctor say?"

"He said it might be a false pregnancy, but I didn't tell him the whole truth."

"You didn't tell him about us?"

"No." She looked down. "That's why he thinks I can't be pregnant, but I'm at least two weeks late. That's not like me."

Adam nodded and then pulled Mary Faye to him.

"Listen to me. Until the doctor says you're pregnant, we won't worry about it. Worrying can cause you to be late. Sneaking around with me has to be stressful. I know that's not the kind of woman you are." He kissed her forehead. "Until we know for sure, we won't worry, okay."

It didn't make her feel any better, but he was right. Until they knew for sure...

Adam kissed Mary Faye again, and her arms went around his neck, then his chest.

"C'mon," Adam whispered. He led her to the backseat. They made love for several minutes. It was exactly the kind of release that she needed. Mary Faye laid on top of him and rested her head on his chest.

"And if I am pregnant?"

"We won't worry about that right now," Adam said as he stroked her hair. He kissed her hand and smiled.

Mary Faye could tell that Adam was scared. He was trying to be brave and did not want to make her worry even more. She was relieved that he had not gotten angry, or at least did not show it. She loved him for that.

At 9:40, Mary Faye entered her home through the front door. Her mother was standing in the middle of the living room with a glass of water.

"You have a nice walk?"

Mary Faye jumped and placed her hand on her heart.

"Oh momma, you scared me!" Mary Faye regained her composure and laughed nervously. "Yes. The evening air was nice."

Should she say something as to why she was out walking? Was her mother suspicious? No, she had to play this casual.

"I hope I didn't disturb you."

"No, hon, I just got up for a glass of water, and I heard you opening the front door."

Should have come in through my bedroom door.

"Just wanted to make sure my baby girl was home safe. Surprised you were out walking this late. You really shouldn't be out this time of night. Could be dangerous."

"Yes, ma'am, I know. I'm gonna get to bed."

Etolia approached her daughter and placed a light kiss on the top of her head. She stood four inches taller than Mary Faye's five feet, two inches.

"I love you, baby. You get some rest. Morning and work will be here before you know it." Etolia returned to her bedroom.

Mary Faye got into bed, but sleep didn't come quickly. Adam said not to worry, but she couldn't help it. The first time they had made love, it never entered her mind that she might get pregnant. In January, her period came around just like always. Each time they were together, it was a gamble, but nothing went wrong in February either. But here she was…it's April, and Mary Faye was two weeks late. Tears rolled down the side of one cheek. Again, she thought about the Bible verse, Your sin will surely find you out.

Please, God. Please forgive me.

Mary Faye didn't drink, smoke, cuss, tell dirty jokes, or laugh when people did. She played the piano and organ for the church, gave her tithes, and loved God. Her reputation had been spotless. By God's Law, she was now an adulteress. If she kept the baby, everyone would know. People might even discover that Adam was the father. So many innocent people would suffer because of her sin. If Mary Faye was pregnant, she could not have the baby. She knew that much.

"Please, God," she whispered. "Please forgive me for what I have done and for what I am about to do. Please."

That night, Mary Faye cried herself to sleep.

Chapter 30

April 12, 1967

Martha Fletcher poured a cup of coffee for her husband. "How do you want your eggs?"

"Over easy," said Adam.

Over easy. Always over easy.

You'd think some morning he'd want the eggs scrambled, or maybe just toast and coffee like they do in the movies. "Or maybe a sweet roll."

"What?" he said.

"Oh, nothing." She broke the eggs into the iron skillet along with three pieces of bacon.

Martha placed juice, toast, and coffee on the table. When the eggs and bacon were ready, she put the food on a plate and placed it in front of him.

Adam suddenly sprung out of his chair.

"I'm sorry." He kissed her on her cheek. "I've got to go. I didn't realize it was so late." He shoved a piece of bacon into his mouth and then tore off a piece of toast and pushed it into his mouth as he swallowed the bacon.

Adam removed his hat from the coat rack by the front door. "I'll see you this evening," he called.

Martha stared at the food. She wanted to throw it at the front door, but what good would it do? She didn't understand what was wrong with him. He barely ate any supper last night — only a couple of bites of breakfast.

She glanced at the wall clock. Adam wasn't running behind. What's going on with him?

"Momma," said the small boy who stood by her.

"Come here, baby. You ready for breakfast?" Seven-year-old Billy moved to his mother and put his arms around her waist. She kissed the top of his head and walked to the counter to prepare a bowl of cereal. As Martha poured the milk, the boy snatched the remaining bacon from his daddy's plate.

-2-

Bumper to bumper traffic lined Highway 31. A lot of people worked in Huntsville and Redstone Arsenal. There were many government jobs with great pay, benefits, and retirement. Redstone Arsenal was the reason Adam had moved to Decatur from Anniston. He needed a better job and a better life. The job was okay, but life really hadn't gotten better. Just more complicated.

A red light caught Adam at the edge of the river bridge. Before it changed, he glanced at the car beside him. Paul Hurst was at the wheel. Four or five others were in the car with him, and in the far back corner, sat Mary Faye Hunter. She was looking the other way.

* * *

Mary Faye didn't see Adam. She still didn't feel well. This morning she felt like throwing up again when she brushed her teeth. Breakfast had been out of the question. She let her mind drift back to the years of her youth. Life had been so much simpler then. The only thing that really mattered then was her music.

"A gift from God," Mrs. Rollo had told her.

Mrs. Rollo had been Mary Faye's piano instructor during her childhood years. She had praised Mary Faye's talent and encouraged her to keep playing. Even after she left Decatur, Mrs. Rollo had occasionally telephoned and spoke kind words to her. Mary Faye's next instructor, Mrs. Fairer, had been amazed at her ability to play the piano.

"Never give up your music, Mary Faye," Mrs. Fairer had said. "It is the one thing no one can ever take from you."

When Mary Faye had placed her advertisement about teaching piano lessons in the newspaper, she also pointed out that she had been a student of Dr. Dorsey Whittington of the Birmingham Conservatory of Music.

Those years had been wonderful. Music. Her gift from God. Almost as if He gave her music to make up for everything else. At least that's how it seemed to Mary Faye.

"Mary Faye, you gonna sit in the car all day?"

"Huh?"

Mary Faye looked around. They were already in the Arsenal parking lot.

She blushed. "No. I don't guess so." She pushed back the car door and got out of the back seat.

The day was bright and beautiful. Birds perched on a powerline whistled. With her lunch bag in one hand, her purse in the other, Mary Faye hobbled toward the office building.

* * *

Rick Overton walked by Mary Faye. He had carpooled with her for a long time, yet he did not really know her. She usually didn't speak unless spoken to, didn't laugh much, and always seemed as if she was more interested in observing people than engaging them.

Rick liked Mary Faye. They were both single. He would have asked her out if he thought she would say yes. Rick also liked to observe people.

Mary Faye did not realize that her relationship with Adam wasn't completely a secret anymore.

-3-

April 22, 1967

Mary Faye sat in an examination room at Dr. Carter's office. She was over two months late.

"Not feeling any better?" asked Dr. Carter.

"No, sir." Her voice was weak and frightened.

"Well, we'll find out what's wrong."

"I have to know...No one else will know what you find out, will they?"

"No one has access to your files outside of this office."

Her voice shook as she spoke. "Please don't put anything in my file about this."

"My goodness, Mary Faye. What's wrong?"

"Promise me."

"All right." Mary Faye had been his patient for years. Never had he seen her behave this way.

"I think I'm pregnant."

"What?"

The facial expression or sound of Dr. Carter's voice did not hide his shock. He soon regained his composure.

"Mary Faye, we have already been over this. You can't be pregnant if you're not sexually active." His eyes bored into hers. "I don't know why you have the symptoms, but..."

"Because I—" She looked away. "Please don't judge me. Just tell me if I'm pregnant or not. Please."

"I would never judge you or anyone else. We'll find

out, and if you are, that will be our secret. No paperwork or no notes will be filed."

She nodded. Sweat beaded across her forehead.

Mary Faye climbed onto the examination table. Several minutes later, Dr. Carter removed his gloves.

"All right," he said as he deposited the gloves into the trash can.

Dr. Carter turned to Mary Faye. She pulled the gown closer to her body and could not bring her eyes to meet his. Instead, she focused on his mouth, waiting for his words.

"About two months, give or take a few days, but probably around two months."

She gasped.

"What happened, Mary Faye? Did someone force you?" Tears streamed down her face. She shook her head and mouthed an inaudible: No.

"Okay, listen. You have three choices."

"Three?"

"Any chance you and the baby's father are getting married?"

Mary Faye shook her head.

"You can keep the baby…"

"No! My parents would die if they knew."

"You could leave town, have the baby, and give it up for adoption."

Mary Faye stared into space as she digested the words. Finally, she said, "And the third choice would be abortion?"

"Yes."

Mary Faye couldn't leave town. Her parents would want to know where she was. And what about work? People would know. She would be the old maid who got pregnant and had to leave. She would be the gossip of the whole town. The shame would kill her parents.

"Can you do that? An abortion?" she meekly asked.

"Mary Faye, I can't. If I got caught, I would lose my

practice. I can't take that kind of risk."

"My parents will never forgive me." She buried her face in her hands and wept. "Please help me." Her shoulders shook as she sobbed.

"Mary Faye, please." Dr. Carter patted her shoulder. "What about your brother? He's a doctor. Maybe he could help."

"I don't know."

"He might know someone, but if he doesn't, I do." Her tear-soaked face looked up at him.

"I'll call him when I get home. But if he doesn't help me, who do you know that can?"

"Don't worry about that. I'll set everything up."

Mary Faye sniffed. "Okay," her voice choked back tears. "I'm so scared."

"I know. It's going to be fine." Dr. Carter patted her hand. "You come see me next Saturday, or I could call you —"

"No! Don't call me." Her mother might pick up the phone at home and wonder why the doctor was calling her. "I'll come here next Saturday."

"All right. Be here at noon."

"Oh, thank you so much, Dr. Carter."

Mary Faye left the office and began her walk home. She didn't want to take a cab. She needed time to think.

"Momma," Mary Faye said as she walked through the front door. Her mother was sitting on the sofa with a Sunday School book and pen in her hand. A Bible was in her lap. She was preparing a lesson for the next day.

"I've decided to ride the bus to Birmingham to spend the night at Jimmy's."

"Well, that's kinda sudden, ain't it?"

"It'll be fine. I could go to church with them. It'll give me a chance to spend more time with my little nieces."

"Well, okay. Go call him, so he'll know that you're coming."

"Okay."

"And you'll need to get someone to play the piano for you in the morning."

"Yes, ma'am," Mary Faye replied as she took her things to her bedroom and started to pack.

-4-

At 3:15 pm, Mary Faye was on a Greyhound in route to Birmingham. The trip would take a little over two hours. Birmingham was known as The Magic City because of its fast growth and ultimately became the largest city in Alabama. Mary Faye knew the area well because she had lived there for two years in the early 1950s as a student at Birmingham Southern. She had visited her brother before, but today she was terrified. Mary Faye prayed that Jimmy would help her. The idea of a stranger touching her was disturbing.

Jimmy Hunter watched his sister step out of the cab in front of his house. In her hand was a small overnight bag. He hurried out to meet her, pulling money from his pocket to pay the taxi driver. He captured the overnight bag from her hand. "C'mon in," he said as they sauntered up the sidewalk.

Mary Faye slipped her arm around her younger brother. Hopefully, when Jimmy realized how desperate she was, he would help her, whether he performed the abortion himself or brought in one of his doctor friends.

When they reached the porch, Mary Faye turned to him. "I love you, Jimmy."

He squeezed her shoulder.

"And I love you too. C'mon in."

Jimmy held the screen door as Mary Faye entered into the house. Her nieces ran to greet her, as well as Jimmy's wife, Sally.

"Mary Faye, it's so good to see you," said Sally.

They sat down and began to talk, as the nieces clung to Mary Faye's neck. The conversation covered many subjects, but the one area that wasn't mentioned was Mary Faye's pregnancy. It would have to wait.

Soon after supper, Jimmy sent the children to bed. Sally Hunter regarded Mary Faye tenderly. She loved her sister-in-law. She also knew that Mary Faye didn't come to Birmingham often for a visit and would want time alone with her brother. Sally understood that they had always been extremely close. Jimmy told her that as children, he had always protected Mary Faye if any of the other children were mean to her.

Jimmy had always been a source of encouragement for Mary Faye, whether it was her music or her job. The one area that he could not impact was her social life. It was as if Mary Faye was content to live her life as a single, working woman. She didn't discuss relationships. She had never even had a boyfriend.

"Mary Faye, I'm tired and think I will go on to bed," said Sally. "The guest room is ready, so feel free to make yourself at home. I'm sure Jimmy will want to talk half the night. You know how he is." Sally leaned over and kissed her husband's cheek.

"Goodnight, Sally," said Mary Faye.

Yes, she needed to talk to Jimmy, but not the carefree conversations of the past. She waited until the bedroom door had closed. Even with the door closed, Mary Faye feared her voice would carry, and Sally might overhear her dreaded words.

"I need to talk to you. That woman at the Arsenal—"

"Mary Faye, I don't know why you're so obsessed with that woman. She's—"

"She's me."

Jimmy stared at her. He was speechless.

"Did you hear me, Jimmy? She's me."

"You're pregnant?" Jimmy finally said, staring at her

in disbelief.

"Yes," Mary Faye whispered. She swallowed. The lump in her throat swelled. She swallowed again. "I'm so afraid."

"But…you can't be pregnant."

"I am. I went to the doctor."

Jimmy stood up and paced the room.

"Who is the father?"

"Shhh! Keep your voice down."

Jimmy glanced over his shoulder. The bedroom door was still closed.

"I can't tell you. It won't change anything."

"No, but I'd like to punch him in the face."

"That wouldn't change anything either."

"It would make me feel better. Did he rape you?"

"No."

Jimmy pounded the arm of the chair with his hand.

"Who is he? Why won't he marry you?"

"He can't. Wouldn't matter. People would still know I'm pregnant. It would kill momma and daddy." Her gaze dropped to her hands. A large tear fell onto her right hand. With one hand, Mary Faye wiped the tears from her face. She met her brother's eyes.

"Everyone would know the church pianist had to get married. The gossip would destroy momma and daddy. Their old maid daughter had a shotgun wedding." She sniffed. The tears would not stay at bay. They spilled onto her hands again.

"I can't believe this is happening. So, this guy just walks away without any punishment while you go through this alone?"

"No, he's not just walking away without suffering through this. He's worried about me. He doesn't want to do this, but he had no choice."

"I bet he has his kids too, doesn't he? How many times did he say he could never leave her and the children?"

Mary Faye dropped her eyes again. Only once, she thought to herself, only once. But there was no point in saying that. She didn't want Jimmy to think bad about Adam. It wasn't just his fault.

"Jimmy, he's not a bad man. It just happened. I love him. I never thought of it as an affair. An affair is what people do that move from one lover to the next. It's not like that. I never realized how deeply a woman could love a man and how easy something like this could happen. I know he loves me. He would have married me in the beginning if he had been free, but there was no way he can leave his wife." She wiped her face again. "None of that matters now."

It was time to ask the question Mary Faye had come to Birmingham to ask.

"Will you help me, Jimmy? You know I can't have this baby. I can't live through the shame, risk my job, and his job. Worst of all...see the look on momma's and daddy's face when they find out I'm pregnant. I can't." She looked down again. "I just want to know if you will help me."

"How?"

"I can't have this baby."

Jimmy didn't respond.

"Please."

"What are you asking, Mary Faye?"

"Abortion."

He shook his head. "No. I can't do that, Mary Faye."

"But I can't have this baby."

He shook his head again. "I can't."

Jimmy sighed heavily. As much as he loved his sister, he could not murder a baby. He could not forsake his oath to save a life, not destroy it. He could not break that oath.

Jimmy looked away, glanced at the pictures of his daughters sitting on the table by the sofa. He could not take a life.

"Jimmy, will you think about it tonight before you give

me an answer. Maybe you can see where I'm coming from, understand my predicament. If I could, I'd just run away..."

"No, you can't run away. Think about momma and daddy."

"Oh, no, Jimmy, I wouldn't do that. I just mean if I could. I'm scared. Never had a problem that only seemed to have one solution. It's not a matter of right or wrong. God in heaven knows I've already done everything wrong."

Mary Faye's voice trembled. Her shoulders shook with heavy sobs. Jimmy draped his arms around her. She buried her face on his shoulder and wept.

He kissed the top of her head, patted her back, but Dr. James Webb Hunter already knew he would not help his sister kill this baby. It had nothing to do with love, worry, concern, or even his parents. It had everything to do with the oath he had taken. He could not break that. If he broke it, would it be okay to break it again for someone else? If an oath is broken, does it annul the vow completely from that day forward? He didn't expect Mary Faye to understand any more than he could understand why she allowed herself to be in this situation in the first place. What about all the rules she had lived by her entire life? Did that mean anything now?

As if she could read his thoughts, she whispered softly into his shoulder. "I love this man more than anyone in my life." Mary Faye raised her head. "I used to wonder why a woman would allow herself to get pregnant, wonder why they didn't wait for marriage. I honestly did not know that I could love a man like this because I had no idea what it felt like. I chose him over what's right or wrong. I chose him over God's Word, knowing that it was a sin. But I love him so much— "

"No, Mary Faye! No! You're just making excuses. Just like everyone does! But you ain't everyone else. You're Mary Faye Hunter. You're the golden child. You never sin.

Not a wild bone in your entire body. You never even drank a sip of beer or smoked a cigarette. The worst word you ever said was 'darn.' You're the yes ma'am, no ma'am girl. What went wrong, Mary Faye? What went wrong?"

"Wrong? Wrong! Have you ever thought that maybe I never slipped up because there was nothing there to tempt me? I'm not the party girl of the block, you know. Maybe I would have got pregnant at seventeen if I'd had a boyfriend, but there were no boyfriends. You can't fall to temptation when there is nothing there to tempt you!"

Mary Faye inhaled deeply, and as she exhaled, so did the words, "Oh, Jimmy. I fell in love."

She wandered nervously around the room. "I would love to have my own home, children, with a loving husband. But there never was anyone..."

"So, you decided to take someone else's."

Mary Faye was stunned. She searched Jimmy's eyes. *How could he say that?*

"I'm sorry," he said.

"No, you aren't. You're right. He belonged to someone else. I knew that. But when I was with him, it was as if there was no one else in the world. I could not even hear the voice of God, even though I knew it was wrong. My guilt was pushed away. I saw no one else's hurt, the pain that it would create if we were found out. But..." She turned to Jimmy. "We had no plans of being caught. I guess the joke is on us, huh?"

Jimmy approached Mary Faye, but she moved away and circled the room like an animal in a cage.

She stopped. "Do you know of anyone who would do the abortion?"

Jimmy knew of no one personally who performed abortions. It was illegal. Doctors could lose their license, or worse, go to jail. He turned away and shook his head.

"I'm sorry, Mary Faye. I truly am." Jimmy said. He took her hand. "If I could help, I would. Maybe you could have the baby and give it up for adoption."

"I would never be able to set foot in that church again. Momma and daddy would be so disappointed."

What was he thinking?

She would be the gossip of the town. Even people who didn't know her would be gossiping about the unmarried church pianist who got pregnant.

"There are some doctors or nurses, I don't know them, that will do abortions. There are also bad people who do abortions, but Mary Faye, that's very dangerous. Women have died or were never able to have a baby again."

"I don't guess it would matter if I could never get pregnant again, does it? It's not like I'm about to get married and have a house full of kids, is it?" she said sarcastically.

"Are you sure that you're pregnant?"

"I saw Doctor Carter this morning. He said I was about two months. Jimmy, please."

He didn't respond.

"Jimmy," said Mary Faye as she moved closer to him. "Don't decide tonight. Think about it. Tell me in the morning."

"No, that wouldn't be fair to you. I know my answer. There's no need for you to lie awake, thinking I might change my mind. I can't. I won't do this."

"Do any of your doctor friends know of—"

"No. I won't ask them. But I will go with you tomorrow to tell momma and daddy if you want me to. We will face them together." He caught her and hugged her tightly. "Together, okay? All you have to do is say the word."

She bit her lower lip. He just didn't understand. She could not have this baby. It would destroy so many lives if she did—her parents as well as hers. No one would ever know who the father was. She could keep him a secret, but what about everyone else? What about the baby?

Brought into this world as an illegitimate baby.

She would not allow her child to suffer taunts from other kids, gossip, tormented by statements like, Who's your daddy? You ain't got no daddy. Neither the baby nor her parents should pay for her sins. It was as if the whole town would pay for her sin. God's Name would suffer for what she had done as people would bring up they had thought she was a good Christian woman.

Christian church pianist? Ha! What a laugh.

There would be no end to the talk and the pointing. Never again would Mary Faye or her parents be able to hold up their heads in town. Forever she would be the church pianist who had a baby out of wedlock.

"Get some sleep," she said. She looked up at her handsome brother. "You're the golden child, not me. The doctor with the nice family. Momma and daddy are very proud of you."

"And you too."

They wouldn't be if they knew the truth.

Jimmy tapped her chin. "Truth be known, I guess we both got a little smut on our face. Won't stop their love though."

"I know. But they just couldn't handle this. They just couldn't."

"What are you going to do?"

She reached up, kissed his cheek. "Goodnight." A weary smile touched her lips as she patted his cheek.

The next morning they went to church. Afterward, they ate lunch. The baby wasn't brought up again, and around 2:15, Mary Faye got on the northbound Greyhound for Decatur. That night Mary Faye cried herself to sleep again.

Chapter 31

Monday, April 24, 1967 - Morning

When Adam passed Mary Faye, he winked at her. She winked back. A thrill rushed through her. That wink meant only one thing. At 11:45 she left the building and crossed the parking lot to his car. He was waiting for her. She hurried into the car, and he drove out of the parking lot toward the highway. He took her hand.

"I knew we needed to talk," said Adam. "I was afraid we might not be able to get away tonight. What did the doctor say? Are you—"

She nodded. "He said about two months."

Adam briefly closed his eyes and shook his head.

"I'm so sorry, Mary Faye. I'd marry you if I could."

"I know."

"I can't leave her...she's the mother of my children."

"And I'm pregnant with your baby," Mary Faye replied. Desperation filled her voice. For a moment, he thought she was going to burst into tears.

"I know," he said. "Give me time to think. We'll come up with something."

Mary Faye knew what Adam meant. There was only one solution now. She could not have a baby, no more than he could leave his wife. They had a problem, and marriage wasn't the solution. Even if he was single and could marry her, people would still know she was pregnant when they got married. That wouldn't work. It would break her parents' heart if they thought she wasn't a virgin.

Real Christian women don't have premarital sex.

How many times had she heard that? All throughout high school, even in college, and especially in today's world when it seemed more young girls were having sex in this so-called free love movement.

But not her. Mary Faye was no teenager. She was a grown woman. Women knew what they were supposed to do in dealing with right and wrong. Teenagers can make a mistake, but not a 33-year-old woman. She had broken one of society's most important rules. The Bible would call her a harlot. Today she would be called worse by her church family and co-workers. They would whisper about her behind her back. She wouldn't be allowed to play the piano at church. People would never ask her to play at weddings or concerts. Her whole world would be over.

Repeatedly, Mary Faye wrestled with all the thoughts and fears. The same words pour over her brain. And the results were always the same. She couldn't have the baby.

"Mary Faye?" Adam whispered. "Did you hear me? I said I'd think of something." He squeezed her hand as he pulled the car into a wooded side road. He turned to her.

Mary Faye gazed into his bold blue eyes. No one has ever stirred her the way this man had. Adam was the love of her life…the only love of her life.

"Yes, I heard you. There's only one thing we can do. We both know what that is."

He nodded.

"Dr. Carter said he might know someone," she said.

Adam wiped his eyes, and then massaged his temples.

"Maybe your doctor can find someone that knows what they're doing and keep everything quiet."

Mary Faye nodded. Adam slipped his arm around her waist. Mary Faye laid her head on his shoulder.

"Listen to me closely," he said. "You being pregnant doesn't change the way I feel about you. Mary Faye..."

Adam began to cry. Mary Faye sat up straight and put her hand on his cheek.

"I love you," he said. Tears rolled.

Her heart squeezed. In the past, Mary Faye had desperately wanted Adam to tell her that. Fear had now dampened the joy of hearing those words, yet she still wanted him to say it over and over again.

Mary Faye pulled Adam to her. She lightly kissed his cheek.

"I love you with every fiber of my being," she said.

"I know," he said and kissed her lips. "There something I want you to know. I'm not proud of being a cheating husband, and I have never done anything like this before. Honestly, I can say that I have never loved a woman like I love you. I can't walk away from you. You cannot spend the rest of your life being my mistress, but I can't spend the rest of my life wanting you beside me and not having you there."

What was he saying? Marriage?

Mary Faye did not ask. Instead, they embraced in a long kiss. He released her, then glanced over his shoulder.

"We best get back to work. When do you see the doctor again?"

"Saturday afternoon."

"I'll come to the church around 2:00. You can tell me what he said."

"Okay." Mary Faye nodded. She squeezed his arm as

he started the car. Before they reached the end of the dirt road, she moved away from him and sat on her side of the car. Their eyes scanned the area as they drove back, but they saw no one as they returned to the building. No one saw them…or so they thought.

Chapter 32

Saturday, April 29, 1967 – 9:05 am

A wave of nausea rushed over Mary Faye's body as soon as she placed her feet on the floor. She ate a saltine cracker, but it was too late. Mary Faye rushed into the bathroom where she immediately lost the cracker and last night's supper. She hoped her mother did not hear her being sick. Mary Faye checked her face in the mirror. At least she didn't look as bad as she did that first morning. Maybe her body would settle down. She touched her stomach. There was a baby there, but she couldn't think like that, couldn't think about it as a person. It wasn't really a baby yet, but she didn't believe what she was saying to herself. It was real, alive, and it was growing.

The knock on the bathroom door jolted Mary Faye. "Ma'am?"

"Your breakfast is on the kitchen counter. I'm going down the street to see Mrs. Penn."

"Okay. I'm going to be late today. After the hairdresser, I plan on doing a little shopping, then going to the church."

"Okay, dear."

She was shopping all right.
Shopping for an abortionist.
In the kitchen, a saucer with three pieces of bacon, scrambled eggs, and a biscuit sat near the stove. Mary Faye grabbed a cup from the cabinet and poured coffee into it. She only ate the biscuit. Her stomach would not handle any heavy food. After eating, she showered and left the house.

* * *

"Mary Faye," said Marjorie Morris. "Do you want your hair set up today?"

"No, ma'am. No wedding today. Thought I'd just have it done in soft curls resting on my shoulder."

"Okay, hon." The woman began to wash Mary Faye's hair. "How're things going at work? Okay?"

"Yes, ma'am. Just the same old routine."

Except for when I see Adam, then my heart soars to the ceiling and wants to dance across the building.

Of course, Marjorie didn't know about Adam. No one knew his name, not even Dr. Carter or Jimmy.

* * *

Paul Hurst sat at the kitchen table and drank his last cup of coffee for the morning. He waited for the morning dew to dry before he mowed the yard. The newspaper was in his hand. On page seven, next to the last page was the section for all the church services in Decatur and the surrounding area that wanted to let people know their church was opened to visitors or those looking for a church home. Central Baptist had the largest advertisement. Seeing it made Paul think about Mary Faye.

"You won't believe what I saw at work the other day," said Paul.

Madolyn was washing the breakfast dishes. "What?" she said without turning around.

"I saw him wink at her."

"Who?"

"Mary Faye and that fellow at work. He walked right by her and winked, and she winked right back."

"You ever winked at a woman?"

"Not since I've been married and I would never wink at one at Redstone."

Madolyn turned and grinned. "You've never worked at Redstone and not been married."

"You know what I mean."

"I think you're making too much out of this."

"Would you ever think Mary Faye Hunter would wink at a man?"

"No."

"Well, she did." Paul Hurst unfolded the newspaper and began to read.

-2-

Dr. Carter had known the shy woman for many years. Mary Faye's hip had brought her to him. Hip Dysplasia. In other words, her hip joint was partially dislocated because the socket didn't fully cover the ball portion of the upper thigh bone. Mary Faye had not shown any symptoms until she was a teenager. Gradually, the condition worsened. He could sympathize with her since he too walked with a limp. Dr. Carter had been her doctor for several years and knew her family very well. Mary Faye Hunter was the last person he would have ever imagine being pregnant.

"What have you decided, Mary Faye?" Deep down, Dr. Carter knew, but he wanted her to say it before he made any phone calls.

She sat in front of his desk in his office.

"I have no choice. I have to get an abortion. If no one

else were involved, it would be different, but it's not just me. My parents, the church—so many people would be hurt. Even people at work. Oh, Dr. Carter..." Tears streamed down her cheeks. "I have no choice!"

Mary Faye's shoulders shook as she buried her face in her hands.

"If you want, I can call the guy for you."

She looked up. Her hands were wet with tears. "I'm so scared."

"I know." He took her hand. His bedside manner was gentle, caring, yet he also had a dark side people usually didn't see. He had always said the act of abortion was simple. In his opinion, it shouldn't be illegal. Most people didn't know his belief on the controversial subject. Dr. Carter was in the heart of the Bible Belt. People were conservative and very religious.

"We'll take care of this," said Dr. Carter.

He saw a genuine fear in Mary Faye's brown eyes. Her body trembled. Her face pale with streaks of pink.

"Mary Faye, listen to me. You aren't the first woman to have an unwanted pregnancy, nor will you be the last."

"But...I'm Mary Faye Hunter. My family is well known in this town. Do you realize I play piano at Central Baptist? The big church on Fourth Avenue and Grant Street?"

Doctor Carter smiled. "Have you ever thought about how many women had abortions, and that they might be prominent members of the community? Forget about everything and everyone except what you want to do. You can have the baby, give it up for adoption, or have an abortion. Don't convince yourself that you only have one choice."

His voice was soft, gentle as if he was soothing a child who was going to have his tonsils removed. Tears rolled down her cheeks.

"You don't have to make the decision today if you

don't want to, but it has to be soon. You're already about two months."

"I can't have this baby. I have no choice. My parents—oh, it would kill them."

"Okay, then...the decision has been made. When it's over, this will all be just a bad memory. You can move on with your life. In fact, since you're now sexually active..."

Mary Faye blushed. She had never thought of being sexually active.

"...we can make sure this doesn't happen again." Doctor Carter smiled.

He handed her tissues as he talked. "Mary Faye, here, wipe your tears. It will all be okay. I'll call the man."

Mary Faye wiped away the tears and nodded. "Okay," she whispered.

"You call me tomorrow."

"It'll have to be done on a Saturday. I work on weekdays. I go downtown every Saturday for a hair appointment." She sniffed and wiped the tip of her nose. "How long will it take?"

"About 15 or 20 minutes. Not long."

"Will this man...will he tell anyone?"

"Oh, no. That's the last thing he'd want to do. He could get into big trouble. No, he'll keep it a secret. You have nothing to worry about there."

"Who is he?"

"Does it matter?"

Mary Faye's face dropped.

"Something wrong?"

"No...no...I mean...just the idea of some stranger who will see—"

"Just think of it as a doctor's examination." He studied her closely. "If you'd rather go to someone out of town, I know of some women in Huntsville and Florence, but the man that I recommend, I've known a long time. Should I just call him?"

What difference did it make? An abortionist would kill her baby and her secret. They would both be murderers and couldn't snitch on the other.

"Yeah, sure."

"I'll go ahead and call him now." He dialed a number. "Yes, this is Doctor Carter. There is a woman here that needs help. When? Just a moment."

Dr. Carter glanced at Mary Faye then checked his desk calendar. He pointed to May 6 and raised a questioning eyebrow to her. Mary Faye nodded.

"Okay," he said into the phone. "How about May 6? She will need you to pick her up." He covered the mouthpiece. "Where?" he asked her.

"I'll be walking toward Second Avenue on Johnston Street. I'll have on a light blue headscarf with a white blouse and orange skirt." Her mother had made her the outfit a few weeks ago, but she didn't tell him that.

Dr. Carter's head moved in agreement as he relayed the information. "Time?" He looked at Mary Faye. She mouthed the word, noon which he repeated into the phone.

"Okay, you got all that? Saturday, May 6 at noon on Johnston Street," he said.

The beauty shop was on Grant Street, but Mary Faye didn't want anyone there to see her get picked up. Too many windows. Johnston was just one block over.

Mary Faye started to stand, but she waited for the doctor to hang up. The doctor replaced the receiver.

"See? It's going to be fine. Just make sure you take three hundred in cash."

"All right." Her voice was barely audible.

"Mary Faye, don't worry, I think you're making the right decision under the circumstances."

"Thank you." Mary Faye stood. Dr. Carter had been a big part of her life for the last ten years, ever since he first came to Decatur from Virginia. She was comfortable with him. Dr. Carter also limped, but he had to wear a heavy brace on his leg. He had joked with her many times that she was lucky not to have to contend with a brace. Over the years, her hip had gotten worse. Not only did she have a limp now, but there was some pain as well. One hip projected higher than the other, which caused Mary Faye to swing her leg as she walked.

    Dr. Carter patted her shoulder. "Everything is going to be fine. Trust me."

    She had to trust him.

Chapter 33

Thursday, May 4, 1967

The night was as black as a coal mine. Just like Mary Faye's mood. Dark. They sat in Adam's car in their favorite spot near the river right off Mussle Camp Road. This used to be his place to fish, but now it was their place. She calculated that it was this spot the baby had been conceived.

Mary Faye pushed herself up against his firm chest.

"Make love to me," she whispered. She had never said that to Adam before.

"Now?"

"Yes."

"Don't you think we should talk?"

"No." She dropped her head slightly. Her words soft, low. "Not right now." She lifted her eyes and looked into his. "I want to hold you in my arms and feel you as close to me as possible." Her voice broke. A large lump had formed in her throat. Tears shimmered in her eyes. "I love you so much, and I'm so afraid."

"Baby..." Adam held her face in his hands and kissed her softly on each cheek, then her eyes, and lips. "I love you too, baby. I never meant for this to happen." His breath was in her mouth.

Mary Faye slipped her arms around Adam and kissed the side of his neck, then moved to the hollow of his throat. She unbuttoned his shirt and kissed his chest tenderly, as her hands stroked his shoulders.

Mary Faye caught the back of his head as she firmly kissed him. She moved to his lap. "You may not ever be able to marry me, but right now, at this moment you are mine. I love you. I have your child inside me."

They made passionate love. More intense than even the first time. Afterward, Mary Faye snuggled against Adam. They discussed the plans that would destroy what their love had created.

Chapter 34

Saturday, May 6, 1967

Sunlight slipped into the bedroom between the curtains. Then it was gone. Mary Faye got out of bed, went to the bathroom, and then entered the living room.
"Momma?"
Mary Faye entered the kitchen. To her surprise, no one was there. There was a note on the table.

Sausage and biscuit on counter. Coffee in pot, milk and juice in refrigerator. I'm at the eye doctor. Should be back shortly. Love, Momma.

Mary Faye remembered her mother saying something about the eye doctor last night but really had not paid close attention. She put down the note and turned to the kitchen counter. Mary Faye wasn't very hungry, but at least she didn't feel nauseated. She poured a glass of milk. The cold milk tasted good, refreshing. She then placed two small sausage links inside her biscuit and took a bite. Her stomach felt settled today. If Mary Faye didn't know any better, she would have thought it was all just a horrible dream. A stomach bug for the last few weeks, anything but pregnancy.

Mary Faye returned to her bedroom and dressed. Underneath, she wore a bra, panties, slip, girdle, and stockings—the whole nine yards. White blouse and the orange skirt fit her perfectly. Beige leather flats covered her feet. She powdered her face with light make-up and added a hint of lipstick. The last thing she put on was her watch. She removed her billfold from her purse. It was 10:10 when Mary Faye left the house.

Etolia had finished her appointment at the eye doctor and was almost home. Mary Faye stepped off the porch and followed the walkway to the end of the front lawn. A minute later, mother and daughter met on the sidewalk a few houses down.

"That skirt looks pretty on you, Mary Faye."

"Thank you, momma. You did a great job on it. Fits like a glove."

"Thanks, hon. Would you please pick up some instant potatoes for me at the A&P? I decided to fix them tomorrow for dinner. I might bake a ham. Haven't decided yet."

"Okay."

"Are you feeling all right? You look a little pale."

Mary Faye laughed. "I'm always pale, but yes, I'm fine."

"Well, okay. You be careful. If it starts to rain, you be sure and take a cab home."

"Yes, ma'am. Maybe it will hold off till later this afternoon."

"Maybe so. See you after 'while."

They parted company. Etolia waved to her daughter before she entered the house, but Mary Faye had already turned and didn't see her.

At 10:28, Mary Faye entered the House of Beauty on Grant Street. Marjorie Morris greeted her as she came through the door.

"Mornin', sugar. C'mon in." Marjorie adjusted the chair for Mary Faye as she sat down.

"Whatcha got in mind today...up or down?"

"Let's go up today."

Marjorie ran a comb through Mary Faye's hair.

"You got another weddin' this afternoon?"

"No, ma'am, not today."

I've got something else to do.

"But I would like tight curls and a lot of spray. It's kinda windy outside."

"Yeah, I noticed that. Looks like the rain is comin'. Maybe a storm."

As the beautician work on Mary Faye's hair, they chatted mostly about the weather. While under the dryer, Mary Faye read the latest copy of Redbook magazine. By 11:30, Marjorie had Mary Faye's hair combed out, curls pulled up, sprayed, and then sprayed again. Mary Faye paid Mrs. Davis at the register and left the shop.

A&P Supermarket was one block over on Johnston Street. Mary Faye purchased the instant potatoes and was once again on the street in less than five minutes.

-2-

1:30 pm

"Webb Hunter, please." Etolia held the phone tightly.

"Let me check to make sure he's not with a customer," said the receptionist.

A minute passed, then her husband's voice came across the line.

"Etolia?"

"Webb, there's something wrong. Mary Faye hasn't come home yet."

He didn't like the tone in his wife's voice but knew he

needed to be calm. "She's probably at the church."

"That's what I thought at first, but she should've been back by now. Mary Faye would've called if she was going to be late. She always calls if she's going to the church to practice the piano. She had that hair appointment at 10:30. I asked her to run over to the A&P, but that would only take a few minutes. She's had plenty of time to get back home."

"I know, but—"

"She doesn't have a wedding to play for today. Mary Faye would have called."

Webb knew that Etolia was right. Mary Faye would have called.

"Did you call the church?"

"Yes, but no one ever answers that phone on Saturday. It's in the secretary's office."

"I'm coming home. On the way, I'll stop by the church."

"Thank you, dear. Please hurry."

-3-

1:45 pm

"Hey, Doc, your lady didn't show."

"What?"

"Yeah, I drove around for over twenty minutes, going up and down Second Avenue and Johnston, looking for her. She was a no show."

"That surprises me."

"Well, I had to leave. Couldn't afford to be seen prowling up and down the streets."

"Yes, of course. I understand."

"Well, when you see her, you can let her know she owes me twenty bucks for my trouble."

"Yeah, I'll tell her."

Dr. Carter hung up the phone.

What happened to Mary Faye?
He was positive that Mary Faye would go through with the abortion after she had left his office last Saturday. Maybe that boyfriend of hers decided he would marry her after all.

Chapter 35

Webb Hunter rushed through the front door. Etolia sat at the kitchen table with a small flowery notebook in front of her. He knew the book held phone numbers.

"I've called everyone I can think of," said Etolia. "I called the beauty shop. They said she left there around 11:30. The A&P clerk said she was in there."

She looked up, tears in her eyes. Webb's concerned eyes met hers.

"I think we ought to call the police," she said.

"First, call all of her friends."

Mary Faye didn't have a large circle of friends outside of church. Etolia searched through the book. She began to call every church member she knew. By 2:00, the house was buzzing with friends of the Central Baptist family.

"Webb, Don and I will go search every room in the church building," Charlie Hammond said. Both were members of the church. Charlie was married to Etolia's sister, Bertha.

"Good. Thank you." Webb's voice tensed as anxiety spread across his face.

This wasn't like Mary Faye.

Webb waited until 4:00, then called the police.

A few minutes later, Webb dialed Jimmy's number in Birmingham.

* * *

The sound of the phone invaded Jimmy's sleep. He stirred in his recliner. His brain processed the ringing, but his body wanted no part of the sound. Jimmy had prescribed himself peace and quiet after a grueling 12-hour shift in the ER last night. He had gotten home shortly after 3:00 am.

Sally and the girls were at the grocery store. A sports show was on TV, but the volume was low. Less than five minutes later, sleep had captured Jimmy.

Now the phone demanded his attention. Probably the hospital calling him to come back in.

Not gonna happen.

This was his weekend off. If Jimmy did not rest, he would never be able to handle the following week.

He reached for a small throw pillow to quiet the phone, but his hand knocked off the receiver.

Ugh! Might as well answer it.

"What?" he demanded.

The line was quiet. He started to hang up when he heard a faint voice.

"Jim—Jimmy, is that you son?"

"Daddy?" Jimmy sat up. "Yeah—yes sir, it's me." Horror suddenly rushed through his bloodstream. Something was wrong. He heard it in his father's voice. Jimmy was fully awake.

"Daddy, is everything okay?"

"It's...Mary Faye. Jimmy, son..."

Jimmy shut his eyes and waited for the impending words.

"She...she didn't come home."

"What do you mean—didn't come home? Home from

where?"

"She went downtown. Never came home." Webb's voice quivered. He took a deep breath. "We've been searching for her over three hours, and...nothing."

"Did anyone see her downtown?"

"Oh, yes. She kept her hair appointment. Went by the A&P for your momma, then...just vanished."

"No one just vanishes."

If his father could have seen him, he would have noticed all the color had drained from Jimmy's face.

Did Mary Faye leave town? No, she wouldn't do that. Did she find someone to do the abortion? No. She wouldn't know where to begin. Someone had to help her. What about the baby's father? Would he harm Mary Faye? Who was he? Jimmy didn't know what this man was capable of, other than using a young woman's innocence against her.

Surely the man wouldn't harm her though—or would he? Where could she be?

"Jimmy? I said your momma wants to talk to you."

"Oh, okay, daddy."

"Jimmy," said Etolia.

"Yes, momma?"

"Can you come home?"

"Yes ma'am, of course. Sally and the girls are at the grocery store, but just as soon as they get home, we'll get things together and head to your house."

"Okay, hon. Y'all drive careful," Etolia said. Her voice sounded strong, but Jimmy knew she was trying to be brave for him.

Sally came through the door just as Jimmy hung up the phone.

"Sally," Jimmy called. "We need to leave soon. My parents need me."

"What's wrong?" Sally stepped into the living room with Meg and Beth close behind her. A third child was on the way. Sally was six months pregnant.

Jimmy sadly regarded his family. Sally sensed that something bad must have happened.

"Girls, go into the kitchen and put the groceries away," she said. The children left the room. Sally turned to her husband. "Jimmy, what's wrong?"

"It's Mary Faye."

"What about Mary Faye? Tell me."

"She's missing."

"Missing? What are you talking about? How can Mary Faye be missing?"

"Just what I said. She's missing and we've got to go to Decatur." Jimmy caught her hand. "C'mon." He led her into their bedroom. "Sit down for a minute."

Sally sat on the bed and watched as Jimmy paced the room.

"It's like this…" He whirled to face her. "Mary Faye is pregnant." He blurted out the words as if they were hot coals in his mouth.

Sally's face twisted in confusion.

"What? Are you kidding? She can't be."

"Mary Faye told me when she came here in April."

"I didn't even know that she had a boyfriend. Who is he?"

"She wouldn't tell me his name." Jimmy cleared his throat. "He's married."

Sally's eyes nearly popped out of the sockets. "No…"

"She asked me for help. I told her that I couldn't be involved with an abortion. It's against my morals and ethics as a doctor." Jimmy put his hand on Sally's stomach. "I could never abort a child."

"Oh, Jimmy." Shock spread across Sally's face. "So you think that has something to do with her missing?"

"Maybe. I don't know what to do. Should I tell my parents that she's pregnant?"

"You keep quiet for now. What if she went somewhere for an abortion and got delayed? She could be home any minute."

Jimmy nodded. He couldn't betray his sister's trust. Not now. What good would it do to tell her secret? No one knew the father's identity. Jimmy didn't know where Mary Faye would have gone for an abortion. She could be anywhere. She could also be dying.

He sank down on the bed. "Sally, what if she's somewhere bleeding to death? What can I do to help her?"

"Nothing. You don't know where she is. All we can do is go to your parents. Be there for them. Hopefully, she'll be home by the time we get there."

Thirty minutes later they were on the highway northbound to Decatur. Little was said as they traveled. They didn't want their daughters to overhear any mention of Mary Faye, yet that was all that was on their mind.

Where was Mary Faye? What happened to her?

* * *

A few minutes after Webb had gotten off the phone with Jimmy, a police officer arrived. Webb joined him on the front porch.

"Mr. Hunter, my name is Lieutenant Frank Shafer," said the police officer, as he entered the house. Webb shook hands with him. "Tell me what's goin' on here."

"Our daughter, Mary Faye, hasn't come home yet. We don't know where she is." Webb swallowed hard. The small, slender man's hands were shaking. It seemed as if it took all his will power to not breakdown in tears.

"Your child, how old is she, and what does she look like?"

"Mary Faye just turned 34."

Shafer stopped writing. "Pardon?"

"She's 34-years-old, about 5 foot, 2 or 3 inches. Brown hair, brown eyes." Webb looked down to the officer's hand. "Are you going to write that down?"

"Did you say your daughter was 34?"

Webb nodded his head.

"What makes you think she's missing? When was the last time you saw her?"

"Her mother saw her this morning at around 10:15."

"This morning?"

"Yes."

"Sir, do you think you might be jumpin' the gun here? Most adults ain't considered missing if they've only been gone a couple hours."

"Mary Faye ain't like most adults."

"Oh, I see. Is there something..." Shafer struggled with his words. "Is there something wrong with her?"

"Of course not."

"Excuse me, Mr. Hunter, but I'm a little confused. If your daughter has only been missing for a short time, why did you feel the need to call the police?"

"You don't understand. Mary Faye always calls us if she's going to be late."

"What about her friends, or a boyfriend?"

"She doesn't have any close friends, and she's never even had a boyfriend."

"Never?" Shafer asked.

"Never." Webb moved away from the front door. Shafer followed him into the living room.

"And your daughter isn't mentally handicapped?"

"She works at Redstone Arsenal. My daughter is not some dim-wit that got lost on her way home. She's just a good, decent woman that's missing."

He sat down on the sofa and offered a chair for Shafer.

"I knew something was wrong as soon as my wife called me at work."

"Okay, Mr. Hunter, tell me more about Mary..."

"Faye," finished Webb.

"Yes. Mary Faye."

"She left the house a little after 10:00, and went down

to the beauty shop on Grant Street." Webb repeated the story that Etolia had told him. "She should have been home at 12:30 or 1:00 at the most." He sniffed. "Mary Faye wouldn't go somewhere without telling us first."

"Okay, Mr. Hunter. I'll relay your daughter's physical description to all of our patrol units. That's all we can do at this point, but I'm sure she'll turn up. They usually do."

Webb raised an eyebrow.

"Usually?" Webb stepped into Shafer's personal space. "Listen fella, wherever my daughter is, it can't be a good place. Every minute that goes by without hearing from her increases the chances that she's in danger."

"Mr. Hunter, ..."

"I'm not finished." Webb inched closer to the stoic officer, who refused to back away. "Me and my brothers have done business in this town for a long time as I'm sure you know. I would appreciate it if you handled this situation in a more urgent manner."

Shafer nodded once and thought for a moment.

"I'll talk to the chief. In the meantime, I will personally check out the beauty shop and the grocery store."

Webb backed away from the officer but did not break eye contact.

"Good."

Before Shafer left the house, Etolia handed him a black and white photo of Mary Faye.

"Thank you, Mrs. Hunter. As soon as we find out something, we'll let you know."

* * *

Lieutenant Frank Shafer parked in a small lot adjacent to the A&P Supermarket. He jotted down a few words on a notepad. Five minutes earlier, he had left the House of Beauty. The hairstylist confirmed that Mary Faye had been there for about an hour and left at approximately 11:30.

"Oh, yes, she was here," Marjorie Morris had told Shafer. "Just like always. 10:30 on the button."

Mrs. Morris also had stated that Mary Faye appeared to conduct herself in her usual manner. Nothing seemed out of the ordinary. When Mary Faye exited the building, she had turned to her left.

Shafer exited his patrol car and approached the front doors of the supermarket. Several advertisements hung on the windows. One of the signs displayed an ad for French's Instant Potatoes. Shafer entered the building and was immediately greeted by a young man stacking cans of baked beans into the shape of a pyramid. Shafer read his name tag, *Kenneth*.

"My name is Lieutenant Shafer from the Decatur Police Department. I need to speak to your manager."

For a second, the stock boy looked confused but recovered quickly with a smile.

"Yes, sir. He's in the back. I'll get him for you."

The clean-cut young man strode away through the backroom doors. Moments later, a tall, middle-aged man entered the room adorned with a red apron. He extended his hand to Shafer, and he shook it.

"What can I do for you, officer?"

"I'm looking for a gal that might have been in here a few hours ago."

Shafer handed the photograph of Mary Faye to the manager. His name tag read, *Willie*.

Willie studied the photograph and immediately nodded.

"Oh, yeah. I've seen her. She comes in here often."

"Was she here this morning?" asked Shafer.

"Yes, sir. I think it was about noon."

"How long was she here?"

"Not long. Probably two or three minutes. She bought a couple of boxes of instant potatoes."

"Do you remember how she was dressed?"

"Oh, sure. She had on a skirt and a white blouse. Let's see...a blue headscarf like she had just got her hair done."

"Excellent. Thank you."

Shafer added a few more notes to his pad.

"Is something wrong?" asked the manager.

"She was reported missing."

"Yeah? Well, I hope the poor dear is okay. She's a sweet woman."

The police officer nodded. "If you hear of anything, call the police department."

"Yes, I certainly will."

Shafer went back to his patrol car and drove to the police station. After a brief meeting with Police Chief Pack Self, three patrol units were dispatched to return to the station. Patrol officers were ordered to conduct a house to house inquiry that began on the east side of Sixth Avenue. The units canvassed Johnston, Grant, Jackson, and Sherman Street until they reached the Hunter residence. Most people knew the missing woman, but the majority of them had not seen her that day.

A witness who lived near the corner of Eighth Avenue and Jackson Street said that she was positive that she saw Mary Faye that afternoon.

"I know it was her. She walks by my house just about every Saturday." The witness thought for a moment. "You see, Mary Faye walks kinda slow with a limp."

She smiled. "She's a very sweet girl. I hope she's okay."

The officers thanked the woman and turned to leave.

"It might not be important, but people are always driving slow when they drive down these streets over here. I noticed this one vehicle, didn't really think anything about it at the time, but —"

"Yes?" Shafer said.

"Nothing, just going really slow, that's all."

"Did you notice the make?"

"I'm sorry, I didn't, but I think it was a dark-colored car. I was weeding a flowerbed and just happened to look up, otherwise, would have never noticed. That was also about the time I went inside to get something to drink. Didn't think anything else about it."

The officers thanked the woman and left, moving to the next house, but no one else remembered seeing her that morning.

The afternoon passed with little information to go on. It seemed to Shafer that Mary Faye Hunter had vanished into thin air. It made no sense. Why would anyone abduct a grown woman in broad daylight? Had to be for ransom. Had to be.

-3-

Martha came through the back door, making some noise as she shook herself and stamped her feet. The rain was cold. Why did it rain on Saturday when she needed to go grocery shopping?

Martha placed the groceries on the kitchen table, then went into the living room. Adam glanced at her from the couch as she entered the room. Martha removed the rain cap and shook it slightly. She hung the raincoat on the coat rack by the front door.

"The rain is picking up. Hope it doesn't storm. Are you okay?"

"What?" He looked up at her, but anxiety covered his face like a dark shawl of despair. "Yeah...yeah...I'm fine."

Adam looked anything but fine.

Martha could see concern on his face. He was probably in that place again. It seemed like he was over there a lot here lately. Sometimes she didn't think he wanted to return.

She returned to the kitchen and put away the groceries

and then went back into the living room. Adam had moved to the chair next to the fireplace.

Why? The fireplace wasn't even lit.

"Have you heard about the missing woman?" she asked.

"What?" Adam sprang from his chair. "Who?" He tried to sound calm. "That's too bad." He turned toward the fireplace. His hand swept the back of his head. "Hopefully they will find her. Who did you say it was?"

"I was at the store and heard the name on the loudspeaker. I don't remember it now…let me think for a second."

WHO? WHO? He wanted to shout, but he didn't.

Adam glared at Martha as if he could will the words out of her mouth.

"Well, finish your story," he finally said.

"That's all there is—she's missing. Said she was in the A&P that morning. Even told what she was wearing—a yellow skirt—no, no, an orange skirt."

With a white blouse, trimmed in orange.

"An orange skirt and a white blouse with orange trim around the collar." She turned back toward the kitchen. Her husband sat down into the chair by the fireplace, his face rested in his hands, deep in thought, but he was not on her mind.

"Hunter," she called from the kitchen, "That was the last name. Hunter. Like the name on that big furniture building on Second Avenue."

Martha had a can of soup in her hand when she stepped to the entryway that separated the kitchen from the living room. She was surprised to see Adam with such anguish on his face.

"Honey," she said gently. "Are you okay?"

"Uh?" Adam looked at her. A deep line rested between his brows. "Yeah…yes, I'm fine."

"What do you want for supper?"

"Doesn't matter...whatever. Doesn't matter."
Oh, Mary Faye, what have I done?
He glanced over at his wife. If only he could tell her, but he couldn't.
I have destroyed everything.
The thought ran wildly through his mind as he tried to decide what to do next.

Chapter 36

Harold Key stood just inside the showroom when he saw a dark blue Dodge Coronet pull into the lot. Probably a '65, Harold thought. Despite the rain, the salesman hurried outside to greet the man.

"Good afternoon," Harold said as the driver got out of the car. "What can I do for you today?"

The driver smiled.

Harold wondered if the man was looking for a new car. The vehicle he was driving wasn't old, but some people wanted a brand new car almost every year just like some wanted a new pair of shoes every fall. They had to have the latest style. Those were the kind of customers that Harold loved.

"Need a new model today? Be glad to put you in a 1967 Dodge in just minutes."

"I'm not looking to buy today," the man said. "Looking for maybe a deal...for you and me. See that little number right there?" The man cocked his head toward his car. "I'd like to sell it."

Huh, thought the salesman. No commission on a buy like that. "You sure you wouldn't want to just trade it in?"

"Nope. I just don't need this one anymore. I'm kinda

in a jam and need some money to pay off some hospital bills. Got too many cars as it is."

"I see. I'll take you to the front office."

"Fine, fine."

The man followed Harold Key across the showroom. There hadn't been a sale yet that month, but it was only the first weekend. *If we buy this guy's car, I might make double commission if I can resell it.*

As they left the showroom, the man turned to the salesman. "I know where to go from here. Thank you for your help—"

"Harold Key. If you ever need any assistance..." Harold removed a business card from his shirt pocket and handed it to the man. "Just let me know."

"Sure thing," the man said. He accepted the card, glanced at it then slipped it into his pants pocket. He entered the front office.

* * *

"Hi, beautiful," the man said as he approached the counter.

Kathryn Mills looked up from her desk. Her husband, Robert Mills, owned the thriving dealership. For the last seven years, Kathryn filled in as his receptionist. Her children were almost grown, and the position gave her something productive to do. She could also keep a close eye on her husband to make sure that he behaved. It was a perfect set up. If she didn't want to come in, she stayed at home. Kathryn had been at home the last two days and needed to catch up on her paperwork. And sometimes Saturday was the busiest day of the week.

"Well, hey there, stranger. C'mon in here. I haven't seen you in a while."

"Yeah, I've been busy." He strutted to her desk and sat

on the edge. "But I'm here today to give you a great deal."

She laughed. "Ha! I've heard that spill before."

Kathryn liked the nice looking younger man propped on her desk. She loved the way he smiled, and his eyes sparkled when he spun one of his lines. He was a talker that could easily woo a woman if he so desired. But Kathryn wasn't worried about him. He was Robert's friend, and she wasn't that kind of woman.

"Where's that no account husband of yours?"

Again she laughed. "Robert," she called out. "Someone is here to see you." She pointed toward an office door. "Oh, he probably can't hear me. Just go on back there." She gave him a warm smile, which he returned.

"Thanks, doll."

* * *

Robert Mills sat behind the desk and signed his name on an order form. When he saw his friend enter the office, the tall and slender man with oily gray hair stood and greeted him with a handshake and slap on the back.

"Just where on earth have you been keeping yourself?" asked Robert.

Robert sat back down and offered a chair to his guest, but the man ignored the gesture.

"Robert," the man said, as he glanced around the room at the dealership plaques on the wall. "I've got you a honey of a deal that you won't be able to turn down."

"What's wrong with it?"

The man chuckled.

Robert Mills snagged a Winston from the pack lying on his desk and handed one to his friend. Both men lit their cigarettes.

"All right," said Robert. "Tell me whatcha got and how much."

The man grinned. "It's a neat, pretty little four-door

1965 Dodge Coronet 440. Not even two years old." Robert glanced inquisitively at his friend, who roamed around the office, inspecting everything on the walls.

"Okay, so what's the catch? Is it a lemon? I don't buy lemons. You know that."

"Dang, Robert. You know that I wouldn't bring you a lemon." He held up his hand as if astonished at the idea. "I just had a little accident with it. I bought it for my wife. She loved it, but this morning, one of our dogs got hit by a car. Well, she just went hysterical on me, so I grabbed up the bleeding dog and put him in the backseat of the car and rushed him to the vet. Poor little guy died on the way there. Now she says I gotta get rid of the car. Said that she would never drive or ride in it again because that's where her poor Boo Boo died. So you see, I need to sell it." He took a long draw off his cigarette. "I ought to make her walk from now on. Whoever heard of getting rid of a car because a dog died in it?" He blew smoke rings toward the ceiling as he talked. "Women are just plain crazy."

Robert laughed. "Can't disagree with that." He got up and approached the man. "Let's get a look at that car."

They walked outside. The blue *Coronet* was parked on the left side of the lot next to the building. As they approached the car, the man flicked his cigarette butt to the ground.

"There's one other thing," the man said.

"Ask me if I'm surprised."

"I cleaned up the blood the best I could, but some of it …well."

"How bad?"

"Bad enough. But hey, my loss is your gain. That's another reason why I gotta get rid of the car. There are bloodstains on the back seat. But I'm sure you got the proper chemicals to get it cleaned up real nice."

"Let's see what we got first," Robert said as he approached the car. His friend was right. The outside looked just like new.

But the interior was a different story.

"My lands, man! What happened? Did you let the dog bleed out in the car?"

"Come on now. It ain't that bad. I'm gonna give you a good deal."

Robert inspected the car like a hawk circling its prey. He turned to his friend.

"Whatcha got in mind?" He stuck his head into the car to read the speedometer. Not bad. Less than 15,000 miles. He might settle for one thousand since he was so eager to get rid of it.

I wonder whose dog he really killed?

"How about five hundred?" asked the man.

He almost choked on his own spit. Robert could easily sell it for two thousand.

"How fast can you turn it over with that kind of profit?" said the man.

"Turn it over?"

"Yeah. Should be a quick turn over, shouldn't it? Could make an easy thousand, couldn't you?"

Something wasn't right here. Robert Mills could feel it.

"Hoyt," Robert called to an employee who was wiping down one of the new cars. "Come over here." The man approached his boss. "See this car?"

"Yes, sir."

"I want you to take it around back, give it a thorough cleaning inside and out. A dog died in the backseat. I want it spotless, ready to be on the lot in an hour. Can you handle that?"

"Yes, sir. It will be as clean as a hound's tooth when I get through with it." Hoyt took the keys and drove the Coronet around back.

The two men returned to the front office.

"Kathryn, get the payment book," said Robert. I just

bought a car." Robert grinned at his friend. "For a bargain too."

Less than an hour later, the Coronet was on the lot with a bright red sales sticker. By 3:45, the car had been sold and was leaving the lot.

"Kathryn, tear out that sales slip and give me the one before and the one after," Robert told his wife as he watched the car leave the lot.

"Okay, but what for?" she asked.

"Nothing. Just a hunch."

She tore out the slips and handed the stack to her husband. Robert went to his office and burned the receipts in an ashtray. He dumped the ashes on a blank piece of paper and then dropped it into the waste can by his desk. When Robert left his office that evening, he flung the ashes into the wind as he drove down the wet streets of Decatur.

Something just wasn't right about that car.

Chapter 37

When the call first came in that afternoon about a woman who had only been missing for a couple of hours, it had sounded ridiculous.

"It doesn't make sense, I know," the dispatcher's voice said over the phone. "But I'm telling you, there is something bad going on here. You'd better check this one out. Sounds bad."

Decatur Police Chief Pack Self held the phone between his chin and shoulder as he made himself a ham sandwich. "What do you mean?" he asked.

He spread a thick layer of mayonnaise onto a slice of Sunbeam Bread then added two pieces of cheddar cheese. There were other things he would rather do on a rainy Saturday afternoon than hang out at the office.

"You better get down there, sir."

He didn't like having anyone tell him where he needed to be, especially coming from a dispatcher. "Who told you to call me?"

"Lieutenant Frank Shafer. He said they have been searching all over southeast Decatur. A woman named Mary Faye Hunter disappeared without a trace."

"Hunter? Is she connected to that big furniture store on

Second Avenue?"

"One and the same. They live on Eighth Avenue."

Chief Self grabbed a Coke from the refrigerator. With the cheese sandwich in one hand, drink in the other, and the phone pinned against his shoulder, Chief Self kicked the refrigerator door closed. "How long has she been missing?"

"About three hours."

Chief Self paused in mid-stride. "This is a grown woman, right?"

"Yes, sir."

"I see." He bit into the sandwich. "I want you to call Detective David Smith and tell him to get over there and find out what's going on."

"Ten-Four."

* * *

Detective David Smith arrived at the Hunter residence at 5:15 that evening. He was greeted at the door by a family member who identified herself as Bertha Hammond, the missing woman's aunt. Concerned family and friends populated the living room.

Etolia sat at the kitchen table, her eyes filled with tears.

"Something horrible has happened to her," she said. "I know it has. Mary Faye would never do this. She would have called us!"

Webb draped his arms around his wife's shoulders.

Detective Smith didn't know what to say, so he mostly listened. If what these people said was true, Mary Faye Hunter would not have left on her own free will. Someone must have taken her.

Just as Smith entered the kitchen, Lieutenant Shafer approached him. For the next five minutes, Shafer briefed Smith on the situation.

"I just found out that some of the members of her church searched Central Baptist for over two hours," said

Shafer. "I was told that Miss Hunter would practice piano at the church almost every Saturday afternoon. But not today." Shafer shook his head. "They didn't find her or any signs of foul play."

Detective Smith nodded as Shafer continued, "She was last seen walking on the corner of Jackson and Eighth Avenue, just a few blocks from her home."

Etolia dropped her head to the kitchen table and sobbed. "She was so close to home...so close."

* * *

When Jimmy and Sally arrived at 811 Eighth Avenue, the curb was bumper to bumper with cars. Patrol cars were also there. The house was almost filled to capacity with policemen, family, friends, church members, neighbors, and people Jimmy had not seen in years. They all had one thing on their minds...finding Mary Faye.

Jimmy found his parents in the kitchen. They looked dazed. When they saw him, Sally, and the kids, their faces brightened. When they hugged him, he wasn't sure that they would ever let go.

* * *

Later that evening, light rain transitioned into a downpour. Every door in a two-mile radius had been knocked on. Only a few people had said they saw a woman who fit Mary Faye's description walking down the street late that morning or early afternoon. They could not offer a lot of information. Two neighbors stated they had seen her on Eighth Avenue sometime between noon and 12:30.

Heavy storm clouds raced against the dark sky. The rain mercilessly continued to pound the landscape. Thunder rumbled, and lightning flashed. Detective Smith sat in the living room with Webb and Etolia. Everyone else had either gone home or cleared out of the room.

"You got to understand our daughter," said Etolia. "Mary Faye's not like most young women. She didn't date. She didn't even have a driver's license. Mary Faye is an upstanding Christian woman." Etolia looked up at the detective. "I know it's hard for you to understand."

Webb sat down beside his wife.

"Mary Faye is a good girl," said Webb. "Never gave us a moment of trouble."

"Is it possible she went somewhere with a friend?"

Webb shook his head. "You just don't understand. Mary Faye had friends, but no one close. She didn't just wander off without letting us know."

The detective nodded. "So, she's been missing since around one?"

Webb nodded.

"And she didn't appear upset, or worried about anything?" asked Smith.

Etolia raised her head and wiped away her tears.

"No, she wasn't worried about anything. The last time I saw Mary Faye, she was walking down the street, going to her hair appointment." Tears flowed down her cheeks.

"Was she supposed to pick up anything besides instant potatoes at the A&P?"

"Maybe a small bag of candy."

Smith wrote her remarks on his pad.

Shafer heard the question. "A clerk at the A&P said she had only bought instant potatoes."

Smith nodded as he transcribed the information.

* * *

The night settled in. Every light in the house was turned on as the police searched every room for anything that might give them a clue. Webb stood in the doorway as they searched Mary Faye's bedroom. Etolia sat on the bed.

Mary Faye had made the bed before she left the house. But then, she made her bed every morning. Her room was always immaculate. Mary Faye despised clutter.

"That door," Smith said as he pointed to the outside door. "Where does it go?"

"To the front porch," Etolia said.

"Is that the way she typically entered and exited the house?"

"Oh, no, she always used the front door just like everyone else does," said Etolia.

"The door was here when we moved into the house," added Webb.

Lieutenant Shafer, who was helping investigators search the room, glanced at the door. The question almost escaped his lips, but he stopped himself.

It's the funeral door. The door for the dead.

He had heard his grandma say whenever there was a house with two front doors that one door was used for the dead to be removed from the front parlor.

So the spirit can leave the room.

Shafer didn't believe in that. He did believe it was a door used for the dead, but he wouldn't dare say that in front of Mrs. Hunter. Etolia shifted on the edge of the bed. Shafer needed her to stand so he could search under pillows and bedding. He just didn't know how to ask her without sounding insensitive. Instead, he approached the missing woman's dresser.

"What's this?" Shafer asked.

"What?" Etolia replied.

"This little ball?"

Etolia joined Shafer next to the dresser. Lying in a dish was a small, red ball. White lines ran through it as if the ball had faded and cracked with age. She rolled the ball over. "I don't know."

"Looks like a gumball to me," said one of the officers peeking over Shafer's shoulder. "Something you can get for a nickel out of a machine."

"Know why she would have left it there?"

"No. Maybe a child gave it to her, and she accepted it to be polite. Mary Faye worked with the youth, and they adored her. She wouldn't have wanted to refuse something like a gumball and hurt a child's feelings."

"Yeah, probably so."

She placed the gumball back in the dish.

Etolia returned to the bed but suddenly felt that she shouldn't sit there. In truth, she could no longer tolerate seeing strangers rummage through Mary Faye's belongings. She had to get out of the house.

The porch swing welcomed her, inviting her to escape from the intrusion. Her mind demanded peace, but there was only turmoil. She examined the street for any movement that might be Mary Faye.

"Oh my God," she whispered, "Where is my daughter?" Gently her foot pushed the swing. "Please...Father, please. Hear my prayer. Please let her be all right."

A car crawled down the street.

Just before it reached the house, it slowed more. Etolia strained to see the driver. It was too dark.

Was it a man?

She moved to the edge of the porch. Her eyes could not penetrate the darkness. Once past the house, the car accelerated. Taillights faded into the night.

Who was that? Probably nothing.

"Mary Faye, oh baby. Where are you?"

Chapter 38

Present Day

The giant plane exposed its white belly as it descended to the runway. A few minutes passed before Jamie Hunter exited the terminal. Brad Golson greeted him with a wave. Jamie stepped towards him, black leather bag in hand. They shook hands. Brad pulled him close for a quick pat on the back.

"You made pretty good time," said Brad.

"It wasn't too bad. No delays. The layover in Houston was only 45 minutes."

"Does it feel good to be home?"

"Yeah, sure." Jamie didn't seem to be interested in small talk.

They dashed through the concourse. Brad struggled to keep up with him.

"You ready to tell me what you found out?" asked Jamie.

"Keep in mind, it's been over 50 years."

"Save the conjecture." Jamie's frustration was evident. "Are you going to give me excuses or tell me what you got?"

"Are you willing to accept this information and not go crazy?"

Jamie stopped. "What's that supposed to mean?"

"I know how you are about your aunt."

"And?"

"Jamie, you have to remember it was a long time ago. It might've been 1967, flower power and free love in California, but this is the South. This is Decatur, Alabama. Things were different here."

"You don't have to tell me that, buddy. I know all about Decatur. What I don't know is...Who murdered my aunt and why?"

"You might want to just let sleeping dogs lie."

Jamie started walking again. His step was swift, jaw set, and tongue silent. Brad picked up the pace to keep up with his friend. Jamie always seemed to be in a hurry. His legs appeared to be longer than they should be for a guy under six feet tall, almost as if they were made to accompany his agitated body.

"Jamie, listen to me."

He kept walking. Jamie was forty, but as stubborn as a five-year-old who wanted a new toy when he demanded to know something or wanted something done. "Jamie! Will you please slow down?"

Jamie whirled. "I know you're going to tell me something bad. It has to be, or you wouldn't be stumbling around with it."

"Yeah, it's bad. It's something you don't want to hear, but you're gonna have to."

Brad thought of himself as a pretty good investigator, and so did Jamie, but the problem was if you want things investigated, you have to be willing to accept whatever turns up even the things you don't want to hear.

"All I know is that someone murdered her," said Jamie. He whipped back around and marched toward the entrance. "Where did you park?" He looked around as if he could find the car.

"Come on. It's over here in Section C."

When they reached the car, Jamie tossed the bag in the back.

"All right," he said as he got into the car. "Tell me."

"Chill out. Let's wait until we get back to Decatur."

Jamie scowled at him but said nothing.

They traveled over the Tennessee River, but when they reached the city limit, Brad didn't turn down the street toward his home. Jamie looked around as if the surroundings were foreign to him, even though Decatur was his hometown.

"Where we goin'?" Jamie's southern drawl that had long since been dormant while living in California had returned.

"There's a man I want you to meet."

"Who?"

"He worked on Mary Faye's case and knows things the public never knew." Brad turned onto 14th Street, went several blocks before he pulled into a driveway. "I want you to be nice."

"What?"

"You heard me. Nice. Let the man talk. Listen to what he has to say. Don't go in there with your mind already made up."

Brad liked facts, not what people wanted to believe. That was the whole point in investigating this case. Not to throw someone under the bus, or over the fence. Whatever happened fifty years ago, let all the guilty parties be exposed. So far from what he had learned, Jamie wasn't going to like it.

"Do you understand what I'm saying? Make up your mind before going in, that you want the truth, not some fairy tale account."

Jamie looked down, then at the small brick house, then over to the car door. "Okay," he finally said. "Okay." They exited the car and approached the front door. Before they had a chance to ring the bell, the door swung open.

"Come on in," said an elderly man. Two small dogs were howling behind him as he shuffled from the foyer into the living room.

Bob Hancock sat in a blue wingback chair in front of the fireplace. A small blaze flickered at the logs. One of the dogs hopped against Jamie's leg and barked loudly. "Hush up, Pedro!" Hancock snapped. "Quit showing out!"

For the first time since he landed in Alabama, Jamie smiled.

"Have a seat." Hancock motioned toward the sofa. Brad and Jamie sat down as the dogs continued to leap at them. In another room, they could hear the television blaring.

Hancock peered at the young dark-haired man sitting in his living room. "So, you're Mary Faye's nephew."

Jamie nodded. "That's right."

"You sure you want to hear this story?"

"Yes, sir. I already know some of it."

"Sure, you do." Bob Hancock reached for his pipe. The 85-year-old retired investigator smiled. "I bet you heard it from your family, didn't you?"

"Most of it."

"Decatur is an old town, and if you're not one of her own..." He smiled. "They ain't gonna tell you everything they know. Most people don't really want the truth, and no one wants the whole truth told about them or their family."

"I want the truth. I've got a right to know."

Bob Hancock narrowed his eyes at the young man. "You think just because you're her kin that you got the right to pull out all this mess...this 50-year-old puzzle?"

Jamie swallowed and looked at Brad.

"Don't be looking at him," said Hancock. He's not the next of kin. You are. This is going to rest on your shoulders. You're the one playing the kinfolks card."

Jamie's shoulders rolled backward, his chin lifted.

"Yes, sir. I'm playing that card because I have a right to know what happened to my aunt. She was my dad's sister. Her murder nearly destroyed him and my grandparents."

"All right then." Hancock smiled at Jamie and darted his eyes to Brad.

"Guess it's time to tell him." Hancock turned to Jamie. "What did you say your name was again?"

"Jamie...Jamie Hunter."

If his memory is that bad, how's he going to tell us anything about a case over 50-years-old?

Brad lowered his head so Jamie would not see his smile. He knew that Hancock was playing him like cat and mouse, checking his reactions.

"All right, Jamie...this is how it went down. It was early May...May 6, 1967. Mary Faye left her house on a mild Saturday morning to keep a hair appointment. She walked from her home to the House of Beauty on Grant Street, then proceeded to the A&P Super Market to get a few groceries, headed home, and disappeared."

"I know all that."

Bob Hancock drew on his pipe. With it between his teeth, he replied, "Of course you do."

He placed the pipe aside and smiled. "Now let's get to the truth of what happened to Mary Faye Hunter."

Chapter 39

Sunday, May 7, 1967 - 7:22 am

Bob Hancock sat at the kitchen table as his wife poured him a cup of black coffee. "Strong as an iron ox," he had told her shortly after they had gotten married. In those days, Bob had poured teaspoon after teaspoon of sugar into his cup. After 13 years of marriage, he drank it straight black.

Betty Hancock set a plate in front of him with two over easy eggs and four pieces of bacon. She placed toast and butter on the table along with a jar of blackberry jam.

"You better be kissing up to momma," she said.

"Let me guess... last jar of jam, isn't it?"

"She's probably got a few left. You might be able to sweet talk her out of one before blackberry season."

"You tell her I said I love her and that jam."

"No sir, I'm not. I don't eat that stuff. You tell her. You're her favorite anyway. I'm sure if you ask her just right, she'll let you have a jar or two. Won't be long till them blackberries are ripe, and then you can get all the jam you want, provided that you're willing to pick them."

Bob spread the jam over the toast. "You know I ain't

got time for that."

Betty grinned. She knew that. Her husband was lucky if he got one day off. Thank goodness he was off today.

"Did you hear that storm last night?" she asked.

"Nope. Slept like a baby. Didn't hear a thing."

"I'm not surprised. You didn't stir, so I didn't say anything."

He nodded. "Good girl. Unless the house is on fire or about to be blown away, let me sleep."

"Well, for a minute there I thought we were."

"Were what?"

"Going to be blown away." She lifted her coffee cup and took a sip. Without setting it back on the saucer, she asked, "We going fishing today?"

"Thought about it."

"Good. We can have fish for supper."

"I figured we were having meatloaf."

"Why?"

"I saw that pound of hamburger meat you got thawing."

"Oh, that's the backup plan. Living with a state investigator has taught me always to be prepared."

Bob winked. "Never hurts."

The avocado green wall phone hanging in the kitchen began to ring.

RING. RING. RING.

"You're not gonna answer that?" Betty asked as she put her fork into her own eggs.

RING. RING. RING.

"No." Bob bit into his blackberry jam toast. "It ain't for me. I'm fishing. That's where I'd be if I had gotten up before seven."

The ringing stopped.

"See?" said Bob. "It wasn't for me. Those people downtown would have kept—"

The shrill ringing interrupted his words. Bob jumped

from his chair and cursed. He grabbed the phone. "WHAT?"

Betty took a small sip of black coffee and listened. She had a feeling that a relaxing day of fishing had just been a pipedream.

"Missing, huh? When? How long? Do what?"

Bob cursed under his breath. Betty shook her head at him. He turned his back so he would not see her disapproving scowl.

"Now you listen here—" He swore again. "I'm not coming down there over some woman who's been missing for only—"

He turned back to Betty and shrugged his shoulders.

"If I come down there and this woman suddenly turns up, it ain't gonna be pretty." He slammed down the phone.

Bob sat back down in his chair. "Might as well finish eating. Nothing I can do right now anyway."

With the meal finished, Bob went into the bathroom. He quickly brushed his teeth and then ran a razor over his face. Betty followed him into the bedroom. She listened to him grumble about losing another day off. She threw the covers up on the mattress and straightened the bedding. Bob grabbed a dark gray pin-striped suit from the closet.

Betty smiled at him.

"You want to ruffle up these sheets before I finish making the bed?" she asked.

"I'll have to take a raincheck."

He stepped around the bed, picked up his wallet, watch, and keys from the nightstand. Betty came around to his side of the bed and tossed the pillows into place. Bob popped her rear.

"You just want to tease me because you know I don't have time," said Bob with a smirk.

Betty laughed and slapped him on the back of the arm.

Bob went to the dresser and rubbed Brylcreem in his hair, and ran a comb through it. Then he slipped on his sport coat. Betty moved up behind him and wrapped her arms around his waist.

"I love a man in uniform." She giggled like a schoolgirl.

He turned to face her.

"I love you, baby," Bob said before he kissed her lips. "I'll see you tonight. Hopefully early."

He stepped to the front door and paused. "And do burgers instead of that meatloaf, with lots of dill pickles and onions."

Bob stood on the carport. He regarded the broken tree limbs that littered the front lawn.

That must have been some storm.

He stepped back inside the house. "Betty, come here."

She joined her husband on the porch.

"What is it?" she asked.

"Look at this yard. I think you're right. We're lucky we didn't get blown away."

-2-

Bob Hancock drove through Decatur as if he owned the small town. He had been in law enforcement for eight years. The day he saw a State Trooper involved in a high-speed chase in his hometown of Scottsboro, Bob knew that he wanted to be in law enforcement. Both cars had been caked in mud.

"That's what I want to do," said a young Bob Hancock.

"What? Be chased by the law?" his friend asked.

"No! I want to be the one doing the chasing."

"Then go to the post office and file the paperwork."

Bob did, and a few weeks later, Betty called him at the Hosiery Factory where he worked. "Honey, you got a letter from the State of Alabama."

"Open it up and see what's in it."

"Well, I'll be. You've been chosen to test for the State Trooper's office."

Bob took the test and passed it with flying colors. He worked his way up to be a State Investigator. He knew his job, and he was good at it. At least, that's what his superiors kept telling him. Now he was in Decatur. The small river town was in the middle of a growth spurt. Plants and factories continued to be built, and the economy prospered. More industry equaled more jobs. More jobs equaled more people. More people equaled more crime.

Bob Hancock entered the Decatur Police Department. Several police officers greeted him as he made his way to the conference room. Bob knew most of the officers on a first name basis, having worked with them for a few years.

State Investigator, Lieutenant E.B. Watts stood in the middle of a conference room with other law enforcement officers.

"Good morning, Bob. Glad you could come in."

"It's not like I had much choice."

A few of the officers snickered.

Watts smiled like he had just bit into a lemon. "We appreciate your dedication."

"I was supposed to be fishing, but I guess the fish won't mind. Did you boys get any damage from that storm last night?"

"No," David Smith answered. "That's what we were talking about earlier. The Star Lite Motel lost part of its roof. Some houses and trailers out around Mud Tavern. Pretty bad storm."

"Sure was," said Watts. It blew into Decatur, passed over Flint Creek before leaving here and going into Limestone and Madison. Someone said it cut a 30-mile path, knocking over power lines, taking down trees, and setting chickens free when it hit a chicken house. You wouldn't have caught any fish today after that kind of storm. Fish ain't gonna bite."

"Tell my wife that."

"Understood, Bob. Can we move on, now?"

"Please do."

"I think you'll soon realize why we called you in today. This case makes no sense at all."

"Can't argue with that."

Bob pulled out a pack of Camels from his coat pocket and slid out a cigarette. He flipped his Zippo lighter lip, twirled the wheel, and the blaze shot up. He touched the flame to the tip of the cigarette. Bob blew smoke from his mouth, but the last of it exited through his nose. Normally, he didn't blow smoke from his nose. He viewed it as an uncivilized gesture. Something teenage boys did to look tough or express defiance. Under the circumstances, exhaling smoke out of his nose seemed most appropriate due to the foolishness of calling in the whole department over a woman who decided not to come home yesterday.

"She might sue the whole department when she discovers that she can't even leave for one night without having a search party looking for her," said Bob.

"Bob, this case is nothing like we've had before."

Bob glared at Watts. Both men were state investigators and partners, but Watts held rank. Bob was still a sergeant. Everyone in the room knew that the two men were not close. There was a familiar saying among the fellow officers. It's like living with papa bear and momma bear. Things will be fine, but you never know when one will roar at the other.

"I was given a little info on the phone this morning," said Bob. "Let me see if I have this right. You're telling me that we're looking for a full-grown woman—not a child, but a 34-year-old woman who's been missing for what—Twenty hours?" Bob wandered across the room. "Have you ever heard of people laying out all night? Spending the night with a boyfriend? You did say she was single, right?"

"Yes, but—" Watts started to say.

"Bob, you don't understand," said Detective David Smith.

"No, I don't. Sounds like y'all have been married too long and don't know what single people do anymore. She might be over at a friend's house or shacked up with a boyfriend."

"Not this one," Watts said. "This girl—woman is different."

"Mentally retarded?"

"Oh, no, no nothing like that. She's well-educated. Has a college degree, plays piano, and works full-time at Redstone Arsenal."

Bob stopped pacing and put his hands on his hips. He waited for Watts to drop the other shoe. Something didn't make sense. People don't just vanish off the streets of Decatur, Alabama.

"Mary Faye Hunter has an impeccable reputation. She's lived at home with her parents all her life. No car or driver's license. She carpools to work. Plays the piano for her church. The big one over on the corner of Fourth Avenue and Grant Street. Central Baptist."

Watts flipped a page and continued. "It says here that she's a very accomplished pianist. She also played at concerts and weddings. Worked with the youth choir." He looked up at Bob. "You get the picture? This woman's life is church, family, music, and work. No close friends or boyfriend."

"No boyfriend?" Bob Hancock asked. "Is she ugly, or does she have a bad personality?"

"Miss Hunter is just an average looking woman. The report says that she is shy but very polite."

"And sweet," Detective Smith said. "That's the word I kept hearing yesterday. Her hairdresser described her that way as well."

Bob took another drag from his cigarette. "Most women have a boyfriend. He might not be worth a cuss, but they have someone."

"Bob," Watts replied. "You don't get it. Her parents said that she's never had a boyfriend." He pulled out a pack of Winston's from his shirt pocket. "She's the portrait of a perfect old maid." He lit the cigarette with a match. "Course that's not the words her parents used to describe her, but that's what she looks like to me." He blew the smoke upward. "You got any more colorful quips, Bob?"

Bob shook his head. He didn't like the sound of this case. There had to be more to the story. He had been involved in several missing person cases. Most of them were cut and dry. A spoiled teenager runs away from home. Someone impulsively goes on a trip without telling anyone. A person's car breaks down in the middle of nowhere. This one, however, gave Bob an unsettling feeling.

How does a woman disappear on the quiet streets of Decatur in the middle of the day?

No one saw anyone pick her up. There was no crime scene. No obvious clues.

"Based on what you've told me," said Bob, "it sounds like a random abduction. Since there hasn't been an attempt to collect a ransom, I'd have to say the motive would be sexual assault or rape."

"Right," Detective David Smith answered.

"Okay, boys, tell me everything you have right now," Bob said.

Watts provided him with a report and briefed him on the rest.

"We even went back over the church with the pastor after church members had already searched it for two hours," said Smith. "It's a huge church campus with several buildings, but we found nothing that indicated foul play. I personally don't believe she was ever in that church yesterday."

Watts eyed Bob closely. "Now maybe you can see why we have everyone on this case. I agree that she was probably abducted then raped. That's why time is of the essence."

Bob nodded. "Do her parents own that big furniture store down on Second?"

"Two of her uncles do. Harland and Robert. Her dad works as a salesman there. A ransom is still a possibility. We could still get a call from the kidnapper any second. Maybe he thinks the parents own the store and are rich."

Possible, but Bob's instincts told him that something more sinister had happened to Mary Faye Hunter.

Chapter 40

Etolia poured Webb a cup of coffee and sat it in front of him at the kitchen table. They had slept sporadically the night before. Webb had never drunk so much coffee, heard no many voices in his whole life. There had been a steady stream of people coming in and out of their house.

The world felt wet and cold. It had stormed all night. Thunder rattled the windows. Strong winds twisted and bent the trees in the back yard. Rain beat the house mercilessly. Etolia had rolled over next to her husband, his arm around her as she wept.

Was Mary Faye out in this horrible storm?

Etolia cried until she was too exhausted to stay awake. A short time later, she woke. Her heart felt bruised. The only thing Etolia could think about was her daughter.

Now it was 10:00 am — still no word about Mary Faye's whereabouts.

"Webb," Etolia said, her voice soft as if she didn't want those in the living room to hear, not even the birds singing in the back yard what she was going to say to him. It was strictly between her and her husband.

"I have gone over and over every detail of those last moments with Mary Faye. She wasn't upset. She seemed normal." She sipped her coffee. "But I will admit, she didn't eat all of her biscuit and sausage like she normally would have. It probably doesn't mean anything, does it?"

Webb listened intently. "I wouldn't think so. She'd been kinda sick here lately. Maybe her stomach was still upset."

"Wait. I just remembered something. She looked a little pale when we talked on the sidewalk."

"Yeah, well, like I said, she had been sick."

"That's true."

They went over everything that Etolia had already told him. There was nothing there.

"Etolia, you know as well as I do that someone has stolen Mary Faye from us. It makes no sense except for one thing. Money. It's the only reason I can come up with for someone to take her." He squeezed her hand. "When they call us, we'll pay, and Mary Faye will come home." Tears set on the rim of his eyes. "Don't you think so?"

His voice was heavy with emotion. Webb cleared his throat, swallowed, and continued.

"I can't think of anyone who would do this. That tells me it's a stranger, at least to us. They may not be from Decatur, or even from this county. Lots of people come through this town, especially on weekends."

Etolia put down her coffee cup.

"But Webb, if that's true, how are they gonna know who to contact for the money? They gotta know who she is."

Neither wanted to voice the other reasons Mary Faye was taken. It was too horrible to discuss. Rape. Murder. An abduction was one thing. If the ransom was paid, there was still hope that Mary Faye would return home. If she had been taken, the abductor would contact them, demand the money, and this horrible ordeal will be over. Today might be the day they call. It was a conflicting emotion to look forward to a kidnapper's call.

Silence passed between them for a moment. Webb reached out and squeezed Etolia's hand. She regarded his warm, caring eyes. So many years ago, he had pulled his car alongside her as she strolled down the street.

"*Whatcha doin', good looking?*" *he called from the window. She kept walking, refused to acknowledge him, but Webb wasn't discouraged. He eased the car to a crawl and followed her.* "*C'mon, pretty thing, speak to me. I mean ya no harm.*"

She stopped and whirled around. "*Leave me alone.*"

He got out of the car. "*No, darlin', that would just break my heart. I do believe I ain't never seen anything as pretty as you. Not even in the hills of Tennessee.*" *He tilted his hat.* "*My name's Webb Hunter. What's yours?*"

She wasn't going to tell him. Then he said, "*C'mon...tell me.*"

"*Etolia Vest. Now go away.*" *She started walking. He followed. She walked faster.*

"*Darlin', ya need to slow down so we can get acquainted. People gonna think ya runnin' away from me.*"

She giggled.

He walked faster. She finally slowed down. At the corner, she stopped.

"*How 'bout a date?*" *he asked.*

"*I don't want to date you.*"

"*Sure ya do. Ya just ain't got to know me yet. Once ya do, you'll want to go places with me...maybe to the movies.*"

Etolia turned. "*How about church?*"

"*Sure, that too.*"

From that day forward, Webb had been her strong fort that weathered all storms. Mary Faye's disappearance was the worst storm they had ever gone through.

"Mary Faye did the same thing every Saturday,

followed the same path," said Webb.

Etolia nodded in agreement as he spoke.

"Maybe someone noticed how she always went downtown at the same time of day. Her steps would be so easy to notice. It wouldn't take long to catch on. They could have been watching her for the last two or three weeks, then grabbed her."

"But who?"

"I don't know. Could have been anyone. Or it could have been someone who just noticed her yesterday."

"But I know Mary Faye. She would have never got into a stranger's car."

"No, but she would take a cab."

"Yes, and it did rain a little yesterday afternoon. That's the only thing that makes sense...a cab." Etolia suddenly gasped. "Oh! I told her to take a cab—that it looked like it might rain."

Webb caught her hand again. "Mary Faye would get into a cab whether you mentioned it or not. So, don't even think about blaming yourself."

Etolia bit her lip and nodded.

"There was a car last night," she said. "It was a little after eight. I was sitting on the front porch in the swing. It drove by real slow—so slow that I thought it would stop. Going real slow all way down the street and when they got to the house, they just crept by, then sped up and left. You think it means anything?"

"I don't know. We need to tell the police. Do you know what kind of car it was?"

"No...just light-colored."

A faint knock came across the house from the front door. A minute later, Grady, one of Webb's brothers stepped into the kitchen.

"Webb," Grady said. "There's a detective here to see y'all."

Bob Hancock stood just inside the living room with his

gray fedora in his hands. Webb and Etolia greeted him.

"Good morning sir," Bob said, holding out his hand to shake Webb's hand. "Ma'am." He tilted his head to Etolia. "My name is Sergeant Bob Hancock. I'm an investigator for the state police. I'm sorry we have to meet under these circumstances. I'm afraid that we haven't had a lot of luck in finding your daughter. If you don't mind, I have a few questions."

"Of course," Webb said. "Let's go into the kitchen. Not as much noise or people in there. Would you like a cup of coffee?"

"No, but thank you."

"Please, have a seat."

Bob sat at the kitchen table. He studied the couple. They appeared to be in their late fifties or early sixties. It was hard to guess someone's age when they had been through a night like the Hunters had just endured.

"Is there any news at all?" Etolia asked.

Bob's thoughts on the young woman had completely changed in the last few hours. Something terrible had happened to Mary Faye Hunter. It was his duty to find her and hopefully, bring her home alive.

Webb and Etolia told Bob everything they had already discussed with the Decatur Police. Mary Faye had left home, walked to the House of Beauty, and picked up instant potatoes at the A&P.

"You said that you're a state investigator," said Webb. "Does that mean the state of Alabama is now handling the investigation?"

"Not exclusively. The city and the county are also investigating. We are all working as a team to find your daughter."

"Good." Etolia dabbed her eyes with the tip of a napkin she had taken from the table. She squeezed the cloth tightly. Her fingers kneaded the fabric. The pain that consumed her heart was evident on her face. Her baby, her only daughter, vanished as if she had never existed. Why? Her brain screamed the simple question, but there were no answers. What were they supposed to do? Just sit there?

Etolia jumped to her feet. The kitchen chair overturned. "Please," she said, "excuse me." She left the room. Crossed the living room as if she saw no one and made her way once again to the swing on the porch. She sat down and prayed.

"Father in heaven, you know where she is. Please don't let her be afraid. Don't let her be in pain. Please watch over my daughter."

Etolia didn't see Bob Hancock ease the screen door open. He watched her pray, heard her soft *Amen* before he approached her.

"Mrs. Hunter, I have no way of knowing what you are going through, nor would I even pretend to. But I do want to find your daughter. To accomplish that, you're going to have to tell me everything, even the smallest details."

Etolia raised her head, her eyes moist, her lips trembled. "I know everyone here is wanting the same thing. They want her home. I don't know what else I can say that would help."

"Tell me about the night before. Friday night."

"Friday night? We had such a nice time in Huntsville. We went to dinner to celebrate Mary Faye's birthday. Who would have thought 34-years-ago when I held that baby girl in my arms that tonight I would be sitting here on this front porch crying because someone has stolen her?"

Etolia sniffed. She blinked her eyes rapidly, chasing back the tears.

"The night she was born, I cried because the doctor said she had a cleft palate. Can you imagine crying over something that in the long run didn't amount to a hill of beans? Yes, it was hard on her sometimes. Kids made fun of her. What was that compared to this? Nothing."

Etolia attempted to take a deep breath, but her lip

quivered during the intake of air, making it sound as if she would burst into tears.

"Did she give any indication she might have been upset about anything?" asked Bob.

"No. She ate a good meal. In fact, she picked the restaurant. A steakhouse because she knew her daddy loved steak. And instead of birthday cake, she said she wanted lemon icebox pie for dessert." Etolia smiled. "Mary Faye told the waiter that she wanted a great big slice. When he returned with her pie we all laughed at the size of it. She ate every bite of it too."

The smile melted away.

"Mrs. Hunter, what about Saturday morning when you saw her? Exactly where was she when the two of you met on the sidewalk?"

"Not far from the house. On the same block. Everything was fine when I saw her. Mary Faye said she would pick up those potatoes for me right after her appointment with the hairdresser."

"So she didn't get anything but the potatoes?"

"No, I don't think so. We didn't discuss buying anything else. Sometimes she would buy a small bag of candy."

Etolia paused. For a moment she was in deep thought.

"Last night a car crept by here. I was sitting on the porch, and this car...I don't know if it means anything, but it came by very slowly. After it passed the house, it sped up." She searched his eyes for hope. "Could it mean something?"

"Perhaps. Then again, maybe not. Someone may have heard that Mary Faye was missing and their curiosity got the best of them."

Etolia stood. "I don't know what else I could tell you."

"Just keep thinking. If anything...and I mean anything comes to mind, you let me know. Don't think it might be insignificant. You let me decide what's important. Okay?"

Etolia nodded.

"Mrs. Hunter, this is going to sound strange, but we're gonna have to search your crawlspace this afternoon."

"What? Are you telling me you think she is under our house?"

"No, ma'am. Just a formality."

"Are you not just looking there because you don't know where else to look?"

"The more places that we can eliminate the faster we're going to find Mary Faye. Trust me."

"Okay. I'll tell Webb so he will understand why there are men crawling around under our house."

"Ma'am, also know we are looking everywhere. There's a rescue squad that will be searching the river. A plane is going up as well to get aerial shots. The river isn't that far from Eighth Avenue. That doesn't mean she is in the river, it just means we are searching everywhere. We are also talking to anyone who might have any information about where your daughter might be."

"Thank you." Etolia turned and went back into the house to find Webb, to tell him the noise he will hear is someone under the house looking for their daughter. She would have to explain it to him tactfully.

-2-

"Come," she said.

"Where?"

"I want you to dance with me."

Mary Faye held out her hand. Adam reached for the small hand with the long delicate fingers. Just before their fingers could touch, she was gone.

Adam jolted awake. He checked his surroundings. Adam was sitting in the living room by the fireplace. He was alone. His wife had gone to church. He had a dull headache and decided to stay home. There had been very little rest last night. Sleep had brought her to him, but reality stole her away.

Chapter 41

Monday - 8:30 am

Bob Hancock didn't know what he would find at Redstone Arsenal, but no one was perfect. Maybe if he could talk to the right person, he might discover something about Mary Faye that would give him a lead. Her parents could not possibly know everything about their daughter. If Mary Faye had any secrets, Redstone was an ideal place to start looking. It was a safe distance away from the prying eyes of her parents and the scorn of church members.

The first person on the list to speak with was the supervisor of the department. Like Bob, Adam Fletcher had served in the Korean War. Fletcher had been at Redstone for the last four years and transferred to Mary Faye's department a year ago.

Sergeant Bob Hancock and Detective Ernest Bowman stood in Fletcher's office. Bob told the supervisor the bad news.

"Miss Hunter has been missing since Saturday afternoon," said Bob. "We're here to speak with her co-workers to see if they know anything."

Adam Fletcher inhaled deeply and nodded.

"I would first like to see her desk," said Bowman.

"Yes, of course," said Fletcher. This way." Adam Fletcher led him to Mary Faye's desk just outside his office. "This is it." He pointed to the desk.

Detective Bowman began going through the drawers, searching through papers. "What about this date on the calendar? Got any idea what it means?"

Adam glanced at the large desk calendar. For the month of May, there was only one date marked. Saturday, May 6. It was circled in red ink.

"I have no idea at all," said Fletcher.

"Maybe one of her friends might know," Bowman replied. His eyes traveled over the room. "Which of these ladies would you say she was close with?"

"I'm not really sure. I have noticed her eating lunch in the cafeteria with a few of the women from this department. Let me think for a minute...Oh, yes. Louella Ketchum. Her desk is the first one as you come through the door, and two desks over from her is Joyce Wallace. Andrea Brown is next to Joyce."

"Okay. If you would, bring those women to your office."

After a quick word, all three women followed Adam Fletcher back to his office. They appeared to be confused. Apparently, the news of Mary Faye's disappearance had not yet reached them.

Webb had called Paul Hurst on Saturday night. He told him Mary Faye was missing. Paul and Madolyn visited them on Sunday. They asked if there was anything they could do. Madolyn had brought a baked ham. She put it on the dining room table beside the one that Etolia had planned to bake before Mary Faye disappeared.

The men in the carpool had discussed Mary Faye on their way to work that morning. They decided to keep quiet about it once they arrived at work. They figured the cops would be coming and it wouldn't be wise to stir up anything.

"Just a few questions ladies," Bob said as they came into the room. "First, please give us your names." Each woman complied. Detective Bowman wrote the names on his notepad.

"I am Sergeant Bob Hancock from the state police. This is Detective Ernest Bowman from the Decatur Police Department. My understanding is that each of you knows Mary Faye Hunter pretty well."

The women exchanged glances, then nodded. They all continued to look puzzled.

"When you were working with Miss Hunter last week, did she say or do anything out of character?" asked Bob.

"No, she was just Mary Faye," Louella replied. "Mary Faye, like you said was a co-worker, but she was also a very private person."

"How long have you worked with her, Mrs. Ketchum?" Bowman asked.

"She's been here longer than me. I started back in 1960."

It never fails, Bob thought. He asked a simple question and in return, got a loaded answer.

"Did Mary Faye confide anything to you?" asked Bob.

"It's not like we are close friends," said Louella. I mean, we work in the same office and eat lunch together. That's about it."

Joyce and Andrea nodded in agreement.

"She was friendly once you got to know her," Joyce said, "but Mary Faye didn't say a whole lot unless someone mentioned music or travel."

"She likes baseball," said Andrea.

"What?" said Bob.

"Baseball. She went to see the Yankees play one time."

"When? Who did she go with?"

"It was a few years ago, but I know she was with her parents. She traveled to a lot of places with them. I don't think she ever went anywhere without her parents."

"Does May 6 mean anything to y'all?" Bowman asked.

The women shook their heads.

"Why?" asked Joyce. "Should it?"

"It's circled on Miss Hunter's calendar."

"Maybe she had to play for a wedding or concert," said Joyce.

"Is Mary Faye in some kind of trouble?" asked Louella. "Whatever it is, Mary Faye is innocent. That girl never does anything wrong. You talk about a woman who is above reproach, that's Mary Faye."

"She's missing," said Bob.

"Missing!" Louella shouted. Shock spread across her face.

"How can she be missing?" asked Joyce.

"Miss Hunter was last seen walking home after she left the A&P Super Market."

"Oh, my gosh!" Andrea said. "Where can she be?"

"That's what we're trying to figure out."

"I know this much," Joyce said, "Mary Faye wouldn't have left on her own. She couldn't do that to her parents. She's just not that kind of person. Mary Faye is a very sweet woman."

Sweet. Nice. Good Christian woman.

Same words over and over. There was no doubt in Bob Hancock's mind that the woman had met with foul play. Ernest Bowman leered at Bob as if to say, We told you so.

"Thank you, ladies." Bob dismissed them back to their workstations. After they left the office, he turned back to Adam Fletcher. "Is there anyone else here that might know Mary Faye on a personal level?"

Adam Fletcher swallowed hard. "Not that I'm aware of."

"She rode in a carpool," Detective Bowman said.

Bowman flipped pages in his notebook. "Paul Hurst, Rick Overton, Almon Hensley, and Stephen Harkins. We need to speak with each one of these men."

"Yes, sir. Come with me." Fletcher led the detectives to the warehouse.

As soon as the men left the clerical department, Louella hurried over to Joyce and Andrea .

"Okay, you two. Do we tell what we've noticed in the last few months?"

"No!" Joyce hissed. "All we have seen was her talking and laughing a little. We have nothing else to go on. It could ruin his life...might lose his job if they brought him in for this."

"But what if they were having an affair?" Louella asked.

"Do you honestly believe Mary Faye would have an affair with a married man? This is Mary Faye you're talking about."

"She's right, Louella. It would be so wrong if we pointed the finger at him and turned out to that he's innocent. Think about his wife and kids." Andrea shook her head while she talked.

"But they said anything," Louella said.

"You know how cops are," said Joyce. They will tear a person apart if they think there is the smallest thing there. Then when there's nothing there, the person is left in tatters, and they move on to someone else. No, if we had something tangible, something that proved he was involved with her, then yes, but just because two people talk and laugh together, no. Too much at stake." Joyce shrugged her shoulders. "If you want to toss out the name, go ahead, but I'm not."

"Okay," Louella said. She returned to her desk. She thought about the young man she often saw talking to Mary Faye Hunter.

-2-

CJ Cantrell waited on Joyce as she walked out of the clerical office. He followed her down the hallway to the exit. Before she reached the door, he caught her. "Joyce." She looked over her shoulder. "Can we talk?"

"Sure," she said.

"What have you heard about Mary Faye?"

"She went missing Saturday afternoon right after she left a grocery store. Someone must have taken her."

"But why? Why would anyone take Mary Faye?"

He held the door for Joyce to pass through. She looked at CJ closely, searching his eyes.

"There's been talk...You know that, don't you?"

"People always want to talk. Talk about things they know nothing about."

"I know. And talk can get people in trouble. Hopefully, they'll turn every stone to find her. Mary Faye doesn't deserve this."

"No, she doesn't," said CJ. "She's a good person."

* * *

"They made me very nervous," Rick said as the carpool headed back to Decatur that evening.

"Why?" Paul asked.

"I'm the only single man in this carpool. I don't want them thinking that just because I'm single and Mary Faye is single that there's a connection."

"They won't think that," Almon Hensley said.

"What do y'all think about the one she talks to in the hallways, laughing and talking?" asked Paul.

Paul did not want to say his name. He knew the others had seen it. Everyone had seen it, but would anyone identify the man to law enforcement?

"That may not have anything to do with her disappearance," said Stephen. "Mr. Fletcher could lose his job. We don't have any reason to believe he would harm her. Sounds to me like someone just took her, for whatever reason."

"I don't think we need to be spreading office gossip," said Paul. "We don't have anything to report other than we saw them talking and laughing. I'll admit, that's not like Mary Faye. She's not one to be flirting with anyone. It's kinda odd how they would go off by themselves and talk, but that doesn't mean he had anything to do with her missing."

Paul Hurst drove across the Kelly Memorial Bridge. For the next couple of minutes, the men were silent. Finally, Almon broke the ice.

"All we can do is wait. See if anything else comes up. If nothing happens, we keep quiet. If the police find something that connects Fletcher to Mary Faye, then we'll speak up. Until then, we say nothing. It's not just about protecting him. This is also about Mary Faye. She doesn't need her reputation ruined."

-3-

"You seen this?" Rusty Cole flipped the newspaper page around. "That's Mary Faye Hunter. Says she's missing. She's connected to that store downtown—Hunter Furniture Store."

Phillip Pierce scanned the pages but didn't read the article. "What's it saying?"

"Just what I said—they're lookin' for her. She's missing."

"Let me see that," Marty Tyler said. He glanced at the photo before he read the article. "Huh." He gave the newspaper back to Rusty. "Never know about people, do you?"

"Whatcha mean?" Phillip asked.

"Maybe she got tired of Decatur."

Phillip turned away, grabbed a rag, and dusted the

dashboard of the ambulance. "They got any idea why she left?"

"Don't think so," Rusty said. "When y'all get through cleaning the inside of that ambulance, make sure there's no trash left in the floorboard either."

Phillip nodded. "Guess they'll be searching everywhere for that girl."

"Probably," Rusty Cole said as he took his newspaper and went back into the office.

"They won't find her."

"What?" said Marty.

"They won't find her."

"Why you say that?"

"Because they don't have a smoking gun."

Chapter 42

Monday, May 8, 1967 - 4:33 pm

Dr. Carter held the newspaper tightly in his hands. A small section on the front page told about a missing young Decatur woman. According to the article, she was last seen at the A&P on Johnston Street. A brief description was given. He read it closely. They didn't mention her innocent smile or her warm personality, he thought. The photograph of her wasn't good at all. It did not reveal the twinkle in her eyes when she talked about music. It was just a face. The photo made her look hard, cold, and aloof. Dr. Carter put down the newspaper. A minute later, he picked it up again and re-read the article. When Dr. Carter finished, he slapped the desk with the folded paper.

There was nothing he could do. He couldn't tell anyone Mary Faye was pregnant. That information would not help the police find her. It might only make things worse for everyone. That was the last thing he needed. Thank goodness there was no paperwork filed about Mary Faye's pregnancy.

Dr. Carter threw the newspaper into the wastebasket.

Chapter 43

Monday, May 8, 1967 – 5:22 pm

At 811 Eighth Avenue, people were in the living room, kitchen, porch, and in the yard. People conversed, but to Webb's displeasure, some laughed. Obviously, the source of the laughter had nothing to do with Mary Faye. Still, it was a somber time, not a party. Etolia reminded him that everyone was there because they cared. He knew why they were there, why they brought in food, why they consoled him, but when Webb heard someone laugh, he felt disrespected.

Detectives had been there earlier as well as the Chief of Police, Pack Self. They had more questions. Everyone wanted to know the same thing.

Did Mary Faye say anything about going on a trip? Who were her current friends, best friends, old friends, enemies?

The questions seemed endless. No one seemed to have any answers as to what happened to their daughter—only speculation. Still no ransom call or letter. Surely, if she had been taken, someone would have called demanding money.

Instead, there was nothing.

"Webb, why don't you eat a bit," said his brother, Robert. "You've got to keep up your strength."

"Did you know they dragged the river yesterday?" asked Webb. Then they flew a plane over the entire area. Said it was just protocol in this kind of investigation. How are they gonna see anything from way up there?"

"Oh, you'd be surprised what they can see, Webb. They know what they're doing."

"Must not...they haven't found her yet."

"No, but they will. C'mon and eat a bit."

"I just can't, Robert." Webb shook his head slowly. "Just can't." He sighed. "They even searched under the house for her. Did you know that? Craziest thing I ever heard of. Again, they said it was just protocol. Where has all of that nonsense gotten us?"

Robert nodded. "I see what you mean, but they are doing everything they can to find her, and they will. Just got to keep praying that Mary Faye will be home soon."

Webb shut his eyes and sighed again. He listened to everyone chatting and waited for the next person to laugh so he could unleash all the pent up frustration on them. This wasn't a party. Mary Faye was missing. He did not say the words aloud, but his mind kept pushing them forward. Mary Faye could be dead. Wherever she was, he knew she was in enormous danger.

Webb sat down at the kitchen table. Jimmy entered the kitchen behind him.

"Daddy," he said. Jimmy put a hand on his shoulder. "Momma is worried about you. She said you hadn't eaten much since Saturday. You know that's a bad idea."

Jimmy and his family had arrived early Sunday morning. He listened to what the police were saying, and everyone else, but he didn't tell them what he knew. There was no way that Jimmy would ruin Mary Faye's reputation. If she could come home, she would. He feared that she was dead. Jimmy wondered if she had decided to see a back alley abortionist. But he couldn't say that. If he was wrong, it would destroy his sister's reputation, break his parents' heart. The very thing that Mary Faye was attempting to prevent. What about the married man who had gotten her pregnant? Maybe they ran away together and started a new life. Nonsense. Even if Mary Faye did that, she would have at least told him about it. Besides, she would never intentionally hurt their parents no matter how much she loved this married man.

Maybe he killed her.

Mary Faye had served her purpose and became too much of a liability. She had complicated his life, and he was afraid that Mary Faye was going to tell his wife everything, including the pregnancy.

If only I knew who this guy was. Why didn't I make her tell me?

"Every time I put a bite of food in my mouth," said Webb, "I think about your sister, wondering if she's got any food. Wondering if she's hungry, scared..." Webb's voice faltered. He looked at his son weakly and tried to whisper something to him. Jimmy had to lean in to hear.

"Son...I'm afraid. I'm so afraid...that...she's gone. That she's...dead." Tears flooded his eyes, ready to spill. He didn't want Etolia to see him cry. Webb covered his face and sobbed quietly. Jimmy put his arm around his dad and shielded him from everyone's view.

"No, daddy, don't say that." Jimmy patted his back. "You got to believe she'll be coming home soon." Webb did not look up but nodded. "And you have to eat. Doctor's orders."

Webb smiled up at Jimmy. He picked up a piece of ham and put it inside a roll, making a sandwich. Jimmy suddenly realized that he was also crying.

The phone rang six times before a man's voice came across the line. "Hello."

"I tried to call you earlier," Dr. Carter said.

"Oh, so that was you who hung up."

"I had no desire for your wife to wonder why I was calling your house." The man on the other end of the line did not respond. "You still there?"

"Yeah, I'm here."

"You read that article in the newspaper?"

"Yeah, I saw it. What about it?"

"She's missing."

"Whatcha want me to do about it?"

"I need to know if something went wrong. Tell me the truth."

"Look, I told ya, she was a no show. Now we know why."

"You better not be lying to me about this."

"And if I was—just what would you do about it? I don't believe you're in any position to be making threats."

"I mean it."

"Yeah, sure doc. But hey, it doesn't matter anyway because I'm telling you the truth. This gal was a no show. I don't know what happened to her. It's not my concern and shouldn't be yours either. We both got a lot at risk here. The last thing we need is for anyone to know you made an appointment for her to…get help."

Rusty was right. There was nothing he could do. If the law ever found out about their little racket, they would both go to jail, and Mary Faye Hunter would still be missing.

"I don't think we should be helping any more women for a while," Dr. Carter said. "If we get picked up for that, they might zero in on us about this missing woman."

Dr. Carter did want Rusty to know how well he knew Mary Faye Hunter or how concerned he was about her well-being. Something bad must have happened to her, and he couldn't help but wonder if his partner had anything to do with her disappearance.

"You do whatever you want, Doc, but I have no intention of passing up on this little business. If I don't do it, someone else will. You do what you want. But naw, it's easy money, and I ain't givin' it up."

"Fine. But for right now, count me out."

Laughter sounded in his ear. "Sure, Doc, but you'll be back."

Dr. Carter hung up the phone without saying bye. He was probably right. For him, it was more than just the money. If a woman wanted to end her pregnancy, she should have the choice. What was the big deal?

But where was Mary Faye Hunter? If Rusty wasn't responsible, then it must have been Mary Faye's boyfriend. But who was he?

Chapter 44

10:00 pm

Paul Hurst lay beside his wife. The room was completely dark.
"They came to the Arsenal today."
"Who?"
"Detectives. Asking questions about Mary Faye. Wanting to know if there was anything out of the ordinary going on with her. I wanted to say something, but I didn't. The fellas in the carpool didn't think it was a good idea either. What if Fletcher had nothing to do with Mary Faye's disappearance? It could ruin his life. His marriage. Just because he talked to her at work. That's not a good enough reason to potentially destroy a man's life."
"But she's not just someone that's missing," said Madolyn. "She's Mary Faye Hunter."
"Yeah, I know. She's a family friend. I've known her daddy for years. Another reason why I should say something."
"Maybe someone else will say something."
"I doubt it."
"What about Fletcher? Maybe he'll volunteer some

information."

"Why would he want to be caught up in an investigation when he's not guilty of something?"

"Paul, I don't believe Mary Faye was having an affair with a married man. That's just not Mary Faye. Stop worrying about whether you should or shouldn't say something."

"You're probably right. I just wish they could find that poor girl."

"So do I." She rolled over and slipped her arm around his stomach. "You need to get something else on your mind and get some sleep."

Paul patted her arm. Sleep didn't come easy, but finally, it carried him off to a world where the river flowed, and the fish were jumping. A faint outline of a woman stood on the bank as if she were watching the fish.

"I had the craziest dream last night," Paul said the next morning. "It was about fish, the river, and I don't know if the woman was supposed to be Mary Faye, but some woman had stood by the riverbank. I guess it was because I had her on my mind and one day we were all talking about fishing on the way to work."

"I'm not surprised," Madolyn said. "The way you were wrestling with what to do about Fletcher." She filled his coffee cup.

"Probably so." He drank his coffee.

-2-

"Did you know that woman that is missing?" asked Martha.

"Yes. In fact, she worked in my office," said Adam.

They were sitting at the kitchen table. A plate of food was in front of Adam, but he wasn't hungry. He cut the eggs, moved them around, but instead of eating them, reached for his coffee.

"Detectives were in my department yesterday asking everyone questions. No one seemed to know anything. At least I don't think they did."

"So very sad. I was reading the article in the paper. Sounds like the police don't have a clue where she is."

Adam sipped his coffee and kept his eyes on his plate.

"Makes you wonder how she could just vanish. Would she have left town?"

"Oh, no. Not her. She wasn't like that."

"Huh. You never really know people. How are you handling all of this?"

Adam made eye contact.

"What do you mean?" he asked.

"Haven't you missed her?"

Adam put down his fork and sat up straight.

"Why would I miss her? I barely know her."

Martha did not like the look in Adam's eyes. She had seen that cold glare many times when he had daydreamed about the Korean War.

"No, honey. I didn't mean it like that. I meant that you had missed her productivity. Losing a good employee affects the entire department."

"Right. Yeah, I did have to make some adjustments, but I think everything will be fine."

"Well, I hope she's okay."

Adam Fletcher nodded. "Yes, me too." He took a bite of the eggs, then pushed his plate away. "I've got to get to work." He leaned over, kissed his wife, and went out the back door.

Martha picked up his plate, tossed the uneaten food away, and put the dish in the sink. She loved her husband, but sometimes his moods drove her mad.

They had gotten married after his tour in the military. Martha had thought she knew him well, but until you live with a person, you do not really know them. That's how it was now. Sometimes Adam was great. Other times, the opposite. Marriage wasn't a fairy tale. Find your prince and live happily ever after. That's not reality. Love is mysterious. What makes someone fall in love with a certain person? What keeps that love alive? Was it predestined?

"I don't know anymore," she said to herself as she turned on hot water for the dishes. "Maybe I never knew." She glimpsed at her reflection in the plate before she placed it into the water.

-3-

CJ Cantrell turned his 1966 Ford Mustang onto Sixth Avenue and hit every red light before he reached the Steamboat Bill Bridge heading east to the Arsenal. He wasn't in the best of moods. He was worried about Mary Faye. Everyone who knew her, knew Mary Faye did not run away. Something horrible must have happened to her. Worrying about her had put him in a somber mood. CJ had already snapped at his wife this morning. They ended up having a big argument, but now he couldn't remember what it was about.

"What's the matter with you?" she had demanded.

CJ didn't have an answer. Joan knew about Mary Faye's disappearance, but she didn't know that CJ was good friends with her. He never told her about Mary Faye being at the Fort to hear his band. Or the record he bought her. No one did. And that was how he wanted to keep it. When those cops came around with their questions, he didn't know what to say. Sure they talked, but that wasn't any of their business. He wasn't going to tell them anything.

A car horn blasted. The light had changed.

"All right!" he shouted into the rearview mirror, glancing at the Chevy behind him. It was then he realized it was Mr. Fletcher. Great. Have an argument with his supervisor first thing in the morning before he can even clock in.

Just what I need.

The Mustang scooted under the light and over the bridge. Maybe Steamboat Bill had the right idea. Just sail down the river on a steamboat, stopping at different towns, loving all the women, and never having any real roots. Guilt quickly rushed over him. No, he wouldn't take anything for his family. There are times when that's all a person has left.

Chapter 45

Tuesday, May 9, 1967 – 7:34 pm

Rick Overton's home was quiet. Through the front window, Bob Hancock and E.B. Watts could see the dim, grayish blue light coming from a TV. Shadows flickered.

Overton lived alone. He was going through a divorce, but something else had caught their eyes. Overton had been arrested a couple of years ago for making a death threat.

Watts rang the bell.

The front door creaked open. A nervous face appeared from the darkness.

"Rick Overton?" asked Watts.

"Who's asking?" replied the man.

"I'm Lieutenant Watts and with me is Sergeant Hancock. We're with the state police."

The man nodded and looked away.

"Come in," said the man.

They followed the man across the foyer into a small dining area. They all sat at the table.

"We're sorry to bother you this evening, Mr. Overton," said Watts. We need to ask you a few questions about the disappearance of Mary Faye Hunter."

Watts glanced around as if he wanted to search everything.

"Yes, of course," said Rick. "I'm afraid I wouldn't be much help to you. I only know her from the carpool."

"Yes, sir, we understand that," said Watts. "We would still like to ask you a few questions."

"She might have said something that seemed to have no significance at the time," said Hancock, "but maybe it would now."

"I don't know what that would be."

Bob leaned forward. "Did Mary Faye mention anything about May 6? For any reason at all. That day was circled on her work calendar."

"May 6? No." Rick ran his hand over his hair down to the back of his neck. "May 6...That was last Saturday, the day she disappeared?"

"Yes, sir," Watts replied.

"No, no...I don't remember her saying anything about that particular day." Rick thought for a moment. "Maybe a wedding? She played piano at a lot of weddings."

"No, it wasn't a wedding." Hancock scanned the room. "You live here alone?"

Rick blushed and looked down. "Yes. I'm currently going through a divorce."

"I see." Hancock's eyes continued to roam, and then settled back to Overton. "You ever ask Mary Faye out?"

"What?" Rick sat up straight. "No. Never. Mary Faye was a fine Christian lady—"

"You don't like fine Christian ladies?" Hancock asked.

"Wait...No. No. Don't put words into my mouth. Look here, I told y'all that I don't know anything about this. I don't know her friends. I don't think Mary Faye had any close friends."

Oh, yes she did, but there was no way I was going to say that.

Lieutenant Watts stood and swaggered around the

room.

"You know," said Watts. "You can learn a lot about a person just by observing his surroundings."

Several books were lined across a shelf. Sports magazines were piled on a table by an overstuffed chair. Nothing to indicate a female lived there.

"Who's your girlfriend?" asked Watts, with his head cocked.

"Girlfriend?"

"Yeah. Does she know Mary Faye?"

Nancy. How would they know about Nancy? Church. That's it.

"I'm seeing someone. It's nothing serious. She goes to the same church as Mary Faye."

"What's her name?"

"Nancy. Nancy Wilbroughs."

"She knows Mary Faye?"

"Yeah. Nancy sings in the choir."

Beads of sweat were forming under Rick's lips.

Rick stood. "Look, I don't know any more than anyone else does about Mary Faye. " Rick shoved his hands into his pockets.

Watts noticed the movement. He kept his eyes on Rick's hands. He didn't believe the man was dangerous, but the man was jittery.

"I'm telling you, I don't know anything about her disappearance. I ride in a carpool with her. That's the limit of my relationship with Mary Faye Hunter."

"Okay," Hancock said. "We thank you for your cooperation. Anything that you might think of, just let us know."

Rick Overton removed his hands from his pockets. "Yeah, sure. But like I said…I don't know anything."

Rick followed the investigators to the door. Bob turned back, offered his hand as Watts opened the front door. "Good evening, Mr. Overton."

"Yes...yes, goodnight to y'all."
Rick Overton closed the door.
"What do you think?" Watts asked as he stepped off the porch.
"Nervous little guy, isn't he?" said Bob.
"I'll say. Wonder why?"
"I don't know, but I think we better find out."

Chapter 46

Bob Hancock sat at his desk, shuffled papers, thumbed through notes, and scanned pages he had compiled on the Mary Faye Hunter case. She had been missing for two weeks. The local newspapers and media outlets had tracked her story from day one. A Mother's Day article appeared on the front page of the Decatur Daily detailing the sadness of the Hunter family, and how Mary Faye's mother had looked forward to a Mother's Day spent with her family. Instead, it had been a grief-stricken day for Etolia, searching for any clues that might reveal what had happened to her daughter.

Bob had reports from the other departments that were working the case. Detectives from the Decatur Police Department, as well as the Morgan County Sheriff's Department. Limestone County had been notified as well. They had checked every nearby abandoned building, but there had been no signs of the missing woman.

The Hunter family posted a two thousand dollar reward for any information that would lead them to Mary Faye. Wisely, the reward was only offered for ten days. If someone wanted the money, they had to act fast. Fast with the hope that Mary Faye was still alive somewhere.

Unfortunately, the strategy had not worked.

Bob studied each file. He searched for anything that might have escaped him. They had interviewed dozens of people. Family member, co-workers, church members, neighbors, store clerks. Every place they could think of that Mary Faye had contact with people, they questioned them. But the answers were almost always the same.

As he through the papers, Bob noticed something. No one had spoken with Mary Faye's doctor.

Who was her doctor?

He picked up the phone and dialed a number. It rang only once.

"Hello, Mrs. Hunter, this is Sergeant Bob Hancock. I was wondering if you could tell me who Mary Faye's doctor was?"

"Well, yes," she said. "His name is Dr. Malcolm Carter."

"Can you tell me where his office is?"

Etolia gave Bob the address, and he wrote it on a notepad.

"Mary Faye hasn't been sick." Etolia thought about the headaches, but that was just a headache. Mary Faye hadn't gone to the doctor.

"Just thought I'd check."

"Oh, yes, we understand."

Bob could hear the sadness in her voice. There was nothing he could say that would alleviate her sorrow. He had a few leads, but none of them felt right.

Bob thanked Etolia for her cooperation. He hung up the phone and quickly dialed the doctor's number.

"I need to speak with Dr. Malcolm Carter."

"I'm sorry, he's with a patient," said the receptionist. "Would you like to make an appointment?"

Bob introduced himself and explained the reason for his call. The woman seemed surprised.

"Yes, sir. I'll make sure that he gets your message

right away."

* * *

The receptionist hung up the phone and gave the message to a nurse. A few minutes later, the nurse handed the note to Dr. Carter as he left one of the exam rooms.

"You might want to take this before you see your next patient."

He looked at the note. Without saying a word, he went into his office and dialed the number.

"Hancock speaking," Bob answered.

"Hi. This Dr. Malcolm Carter. I was returning your call."

"Hello, doctor. I need to ask you a few questions if you have a moment."

"Sure."

"I'm working on the Mary Faye Hunter case. I was told that you are Mary Faye's primary care physician."

"Yes, that's correct."

"When was the last time you treated her?"

Dr. Carter had not considered the police would question him, but it did not surprise him either. After all, Mary Faye was his patient. He remained calm. There were no records of her last visit.

"I don't recall off the top of my head. I would have to check my records. If I had to guess, the last time she came to my office was around the first of the year. Just a routine physical. For the most part, she's a strong, healthy, young woman."

"I see. I'll need to verify that appointment."

"No, problem. Just have her parents request them, and I'll be glad to send them over to your office."

"Okay, thank you." The call ended, and Bob Hancock felt he had hit another dead end.

-2-

It was 4:15 pm. Bob Hancock and E.B. Watts waited in their state-issued 1964 *Ford Galaxie* in front of Rick Overton's home. It was hot inside the car. Minimal air circulated. Spring felt like summer most of the time in the South, and today was no different.

"Overton's file was mighty interesting," said Bob.

"Yes, it was," replied Watts.

"But I don't think he had anything to do with Mary Faye Hunter's disappearance."

"Why do you say that?"

"Overton doesn't fit the profile. The only thing we have against him is a quarrel between him and his wife. He might be a hot head, but he's not our guy."

"You may be right, but it's worth a shot. What other leads do we have to follow?"

"True."

"We'll shake him up and see if he stirs."

Bob rolled his eyes at Watts's attempt at humor.

"He might not come straight home," Bob said.

"We'll be here when he does."

"What does he drive?"

"Probably a Henry J. He just looks like a Henry J kind of guy."

Bob chuckled. "And what would that be?"

Before Watts could answer, a car approached and pulled into the driveway. Rick Overton stepped out of the white Dodge. He walked to the porch with his keys in hand. Bob and E.B. exited the vehicle.

"Mr. Overton," Bob called. Rick turned around. Astonishment flashed across his face. The investigators hurried toward Overton. He glanced around as if he was trapped, nowhere to run or hide.

"Just need to ask you a few questions," said Watts.

"I've done told y'all that I don't know anything else

about Mary Faye Hunter." Rick hurried to the front door. "I don't know why y'all keep comin' around here. I barely know the woman."

Rick put the key into the lock. He stepped into the house with the detectives close behind.

"Have you ever been arrested?" Hancock asked.

Rick paused in the doorway.

"Arrested?"

"That's correct," said Hancock.

What did they know?

Rick placed his lunchbox on a small table by the door. How was he going to answer that?

"Why are you asking me that kind of a question?"

Bob smiled. Not a friendly smile. A sly fox smile. "Because I want to know your answer."

The investigator didn't say he wanted the answer. He wanted my answer.

Rick stepped into the living room. The investigators followed.

"Okay. I was arrested once. I'm sure you know that already."

"Want to tell us about it?" asked Watts.

Rick didn't want to discuss it, but if he didn't, that would make him look even more suspicious. His failure to cooperate might imply that he was responsible for Mary Faye's disappearance.

What could he say? He turned his back to the men and rubbed the back of his head in a nervous gesture. "It wasn't a big deal."

"You don't think a death threat is a big deal?"

He turned. "My personal life is none of your business."

"I don't know about you," said Watts, "but I tend to take death threats very seriously. It tells me that you might be an unstable type of person."

"Listen, that whole thing was blown out of proportion. I was angry and I said something that I didn't mean. It was all taken care of in court."

Watts smiled.

"Okay, Rick. Let's get to the point. What we really want to talk to you about is Mary Faye Hunter. Do you know why she is missing?"

"No! Of course not!"

"Then why don't you tell us everything you know about her?" Hancock moved closer to Rick. "Did you ever see anything unusual going on with her? Did she ever complain about someone bothering her at work?"

"No. Mary Faye never said anything against anyone."

"Didn't seem afraid of anyone?"

"No one that I know at work would have a reason to bother her. To my knowledge, Mary Faye has always been treated with respect."

The detectives glanced at each other.

"Honest, fellas. If I knew anything, I'd tell you."

"Okay," Hancock said. "If you think of anything, let us know." He pulled a card from his breast pocket. "Here. My number is on the back."

Rick nodded. When the investigators left, he breathed a long sigh of relief.

Chapter 47

"Cops make me nervous," Rick said. "They were back at my house last night, asking me crazy questions like I know something about Mary Faye."

"It's only because you know her," Paul said.

Rick turned and regarded the other two passengers in the car.

"Have they been to y'all's house?"

"Well, yeah, of course," Stephen replied.

"We've all been questioned," Almon said. "It's only natural since she rode with us every day."

"Yeah, but I'm the only single man in this group. That's why they keep hounding me. Thinking that because I'm not married that me and Mary Faye had somethin' goin' on. That ain't fair."

He shook his head.

"Don't worry about it," said Paul.

He knew Rick couldn't have had anything to do with Mary Faye's disappearance. Paul wished he knew who did.

-2-

August 1967

"How you boys doin'?" Rusty Cole asked as he approached the city patrol car.

"We're good. How're you doing?"

Rusty propped himself against the open car window. He smiled at the two police officers.

"I'm doin'. That's about all I can say. Guess y'all have got that missin' woman case figured out, huh?"

"I wish," one of the officers said. "Course we're not working on the case right now. Ain't nothing going on. It's a dead end."

"What's the latest?" asked Rusty.

"Nothing. We've talked to just about everybody in town, and the only thing we know for sure is that she's a nice woman and would never leave home on her own."

"That sure is a shame," Rusty said.

The younger cop shook his head as he dropped his eyes.

"Just plain sad. Especially for her folks. They're sitting right next to the phone. I heard that they even brought in that psychic, Jeane Dixon. Hasn't done any good though. Dixon told the parents that their daughter was okay, but Mary Faye Hunter would be at home with her parents if she were okay."

Rusty shook his head. "Downright pitiful."

The other officer took a deep breath. His sigh was heavy. "Yeah, it is. No one has any good leads. How can a woman just disappear?"

"Beats me," Rusty said.

The conversation soon turned lighthearted. Rusty decided it was time to move on.

"I gotta get goin'. You boys keep all the crooks off the streets now, ya hear?"

"You know we will."

Chapter 48

The summer dragged on for more than three months in the South. Time is slow, and living is easy are just words in a song. The heat was heavy and sticky. In July, there were popup showers that refreshed everything until the unforgiving summer sun returned. It's almost as if God gave the crops a drink of water as they finished the growing season. Harvest would begin soon. August, on the other hand, was a sultry month that seemed to have no end.

Bob Hancock walked across the sun-bleached pavement to the Decatur Police Department. He had a meeting with Lieutenant Watts and a few detectives from the Decatur Police Department. Mary Faye had been missing for over three months, and they still did not have the slightest idea to her whereabouts. Bob would be leaving soon for Washington, D.C. There was an FBI training course that he wanted to complete so he could continue to move up the ranks. He wished it was today. Get on the plane and leave this hot city and crazy case behind for a while.

The problem was, Mary Faye never left him. Even when the day was over, her presence went home with him. Several members of law enforcement had spoken to every person they could think of, and no one offered anything. The cab driver had been another dead end. Bob had found out that Mary Faye would sometimes take a cab home. He checked with Yellow Cab to see if any of their employees had a criminal record. One of them did. William Oakley had only been with Yellow Cab for a few months. He was originally from Gastonia, North Carolina. He was a career criminal. Burglaries, mostly. No history of violence or sexual assault. On top of that, he had an alibi. At the time Mary Faye Hunter had gone missing, Oakley was driving a passenger to Moulton.

"Bob," Detective David Smith said as Hancock entered the room. "How are you doing this morning?"

"Hot. Mad."

"What's going on?" Smith asked.

"We ain't any closer to knowing what happened to Mary Faye Hunter today then we were on May 6."

Smith sighed. "Unfortunately, I'd have to agree."

Bob took a blank sheet of paper off the conference room table.

"See this?" He waved the paper over his head. "This is where we are. Nothing. We have no suspect. No body. No evidence of foul play. Bob crumbled up the paper and tossed it back on the table. He looked around the room. They were all there — investigators from the Sheriff's Department, Clarence Harris and Jerry Johnson. David Smith, Bob Andrews, and Ernest Bowman represented the Decatur Police. He and E.B. Watts with the state police.

"Anyone got any new ideas on how to approach this case?" asked Watts. "Frankly, we are just spinning our wheels."

No one answered.

"Okay," said Watts. "The only thing I know to do is let those reporters who are always hammering on the door for information, report that we expect to make an arrest soon."

"And?" Bob understood the strategy, but what would

happen when there was no arrest?

"And maybe whoever is guilty will get nervous and slip up."

"And?"

"What're you getting at, Bob?"

"And what happens if he doesn't slip up?"

"Citizens will forget we even said anything. They will move on to whatever else is going on in the news. We're the ones living with this case, not the general public."

"I'm not so sure about that. Seems like there's talk around town. Where is she? Who took her? Do y'all realize there are women who are afraid they might be next?"

"The fear will pass too."

Bob shrugged. Watts was probably right. It always passes. There's always a new case. Someone else gets killed, and Mary Faye Hunter will be pushed off the front pages.

"Go for it," said Bob. "You might as well."

Chapter 49

October 14, 1967

It was a sunny fall morning. The Housers rose early. There were always chores on a farm, but there was also time to enjoy with their grandchildren.

"Dewey, let's go fishing," Omal Houser said to her husband. A plate of hot biscuits was placed on the kitchen table to go with the platter of eggs and sausage. She put a jar of pear preserves on the table. Then poured two glasses of milk for her granddaughters Kim and Connie, next to a bowl of buttery grits. It was 7:30. The house cleaned—dusted, floors mopped, beds made, and now the whole day was free.

Six-year-old Kim ran to her grandmother and hugged her waist. "Is it time to go yet, Mam-Maw?"

"We got a few more chores to finish," said Omal. "While I'm doing that, you and Connie can go outside and dig up some worms. Pap-Paw will load the poles."

"Yay!" Kim shouted. Four-year-old Connie cheered with her sister.

"Need to check on those cows over on the refuge," Dewey said as he ate his breakfast. He spread preserves on the hot, buttered biscuit. In the south, hot biscuits with preserves, jellies, or jam are a staple. Sometimes a leftover cold biscuit and sweet jellies made an excellent snack with a frosty glass of milk.

"We can go over to the boat ramp to fish after checking on the cows," Omal replied.

The Houser farm on North Bethel Road backed against the Wheeler Wildlife Refuge. The rich river land was suitable for any crop. The pastureland was also good for cattle or hogs. They rented land that belonged to the refuge with their son.

By 8:30, they had loaded the car and were approaching the Wheeler Wildlife Refuge. They turned off Highway 67 onto Hickory Hill Road, a road that had many sharp curves. The narrow road twisted up and down small hills as it snaked its path among the trees. About a mile from the highway, they turned onto a one-lane gravel road that went down to Flint Creek. The mouth of the creek joined the Tennessee River. Nearby Susie Hole and Garth Slough were favorite places for residents to fish. A person could easily slide in a boat or fish from the banks.

The creek water was low. The first place the Housers tried to fish did not produce any bites, so they moved on to another spot. Kim and Connie lost interest. They removed their shoes and skipped along the mud flats. They took their long walking sticks. Their grandparents also had walking sticks because they never knew what they might run across in the woods or along the riverbanks. A long stick was a useful weapon against snakes.

Kim and Connie mostly raked through leaves or turned over rocks in the mud. Their grandparents became small figures behind them as the young girls ran along the mudflats. They skipped, poked, and played; lost in a world of adventure that only a child could appreciate.

"Look!" Kim cried out. She bent down and picked up a shiny object.

"What is it?" asked Connie.

Kim turned to face her sister. In her hand, she held a mud-spattered wristwatch. The band was filthy, but the crystal was washed clean by the river water.

"Here. You can have it." She placed the watch on Connie's wrist.

"Wow! It's pretty!"

They trudged across the muddy landscape, searching for more treasures.

"Oh, look!" Kim pulled a red billfold out of the mud. It was dingy, faded, and cracked.

"I'll keep the billfold and you can keep the watch." Kim giggled. "We're rich!"

Kim opened the billfold. It was empty. Someone must have thrown it away. She took her stick, flipped over leaves, small stones, and a few shells. She glanced over her shoulder to her grandparents. She waved to them, but they were so small.

The stick hit something hard. Kim looked at the muddy ground.

It was a bone.

"Connie, look!"

Connie rushed over, but stopped in her tracks when she saw the bones.

"Is that doggy bones?" she asked.

"No," said Kim. "Go get Mam-Maw and Pap-Paw! Hurry!"

Connie was old enough to know that something had scared her big sister. She ran down the mud flat as fast as she could, hollering for her grandparents. Kim peeked at the bones again. Fear gripped her small body. She jabbed her walking stick into the mud to mark the location and then sprinted down the bank behind her little sister.

"We found something! We found something!" Connie yelled as she reached her grandparents.

"Good gracious, child." Omal bent down and smiled as

Connie hurried into her arms. "What are you talking about?"

"There's some bones over there."

"Oh, it's probably dog bones."

"No, Mam-Maw, no."

Kim ran up to her grandmother. She tried to catch her breath. Excitement filled her voice.

"We found something down there!"

Kim held up Connie's arm. "We found this...and this billfold...and—"

"Bones!" Connie finished.

"Dewey, look at this." Omal handed the red billfold to her husband. He studied it closely.

"Where did you kids find this?"

Kim turned and pointed toward the long muddy bank. "Over where I stuck my stick down." Her stick was barely visible from where they stood. "Way down there. See my stick? That's where it's at. C'mon, Pap-Paw! C'mon, Mam-Maw! Hurry!"

The grandparents pulled in their fishing lines and followed the girls across the mudflat. The two girls ran ahead.

"You kids come back here," Omal called. The girls paused until their grandparents caught up to them. Moments later, they approached Kim's walking stick.

"See! See!" Kim shouted. The young girl jumped up and down. "It's right there!"

The stick protruded from the mud next to a skeletal frame.

"Get back," Omal told the girls.

Connie glanced at her grandmother and saw the same fear that had glinted from Kim's eyes.

"We better get the sheriff," said Dewey.

Omal nodded. "All right, girls. Let's get in the car, now."

Kim reached for her stick to take it home.

"No darlin'. Leave your stick. Pap-Paw will get you another one. Y'all go get in the car."

It took approximately 15 minutes to get back to the house and call the sheriff's office. Their son, Allen, was on a tractor when they got home. Dewey told him what they had found. Allen dismounted the John Deere and came into the house. Another 15 minutes passed before two deputies arrived at their home.

"Just where did y'all see these bones?" the young deputy asked. His partner stood beside him and took notes.

"We found 'em," Kim chirped. Omal looked at the child. Kim knew it was time to let the adults talk.

"Flint Creek," said Omal. We were down there fishing, and the children ran across them while they were playing," Omal said.

"All right. Let's go have a look see." The deputy led the way back to the front porch.

Kim and Connie ran to their grandparent's car.

"Hey, come back over here," said Allen. "Y'all better stay home with me."

"Actually," said the deputy, "we might need the girls to show us where they found everything."

"I don't know if that's a good idea. Are you sure that's necessary?"

"I'm afraid so, sir. Don't worry. Kids are resilient."

"Okay, but try not to keep them there too long."

"Yes, sir."

Dewey and Omal approached the Deputy.

"You can follow us," said Dewey.

The young deputy knelt down and smiled at Kim and Connie.

"Would y'all like to ride in the back of the squad car?"

Kim and Connie looked at each other and beamed.

"Really? Can we?" asked Kim.

"As long as it's okay with your folks."

Dewey pulled Allen in close to him. "Let them. It

might keep their minds off this mess."

Allen nodded. "Okay. But y'all be good in there."

The girls leaped and cheered. The deputy opened the back door, and the girls slid inside.

"Kim, Connie," said their dad. "I mean it. I want you to be on your best behavior."

Kim gave him a devilish grin and nodded. "We will!"

The deputies followed Dewey and Omal to Flint Creek. They parked in the gravel lot next to the boat ramp. Kim and Connie were ready to get out of the car, but Omal told them to stay with the nice deputy. He looked back at the kids. This wasn't what he had in mind.

"I think they will be okay here in the car while we walk down to the shore," he said. He wanted to see if it really was human remains.

Dewey and Omal led the deputies down the muddy shoreline until they reached the bones. The young deputy squatted down next to a large ribcage.

The bones were unquestionably human.

"Daryl," the older deputy said, "Get on the radio and call this in as a crime scene. We also need an ambulance."

Daryl hurried back to the squad car and called in the dispatcher. Kim and Connie were playing in the backseat, but stopped when they heard the deputy speak. They grabbed ahold of the cage that separated the front and back. They listened quietly.

The dispatcher answered.

"Requesting a 10-52. Location, Hickory Hill Road at the Wheeler Wildlife Refuge boat launch. We have a 10-67. Requesting a 10-52 at Hickory Hill Road at the Wheeler Wildlife Refuge boat launch.

"10-4," confirmed the dispatcher.

Kim and Connie heard the sirens long before the law enforcement vehicles had arrived.

Chapter 50

"I think they found her!" said Pete Foster.

"What—who?" said Rusty.

"Mary Faye Hunter. We just received a call from dispatch. Skeletal remains were found this morning near the Wheeler boat launch."

Rusty jumped out of his chair. "What! Who found her?"

"I just heard some family found a human skeleton out there while they were fishing. Other items were found that matched up with Mary Faye Hunter. Clothes, watch, and billfold."

Rusty hurried to the door. "C'mon!" He rushed out of the office with Pete and Phillip close behind. The three men hopped into the ambulance and sounded the siren.

They sped down Sixth Avenue then turned on Highway 67. Soon they were on Hickory Hill Road. Trees limbs canopied the street that curved to the right, then swung back to the left. There were a few houses at the beginning of Hickory Hill Road, but the houses were quickly lost as the woods grew deeper. The area was just an undeveloped subdivision with a paved road winding through the woods, creating a perfect place for lovers. After all, it had been dubbed Lover's Paradise among the adolescent residents. Trees surrounded the curvy road until it reached the parking area by the water, which was covered with vehicles that belonged to the city and state police, coroner, sheriff, and deputies. They were all there.

Everybody and his brother, thought Rusty Cole as he exited the ambulance. People crowded the riverbank. Some he recognized as law enforcement, but most were just spectators.

Rusty approached the group of deputies and city policemen.

"What y'all got here?" he asked.

Lieutenant Frank Schafer turned. "They found her."

"Who?"

"Mary Faye Hunter. She's been out there the whole time."

"And no one found her till now?"

"Yeah, crazy."

Rusty nodded then moved a little closer to the creek bank. He peered over to the scene below where men in dark suits discussed something while others were searching the mudflat.

"Y'all sure it's her?" Rusty asked as he glanced back to the officers standing a few feet behind him.

"Well, no, course not, but ain't nobody else been reported missing."

"Hmm."

Rusty turned back to the scene below. The embankment wasn't steep where they stood, but it was easier to go to the boat ramp to access the mudflat. Pete moved toward the water.

"Where are you goin'?" Rusty asked.

"I want a closer look."

"Why don't you go tell McBride we're here and that we'd be glad to help in any way we can."

"Yes, sir, will do." Pete stepped down the

embankment. He followed the mudflat to where the men in suits congregated.

"McBride!" Pete shouted as he approached.

"Hey, Pete," greeted the Morgan County coroner.

Pete saw the bones in the mud. Many times he had picked up dead people off the streets, but this was different. Maybe it was the location. The haunting atmosphere prickled his skin.

"Rusty Cole wanted you to know that we'll help in any way we can."

"You tell Rusty that I said get down here."

Pete hurried back up the creek bank. "McBride wants you."

"Okay, sure." He followed Pete back to meet with the coroner.

The skeletal frame was in a supine position. The skull and ribcage were still attached to the spine, along with the arm bones. The leg bones, however, were several yards away. One leg had on a stocking, which preserved some of the flesh. The other stocking had not been recovered.

"Wonder what happened to it?" Pete asked.

"Washed away, I would assume," McBride said. He turned to Rusty. "When we are through here, take the remains to Guntharp's funeral home."

"You got it, Hoss," said Rusty.

"Sad. Just plain sad," McBride said.

"I'd like to add," said Watts as he approached the men, "murder, plain murder."

"Murder?" Rusty said.

"How do think this woman got here?" asked Watts.

"Maybe it's suicide." Rusty kneeled down. "Don't see no bullet wound to the head." He stood.

"The medical examiner should be able to tell us something once the autopsy is performed," said Watts. "Vann Pruitt will go over every one of those bones with a fine-tooth comb, and whatever there is to find, he'll find it."

"Who found her?" Pete asked.

"See them folks over there talking to the deputies? Dewey Houser and his wife."

"You think she's been here the whole time?" The question came from a Decatur Daily reporter.

"I can't answer that yet," said Watts.

"You got any solid leads?"

"Yes, and we hope to make an arrest soon," Watts said.

Rusty shook his head. He stared at the remains. How could there be any new clues here?

A few yards away, Sheriff David Sandlin waved his arm.

"Watts! Come over here," Sheriff Sandlin called.

Watts approached the sheriff.

"Look," said Sandlin. "What do you make of that?"

Watts squatted. He looked closely, but shook his head.

"I don't know. The hip bone appears to be misshaped. Strange."

"These bones might be our only chance to find out what happened to this woman," Sandlin said.

"I hope not. I don't see bullet holes or any evidence the body was stabbed," Watts said. "Of course, we might learn after the autopsy." Watts looked up toward the crowd of onlookers. "I wonder if the killer is on that bank watching us."

"Wouldn't surprise me," said McBride.

Investigators continued to scour the area. Other than a few loose finger bones, nothing else was found. Clothing had been found earlier tangled in the roots of trees that hung over the creek bank.

"The body may have even close to the bank when the water was high," said Watts. "Could have been caught up in those roots the whole time. Water goes down and the body washes out."

"Possible," said Sandlin. "Sounds reasonable."

"I think we found everything except one stocking."

"Who's going to tell the parents?"

"Give that job to the city police since the Hunters live in the city limits."

Sandlin nodded. "I'll tell Rusty to haul the remains out of here."

Rusty Cole stood over Mary Faye Hunter's bones. The skull and ribcage were prominent, but the leg bones had sunk deep into the mud several feet away.

Pete put down a black body bag and Phillip unzipped it. Delicately, they placed the larger remains in the bag. Once that was done, the silver wristwatch, billfold, clothing, and shoes were placed in evidence bags.

-2-

"Y'all fish here a lot?" asked Sandlin.

"Yes, sir," said Dewey Houser. "A good bit." Dewey and Omal were standing off to the left of where the remains had been found.

"When was the last time?"

"Last time? Omal, when you reckon was the last we been out here?"

"Oh, I don't know, probably not in the last month. It's been a few weeks."

Omal frowned. The situation was so upsetting. That poor girl had been thrown away like she was trash.

"What made you go today?"

"The little ones like to go, and I just told Dewey, let's go fishing. It was just one of those spur of the moment decisions."

"I see."

Watts approached them. "So y'all are the couple who found the remains?"

"Yes, sir. It's that Hunter girl, isn't it?" Omal said.

"Might be," Watts said. "You people come out here a

lot?"

"Well, yes," said Dewey. "Like we were telling the sheriff, it had been awhile, but we don't live that far from here. Our farm is right next to the Refuge."

"Okay. Thank you, sir."

The Housers appeared to be a nice couple. It was obvious to Watts that they were still upset about finding the body.

-3-

"Your daughter has been found. I regret to inform you, your daughter...With sadness I am sorry to say..." the young officer said.

"What are you doin'?" his partner asked.

"I've never informed anyone that their loved one is dead."

"I'll do it," his partner offered.

The young cop was relieved. Then he said, "No, I need to do this. Sooner or later, I'll have to do it. Might as well be today."

His partner nodded. It was one of the most difficult things to do, but it was part of the job. There was no easy way to tell someone that their loved one was dead, especially when the victim came from a well-respected family.

* * *

The sun was sitting low in the western sky. Webb sat on the sofa, watching football on TV. He wasn't surprised when his sister-in-law came over. "Since you're watching football, I'll answer the phone if you get any calls," she said.

That didn't surprise Webb either. Someone always stayed close by the phone just in case news came about

Mary Faye. The phone had not been alone since she disappeared five months, eight days, and four hours ago on May 6. More people began to drift in, but that was normal for a Saturday. Some came to talk, encourage, or to find out if there was any possible news about Mary Faye. Webb continued to watch the ball game.

Etolia saw officers coming up the walkway. Bertha opened the door for them.

"They know," she said. "Someone called a couple of hours ago and said Mary Faye's clothes and belongings had been found. And of course, the remains. That's why we're here."

Bertha opened the door a little wider. Voices floated toward them as if everyone was talking at once.

"I see," said the officer. "We still have to officially inform them."

Bertha led them into the living room where Webb and Etolia were seated on the couch.

"Mr. and Mrs. Hunter, we regret...."

"We know," Etolia said softly. "Our baby is gone to heaven." Etolia erupted into tears. She buried her face into Webb's chest. He stared blankly at the TV screen. Tears welled in his eyes then spilled down his cheeks. Etolia moaned loudly. Webb did not move or make a sound. The pain of losing his daughter had completely debilitated him.

Chapter 51

MARY FAYE FOUND DEAD

The news spread throughout Decatur like a grass fire on a dry August day. When Adam heard the news on the car radio, he pulled over, turned the volume louder.

The skeletal remains of Mary Faye Hunter were found today in the backwaters of the Tennessee River. Miss Hunter had been missing since—

Adam punched the radio off.

He lay his head on the steering wheel and wept.

Chapter 52

Law enforcement continued to search the Flint Creek area for clues. Skin divers were in the water, searching for a potential murder weapon.

"Sheriff, look at this!" a deputy yelled, waving at the men. Sandlin and Watts hurried to the man. They saw a tire track cut prominently into the ground. Leaves were carefully removed from the rut.

"What kind of vehicle do you think made that track?" asked the deputy.

"Too small for a truck or van," said Sandlin. "Could be a small truck."

"I agree," said Watts. "Too small for a truck or van. I don't believe a kidnapper would use a truck anyway." He looked at the deputy. "I need a cast made of that track."

"Yes, sir. Oh, look at this." Next to the track, several stems from a small plant were bent at a 90-degree angle. Some broken. "Looks like a car door closed on it."

"Yeah, it does," Sandlin said.

"What kind of plant is this?" Watts asked.

"I don't know," the deputy said, "but it only grows near the water. I've seen it before. There's little red berries on it in the springtime."

"Hmm." Watts studied the plant.

"And look right here," he said excitedly. The deputy pushed a few leaves away. A small brown paper bag lay on the ground.

Watts picked it up. Underneath was a dingy white piece of paper.

"What's this?" he said as he picked up the paper. "It's a receipt—A&P Grocery. Well, I'll be." He inspected the back. "I guess the bag protected it from the weather."

"What's inside?" Sandlin asked.

"Instant potatoes. French's Instant Potatoes. Mary Faye Hunter was brought here, dumped, and somehow the bag was knocked out of the vehicle," Watts said.

The receipt, and the instant potatoes were placed in a large brown paper bag, and folded down three times.

"Here," Sandlin said to the deputy. "Put this in the trunk of my car." The deputy took the bag, placed it into the car, then returned to search the area again.

"She was right here. There is no doubt about that. Unbelievable," Sandlin said. He looked again at the tire imprint. "This looks like a fairly new tire. You know, I wonder—"

"What?"

"I think we should check every tire store and car dealer see who might have bought tires or traded in a car on the day Miss Hunter went missing. Our guy might have panicked. Maybe there was blood in the vehicle, or he was afraid that someone saw his vehicle when he picked her up."

Watts stepped to the left of the tire track. "Here's the other one. This track's not cut as deep. It would have been easy for someone to pull in here, circled around, then go back out the way they came. Never thought about this place as a dumping ground, but it's secluded enough to get the job done, especially at night."

"No, not at night," the deputy said.

They leered at him.

"Okay, okay," he chuckled, "I've brought a girl here before. This place is called Lover's Paradise for a reason. That's why I don't think it was at night because too many people would have been out here."

"But a lot of people are here in the daytime to fish or have a picnic," said Watts. He shook his head. "More questions than answers. Start with the tire tracks. I don't know if it will help or not, but it can't hurt. We don't have much to work with here."

John McBride walked up behind the men. "They got her loaded up. Sad. A woman like that just dumped like garbage. What have y'all got here?"

"Tire tracks," Watts answered.

McBride examined the tracks. "Think it might have been left that day?"

"Don't know for sure. It was raining that day—and that night. That's when that tornado came through."

"I won't soon forget that," Sandlin said.

They were surrounded by tall trees and dead leaves. It appeared that half of Decatur's residents congregated around the boat ramp and parking lot. Sandlin silently cursed himself for not having the road closed off.

"Benny," Sandlin said to the young deputy. "Call Howard and get that cast made."

"Yes, sir."

"We need a metal detector brought in here to search these woods," Watts said.

Sandlin nodded as the officers continued to check the perimeter for evidence.

-2-

October 14, 1967 – 7:00 pm

The black phone was mounted on the kitchen wall, but

its long cord allowed the phone to reach into the living room. Omal Houser sat on the living room sofa when it rang. Her granddaughters raced into the kitchen to answer the phone. Connie got there first, but Kim wrestled the handset away.

"Hello," said Kim. Instead of waiting for an answer, she stretched the coil cord until it reached the sofa then handed the phone to her grandmother.

"Hello? Yes, this is the Houser residence." She didn't recognize the male voice.

Probably another reporter.

Before today, Omal had never spoken to a reporter. She had talked to enough of them in the past few hours to cover a lifetime.

"Are you the one that found that woman out on the Refuge?"

"Yes."

"You actually saw where she was?"

"Well, yes. Who is this?"

"How did you find her?"

"She was just lying there. What did you say your name was? Are you a reporter?"

"You need to be careful what you say about that."

"What?"

"You heard me."

"Who is this?"

"You don't worry about that. You just be mindful of what I'm saying. You need to keep your mouth shut."

The color drained from Omal's face. Dewey and Allen looked at her.

"I said, who is this?"

"I am a friend of the Hunter family. Everybody knows that woman went out there and killed her own self."

"What! That's crazy."

"You listen to me. Keep your mouth shut."

Click. The phone was dead.

Omal hung up the phone.

"Who was it?" Dewey asked.

"I don't know," her voice trembled.

Dewey Houser could see his wife was shaken as she came back into the living room. Fear gripped her pale face. Omal sank into the sofa. Her terrified eyes stared at the wall. Dewey rose from his chair and eased over next to his wife.

"Omal, what's wrong?"

Dewey and Allen led Omal to the kitchen. The children stayed in the living room and watched TV.

They all took a seat at the kitchen table.

"There was a man on the phone. He kept telling me to be quiet about the body we found today."

Omal repeated to them everything the mysterious man had said. She grabbed Dewey's hand. "I'm scared that he might try to hurt the kids." She turned to her husband and son. "I didn't see anything but those bones and clothes. What on earth does he think I saw?"

"I don't know, but I'm calling the sheriff's department," Allen said.

"He said for me to keep my mouth shut. Allen, I think you better take the girls home. It'll be dark soon." She squeezed Dewey's hand tighter.

Allen grabbed the phone. "I'm calling the sheriff."

Omal started to protest, but Dewey embraced her.

"I think Allen is doing the right thing. That man could have been the killer."

"He could have been in that crowd of people at the creek," said Allen.

"He's right, Omal. He could have seen us talking with the sheriff. Easy to have found out who we were."

"Yeah, I guess so."

"Hello. Yes, this is Allen Houser. My parents are the ones who found the human remains this morning. Well, we just got a call a few minutes ago. Some man told my mother to forget about what she had seen out there." He was silent for a moment. "No, sir, don't have a clue who it could have been. He told her to keep her mouth shut." Silence. "Yes, sir. That's how he put it...keep your mouth shut."

Allen turned to his mother. "They want to talk to you."

Omal accepted the phone. "Hello?"

"Mrs. Houser, this is Sheriff David Sandlin. I don't want you to repeat this story to anyone. Don't tell reporters, neighbors, or even other family members. It could have been a crank call, or it could have been the killer. We don't want the newspaper to find out about this yet. He might call again and provide details."

"But why is he threatening me?"

"He might think you saw something. Maybe he left a clue behind, and we just haven't found it yet."

"But I didn't see anything else."

"Undoubtedly, he's afraid that you know something. Maybe if he calls back, he'll let it slip what he thinks you know. We'll tap your phone just in case he calls again."

Tap my phone? Oh, dear!

"This could also make him want to harm my family," Omal replied.

"Just make sure y'all keep your doors locked. If you have a gun, keep it close by. I don't believe he'll try anything. You aren't a defenseless woman walking alone on the street. I believe you're safe. I'll have one of my men out patrolling next to your land just to be on the safe side."

"Thank you, sheriff."

-3-

Bob Hancock was still in Washington, D.C. After a long day of learning new techniques on how to disarm criminals, Bob was finally able to enjoy some downtime in his dormitory room. At least until his phone rang.

"Hancock here."

"Bob," Watts said. "Our lady has been found."

"What! Alive?"

"No. Her skeletal remains were found."

Bob felt like one of his FBI instructors had just knocked the breath out of him again.

"Who found her?"

"Just a family out fishing."

"Fishing?"

"An elderly couple. Dewey and Omal Houser. You're never gonna guess where they found her."

"Well, if I can't guess, then tell me."

"You know that boat ramp near Hickory Hill Road off Highway 67?"

"Yeah, I've been out there."

"They found her bones lying on a muddy creek bank. Her clothes were all caught up in tree roots."

"Roots?"

"Yeah, when the creek is dried up you can see the tree roots sticking out of the side of the bank."

"Well, I'll be."

"Yeah," Watts said.

"Got any leads on what happened to her?"

"Not yet," Watts said as he unwrapped a pack of Winston cigarettes. "They also found her watch and billfold. Plus all her clothing, including her shoes."

"Any evidence of what happened?"

"Not yet. Vann is checking it out. So far, the cause of death can't be determined. Never would have thought she'd been there."

"Me either. I got two weeks left here before I can leave, but as soon as I'm back in town, I'll hit the ground running."

"Okay. See you then."

"If there is an arrest before I get back, call me."

"Oh, you know I will."

After the phone call, Bob Hancock laid across his hotel bed with his hands behind his head. He stared at the toes of his brown loafers. Questions about Mary Faye floated in his mind.

Who took Mary Faye and why? Rape? Money?

Did the killer panic then decide to get rid of her? How did her body stay submerged? Weighted down, maybe?

Had to be rape.

She didn't have any enemies. Then who? The killer had been bold enough to grab Mary Faye right off the street in broad daylight.

Answers? I have nothing.

The main question Bob had was how did the killer abduct a grown woman without anyone seeing him?

Chapter 53

People had come and gone through the Hunter home all day sending their condolences. Finally, the house was quiet. Mostly, Webb and Etolia had sat silently, too stunned and heartbroken to carry a conversation. Jimmy encouraged his parents to sleep. At 11:00, Webb and Etolia decided to take their son's advice. They were a miserable sight.

That evening, they had wept until there were no tears left. Webb had hardly moved. His mind unable to comprehend the anguish that tore through his heart. Etolia had displayed her misery in a more traditional sense. Her agonized wails penetrated Jimmy's emotional armor and left him defenseless against his own tears. The pain was almost too much to bear.

Darkness encompassed the house. Jimmy and Sally slept in his old bedroom. Their daughters, Meg and Beth, slept on the floor next to his bed. Only two months before, Sally had given birth to their third daughter. They named her Mary Jane, to honor Mary Faye, who at the time, had been missing for almost four months. Sally's mother had agreed to keep the newborn for the next few days.

Jimmy could not sleep. His mind brought him back to the day Mary Faye had come to Birmingham to tell him about her mystery man and the pregnancy. She had asked Jimmy for help and he turned her away. What kind of brother was he?

I should have done something.

Jimmy didn't know for sure if Mary Faye's death had anything to do with her pregnancy, but deep down, he knew. Jimmy buried his face in the pillow and wept for several minutes until he fell asleep.

Etolia laid quietly next to Webb. When she thought that the pain could not get worse, another wave crashed into her like a freight train. The impact crushed her will to live.

"Webb?" Etolia whispered. "How could anyone just throw her away like that?"

He rubbed her arm. "I don't know, dear. I can't make sense of it."

"Do you think she was...taken advantage of? Oh, I pray that didn't happen to her."

For a moment Webb didn't answer. He struggled with his words.

"There seems to be no other reason since they didn't ever ask for money."

Etolia sniffed back tears. "My poor baby."

Webb pulled her closer. Together they cried.

-2-

The phone rang and woke the man who had fallen asleep in his favorite chair. "Hel...hello," the sleepy voice said.

"I know how you are, so I'm just calling you again as a reminder to keep your mouth shut. You understand?"

The man was wide awake now. "Yeah, yeah. I got ya. I ain't gonna say a word. Ya know I wouldn't."

"Like I said...just a little reminder after today. Didn't think they would ever find her, but it doesn't change anything. Keep quiet. They won't ever know what happened."

"I won't say anything."

The caller hung up.

Chapter 54

Sunday afternoon, Roger Youngblood and Morgan County Deputy Jerry Johnson went into the murky waters and stayed until sunset. They found an empty box, but it had no connection to Mary Faye Hunter. A few bones and another billfold were found. They had fished out a mud-covered metal chest, but it was also empty. They combed each section, moving along the creek bank at a steady pace. None of the additional items found proved to be the murder weapon.

On Monday afternoon, Mary Faye's funeral service commenced at Central Baptist Church. Pastor Van Arsdale officiated.

"Mary Faye lived as close to a perfect Christian life as anyone I had ever known," Van Arsdale said. "She was a fine Christian woman. Whoever did this to her must be found."

After the service, Mary Faye Hunter was laid to rest in Roselawn Cemetery, but those who loved her would not rest, nor could law enforcement until whoever put Mary Faye into the Flint Creek was brought to justice.

Chapter 55

E.B. Watts had worked his way to each tire dealer in the area. Finally, he traced the tire tracks to a tire that only fit certain types of vehicles. Watts searched for a full-size car, like a Chevy Impala, Oldsmobile, Dodge, or Ford Crown Victoria. Any big car.

Watts checked every car dealer in Decatur. Hicks Chevrolet and Peek Oldsmobile-Cadillac on Sixth Avenue. Smith Motors was on Oak Street. McRae Motors on Lee Street. Kennedy Motors on Grant Street, and Mills Dodge on Second Avenue. Beginning with May 6, Watts studied every receipt. There was nothing out of the ordinary until he reached Mills Dodge.

"You're saying a man brought in his car and sold it to you that afternoon?" Watts asked.

"Yes. I remember it quite well. It had been the first one I had sold in a few weeks. It was raining. Nice car. We cleaned it up and sold it the same day."

"You sure?" Watts asked.

"Oh, yeah. There was a big storm later that evening. The same night that tornado came through here."

He was right about that.

"Did you know him?"

"No."
"Did the man trade it in?"
"No, just sold it to us. Cheap."
"We need to see the receipt for that day."
"Sure. Come with me."
Watts followed him to the office. A middle-aged woman looked up from her desk.
"This is detective…"
"Lieutenant Watts from the state police, ma'am. I need to look at a receipt for a vehicle that was sold on May 6 of this year."
"May 6? Oh, I'll have to find that book. If you come back in a few days, I'll have it for you."
"Thank you. How about Thursday?"
"Yes, that'll be fine."

* * *

When Watts returned on Thursday, there was a problem with the receipt. The numbers did not match the page in the receipt book. The pages before and after May 6 had been removed.
"What happened here?" asked Watts.
"Oh, I don't know. Something could have got spilled on the book. But that's the receipt for the car."
"But it doesn't match."
"Well, I'm sorry, but that's all we have. Sometimes things happen and the pages don't always line up. It's no big deal."
Watts glared at the woman. What could he say? You're lying?
Watts kept the receipt and left.

* * *

The dark blue 1965 Dodge Coronet now belonged to a

man who worked at one of the plants on the river.

"Sure, I have no problem with y'all looking over the car," said the new owner.

The backseat was removed, and red berries were found in the well.

"Look at that," the owner said. "When I bought this car, it looked brand new. Guess they forgot to check under the seat. You wouldn't believe what a good deal I got on this car."

Oh, I believe it.

* * *

Watts turned in the report on the car. He needed more than proof that the vehicle had been at Flint Creek if he was going to connect the vehicle to Mary Faye Hunter.

"You think this vehicle might have something to do with her disappearance?" Detective David Smith asked.

"Not sure," said Watts. "It's a good possibility. But it's not what you know, it's what you can prove. All we got is a car. Nothing else ties the owner Mary Faye Hunter. Nothing."

Chapter 56

November 1, 1967

Sixteen days after Mary Faye Hunter had been found, Bob Hancock was back in Decatur, Alabama. Wheeler Wildlife Refuge was his first stop. He strolled through the vacant lot, down the path that led to the creek, and along the mudflats.

"Mary Faye, Mary Faye," he said softly. "Speak to me, Mary Faye. Tell me who did this to you. Who brought you here, Mary Faye?"

Robins perched on a tall tree branch sang a soft melody of music. They might know, but they couldn't tell him.

Bob searched the deserted creek bank. He moved to the spot where Mary Faye's remains were found. His eyes strained at the location. Were there any clues here at all? They found her clothing, her belongings, everything that she had with her that day.

"Why was one leg covered and not the other? One stocking on, but not the other?"

Bob kept moving. He picked up a small twig and used it to turn over a small stone. Nothing under it, but something was next to it. Bob picked it up and realized that the white sliver was a bone. Probably from a hand.

Mary Faye's hand.

"What do I do with this, Mary Faye?" He stood, peered to his left, then to his right. "How did they get you out here, Mary Faye? Did you know them? Was it a man or a woman? More than one or was it just one man? I need answers, Mary Faye. I need answers."

The only thing that answered was the water sailing down the channel. The robins had left. No boats or fishermen around.

Bob sighed. He was still no closer to solving this case.

"Mary Faye, talk to me, darlin'. I keep getting one thing—you were picked up, brought out here, raped, and murdered. Nothing else fits." He placed the bone in an envelope and stuffed it into his shirt pocket.

Ten days later, Bob returned. He gazed across the Tennessee River and Flint Creek. The water was still down. He returned to the spot Mary Faye was found. The small bone was in a bank envelope. He didn't give it to anyone—no point. She was buried when he had found it. It was almost as if the bone was a part of him. It inspired him.

"Why, Mary Faye? Did you know why?" He surveyed the sky and saw a plane flying toward Huntsville. Cars were rushing along Highway 67 just a short distance across the water. This place was secluded, yet civilization could be seen.

Bob could see the cars and the plane, but he could not hear them. Even the water was quiet—smooth as a plate of glass. A hawk screeched, breaking the silence.

Bob examined the tree roots. Did her body wash up there? After she decomposed, did her bones separate from her clothing? The skull and rib cage were still attached to the spine. The arm and leg bones had not been far from the bank. It seemed that once she was loose from the roots, she washed out, and sank to the muddy creek bottom. The roots kept her clothing. Everything stayed right there in the general area.

Bob inspected the cluster of roots. Water had washed the dirt from several trees and bushes that grew close to the creek bank. "Almost as if you were meant to be found. And everything you had on."

Bob turned his eyes back toward the water. "Okay," he said. "How did they get you out here? Did they put you in a boat, go out to the channel, and throw you overboard?" He crossed the flat. "But that day, the water wasn't low like this. Did they step into the water and fling you across?" Again he stopped. His eyes searching. "That would take two men."

He observed the roots. "Why didn't you rise, Mary Faye? Did they shove you under the roots?"

Bob used a young sapling to pull himself on top of the bank. He looked across the water again. "C'mon, Mary Faye, give me something."

He noticed some small trees were twisted. The tornado from May 6 had hit Flint Creek. Could the storm have pulled Mary Faye closer to the shore, and dropped her where she was found?"

"Could you have been weighted down, but when the storm stirred the waters, moved you closer to the bank?

"Mary Faye, there are so many questions surrounding you, but I promise you, hon, I'll do my best to find those answers." Bob touched the small bone in his coat pocket. "I promise, Mary Faye. I promise."

Chapter 57

December 17, 1967

Etolia ran the last stitch around the little doll dress. She was making the clothes for her granddaughters. Many times she had made clothes for Mary Faye. The days were so empty without her. Etolia had learned the true meaning of God's strength during the last few months. It still didn't seem real. Probably never would, but she knew a new life must be built without Mary Faye. Etolia's life had always been centered around her. Jimmy had his own family, career, but Mary Faye had always been there with her and Webb. So many times they traveled together, had dinner together.

In a week it would be Christmas again. This time last year, Mary Faye had been so excited about Christmas. This year would be hard, but Etolia did not want her grief to spoil Christmas for her grandchildren.

The small dress was put aside. If the police ever found out who killed Mary Faye, Etolia wanted to know what he did to her and why. Until then, she had to keep moving forward. Today, there were sugar cookies to be made for her granddaughters.

-2-

In January, John McBride called for a Coroner's Jury. He needed a cause of death, but at the very least he wanted to know if Mary Faye Hunter had been murdered. State toxicologist, Van Pruitt believed she was raped because one stocking had been pulled off, which didn't really make sense. Then again, a lot of things in this case didn't make sense. In Pruitt's mind, there was only one logical explanation. Mary Faye Hunter was abducted, raped, murdered, and dumped into the creek. Less than an hour after hearing over a dozen witnesses, the jury ruled Mary Faye's death as a homicide with cause of death unknown.

Chapter 58

March 21, 1968

Adam left the house for work. He put in a few hours. Tidied up things. He didn't want to leave anything unkempt. It was too difficult to be at work without Mary Faye. Moments in a quiet corner talking to her had been joyful times. Redstone was now just another painful reminder that she was gone.

Adam left work at noon. He drove to his fishing spot at the end of Mussle Camp Road. There was only one thing on his mind now. Mary Faye. The emotional pain was unbearable. Guilt consumed him. Time did nothing to ease Adam's suffering. Mary Faye left a void inside him. Nothing could fill it.

When Adam reached his destination, he parked next to the gravel shoreline. For a few moments, he sat motionless and reflected on his relationship with Mary Faye. Memories of her haunted him. If he had never kissed her, never made love to her, she would still be alive. She had stolen a part of Adam on the day he had fallen in love with her. Because Mary Faye was gone, she now had all of him. All he could think about was her. Things that once brought pleasure were now lost. Nothing but Mary Faye. Memories of her—and tears.

Emotions stormed into Adam's throat. He gasped for air.

"Mary Faye," he cried. "Oh, my sweet Mary Faye." Hot tears rushed down his cheeks.

How can I go on? I can't. I just can't.

He buried his face in his hands and sobbed.

A few minutes later, he wiped his face. He stared across the river and thought about Mary Faye being in that cold water.

"This is our place, Mary Faye. This is where we went fishing. This is where we made love…"

It was the last place they had made love, and it should be the last place that he took his final breath.

A massive tree had fallen over the water a few months earlier. It was the perfect place to fish. He used to sit on that tree and cast his line right into the water.

Adam stepped on to the tree and walked to the far end. He sat down, and then let his legs dangle just above the water. He opened a bottle of pills and dropped a few into his hand. Without hesitation, he popped them into his mouth and washed them down with a Coke. He waited for a moment, then swallowed more. After Adam consumed all the pills, he tossed the empty bottle into the water. It bobbed like a cork.

"God, please forgive me. I'm so sorry for all of it. Please look after my family. I just can't handle it anymore." He drew a deep breath. "Mary Faye was more than my lover. She was my friend. It's my fault she's dead."

Tears streamed down his face.

"I—I should have died on the battlefield. That way…"

The pills intoxicated his blood. A dark veil slowly swathed over him.

"She'd be alive…Mary Faye…my sweet darl—"

Adam fell into the river.

Water rushed into his lungs. His body offered no resistance. The river carried him farther and farther away in mind and body.

On the front seat of his car lay an envelope addressed to his wife.

-2-

5:30 pm

Adam was late.

He should have been home by 4:30. Adam had not mentioned this morning that he would be coming home late. Which probably made more sense since he had been so moody and consumed with something that he refused to discuss it. Could be the effects of the war, but this seemed to be even worse. Sometimes in his sleep, he called out that woman's name. It worried her. When Martha asked Adam about it, he said it was probably because everyone at work talked about her so much. It made sense, but Martha still thought it was odd.

* * *

It was 8:00. Adam still was not home. Should she call someone? Tell them what? Her husband wasn't home? A little after 9:00, she called her pastor.

"I don't know what to do. Adam could be anywhere, but he could also be hurt. He's been despondent for over a month."

"I'll check the hospital for you," said the pastor. "I'll also check the accident reports."

"Thank you so much."

A few minutes later, he returned her call. "None of the hospitals have his name listed. I checked with the police. No wrecks. No one stranded. No abandoned cars. Nothing.

I guess all that's good news in a way. Give Adam a little more time. Maybe he will show up soon. Keep me informed."

"I will. Thank you."

Morning seemed so far away.

Sometime during the night, Martha finally dozed off. It was a fitful night, filled with horrible dreams of Adam crying out for her. She could hear him but couldn't find him.

Martha woke with a jolt.

It was after 3:00 am. The house was quiet and felt empty. She glanced out the window to see if Adam's car was out there in the darkness. Before Martha looked, she knew it wouldn't be there.

At 6:00 am, Martha got out bed and made coffee.

Still no Adam. What will I tell the kids?

An hour later, she called the pastor again.

"He's still not home."

"Oh my dear, I'm so sorry to hear that. Okay, I think it's time that you called the police."

It had been 24 hours since Martha had seen him. By law, Adam was now a missing person.

Chapter 59

Just before noon, a Wheeler Wildlife Refuge ranger noticed a grey and white 1957 Chevrolet as he pulled up to the gravel shoreline of the river. He figured the vehicle belonged to a fisherman, but after getting out of his Jeep, he noted there was no one on the riverbank. That was odd. No evidence of a boat trailer either. Just a lone car. The ranger examined the shoreline. Nothing.

"Hmm," he said. He walked back to the Chevrolet. Probably just car trouble. He peered into the car. A while envelope lay on the front seat. A name was written across the front. He glanced back toward the river.

The ranger radioed the front office. "Got a possible suicide out here on the north end of Mussle Camp Road where it meets the river. Can't find anyone, but there's a letter on the front seat. Go ahead and call the sheriff's department."

An hour later, deputies arrived. They removed the envelope, but Sandlin advised them over the phone not to open it. Because the envelope was sealed and specifically had a name addressed to it, by law, they could not open it without a warrant.

The owner of the abandoned vehicle was identified.

The dispatcher radioed the name and address to deputies Metcalf and Sparkman. They pulled into the driveway on Cecil Street. Softly, they tapped the front door. Suddenly, it burst open. A frayed, distraught woman stood on the other side. Her ashen face glared at the deputies.
"Have you found him?" she cried.
"Who, ma'am?"
"My husband."
"Who is your husband?"
"Adam Fletcher!"
"I believe this is for you," the deputy said as he handed the white envelope to Martha.

Chapter 60

"So, there you have it, boys. That's what happened to Mary Faye Hunter," Bob said. He placed the pipe stem in his mouth, and drew back on the walnut wood lip. "She was involved with her boss, got pregnant, went to Florence and the abortion was botched."

Jamie and Brad sat silent.

"Of course, there is that other rumor that floated around."

"What other rumor?" Jamie asked, his eyes wide.

"There was some talk that Mary Faye worked for the government."

"We know—"

"Not Redstone. I mean government intelligence."

"You mean as a spy?" said Jamie.

Jamie and Brad exchanged looks of disbelief.

"Well, you know how rumors are. There was one that said that she worked with the Russians—or was it the Germans? I don't know, it's been so long ago. Anyway, they thought she was working with them, giving them information on our government when in reality she was feeding them false information for our country."

"Oh sure," Brad said. "Did she shoot Kennedy too?

That's ridiculous."

"Of course it is, but no one would ever suspect a quiet, church going, shy, single woman to be a spy. No one. All anyone ever saw out of her was playing the piano and going to church. Which is more credible? Mary Faye as a spy or Mary Faye having an affair with a married man, getting pregnant, and having a botched abortion? Neither story fits the description of a young, genteel woman."

Bob drew on the pipe. Tobacco smoke sailed from his mouth.

"The rumor was that Fletcher was her contact to get the information that she fed to the foreign government. Something went wrong, they found out, killed her, and threw her body in Flint Creek. It was a perfect spot to get rid of the body. They thought she would surface, the U.S. government would get the message, but she didn't."

"But why would Fletcher kill himself?" Jamie asked.

"If they were spies working out of Redstone, I'd say the Russians, Germans, whoever they were, killed them both. That's why it was written up as a suicide and accidental drowning. To cover it up."

"Is that true?" Jamie asked.

"Why, heck no. It's just folklore. Rumors surround this whole case. You just have to believe whichever one you want." He stood. "Hold on. I got something for you."

Bob left the room and returned a couple of minutes later. "Here." He pitched a white envelope into Jamie's lap.

"What's this?" Jamie asked.

"The bone from Mary Faye's hand."

"What?" Jamie quickly tossed the envelope to Brad.

Brad laughed. "He's very superstitious."

"Whatever," said Jamie. "I'm not touching it."

Brad removed the bone from the envelope and studied it closely. "Wow."

Jamie shook his head and grimaced. "That's just

morbid. Doesn't any of this stuff ever phase you?"

"It's fascinating."

Bob smiled. "I don't guess I have any more use for it."

"What about the note that Fletcher left for his wife?" Brad asked.

"I never saw the note," Bob said. "The police confirmed that there was one, but I never saw it. A woman called me a few years ago and told me the note said Mary Faye died from a botched abortion. She hemorrhaged and bled to death after some lady did the abortion in Huntsville."

Huntsville?

Earlier Bob said the abortion had been done in Florence. Now he says Huntsville. Which was it? Was he mixed up, or just didn't want to tell everything he knew?

Bob continued. "The woman on the phone said that Fletcher panicked and dumped her body in the water. Guess he thought it would hide everything that happened. Apparently, it was just a horrible accident that snowballed."

"You don't remember the name of the woman that gave you this information?" asked Brad.

"No, I sure don't. I couldn't tell you if my life depended on it. All I remember is that she said that she worked at Goodyear."

Brad's eyes lit up. "The Goodyear plant or the store?"

"The plant. Goodyear Mill."

Brad furrowed his brow. "Rusty Cole's wife retired from Goodyear Mill."

Bob glanced sideways and raised an eyebrow. "Who told you that?"

"Their daughter."

Bob nodded slowly.

"Wait," said Jamie. "Who is Rusty Cole?"

"Rusty was the guy that did abortions in Decatur," said Brad. "He was arrested in 1969 and 1970 for nearly killing two women when he botched their abortions. On both accounts, the charges were dropped because the victims failed to appear in court."

"That's true," said Bob. "I was one of the men that arrested him. We found crude instruments in his home. Coat hangers, suction cups, and tubes."

Jamie shuddered. "That's insane."

"We had him dead to rights," said Bob. "For some reason, no one wanted to testify against him. Maybe they were just too embarrassed."

"Or afraid for their lives," said Brad.

"I don't know," said Bob. "People in those days didn't want stuff like that to get out."

"Maybe Rusty Cole did the abortion and told his wife about it," said Brad. "She might be the lady that called you. She could have tried to cover for him or..."

Jamie leaned in anxiously. "What?"

"Maybe Rusty told his wife that Fletcher's suicide note mentioned that a lady from Huntsville or Florence did the abortion. His wife might have heard rumors about him doing Mary Faye's abortion. If she asked him about it, he could have lied and blamed it on a fictional lady.

Bob blew smoke toward the ceiling. "I don't know," he said. "It's a sad, tragic case. Nothing was ever found otherwise. We had other cases to solve. Sometimes it's too painful to tell the truth, at least to the public. Mary Faye Hunter's case will always be officially classified as unsolved."

Jamie and Brad left Bob's house feeling dazed. There was so much information to process.

"What are we going to do with the bone?" asked Brad.

"I don't know, but it could have some kind of evil curse on it. The way she died."

Brad laughed. "You're nuts."

"I've got an idea. Let's go to the cemetery. The bone should be buried with her."

"Um, you mean next to her, right?"

* * *

At the head of the gravestone, Brad dug a small hole, and carefully placed the bone inside. He returned the disturbed dirt and grass. For a minute, they stared silently at Mary Faye's grave.

"Do you think we really found out what happened to her?" Jamie asked.

"Yes, I think so, but—"

"But what?"

"I still have questions. There are things that don't make sense about the day Mary Faye went missing. Why would she go to Florence or Huntsville to get an abortion when her parents expected her home at 12:30? Why did she walk all the way to the corner of Jackson Street and Eighth Avenue to meet Fletcher? He could have picked her up downtown in an alley or crowded parking lot."

"Things don't always go as planned," said Jamie. "Maybe he was late and she got tired of waiting for him."

"But the timeline doesn't fit. It's possible that the witness who saw Mary Faye on Eighth Avenue was mistaken about the time."

"We'll never know. I could see my shy, gentle aunt being a spy. No one would ever suspect her."

"Don't even go there."

Jamie laughed. "Yeah, I could see that."

Chapter 61

Brad Golson closed his computer. He was pleased with the Facebook page he had created for Mary Faye Hunter. He had spoken to dozens of people related to the case and searched through several documents, probing for any evidence. The truth was finally out there. It had been a laborious journey. Brad struggled with the decision of whether or not to publicly reveal Mary Faye's secrets. Unquestionably, she had made some poor choices. Like so many others, she had fallen prey to temptation. The more she fought against it, the weaker she became. Mary Faye unwittingly put herself in a position that she had no experience handling. She was not accustomed to making mistakes. She had been sheltered from all of the routine troubles and temptations dealt with by most people. But it was one thing to have an illegal abortion, and another to be thrown into the river. Her lover should not have allowed her to die that way.

The phone buzzed.

Another notification.

Since the launching of Mary Faye's Facebook page, Brad received several messages daily. Some were simply interested in a good mystery, while others tried to contribute information.

Brad picked up his phone. The message was short. A woman named Jenny. "May I call you? This is about the Mary Faye case." He punched in his phone number and hit send. A few seconds later, his phone rang.

"Hello," he said.

"Brad Golson?" said a female voice.

"Yes."

"I've been reading your Facebook page. You've done a great job with it. There is a lot of information on there."

"Thank you."

"But there is something missing that you need to know about."

Brad leaned forward in his chair. "You have my attention."

"Mary Faye was murdered."

"Technically speaking, it would have been manslaughter."

"I don't think you understand. She was deliberately murdered.

Brad swallowed hard. Anticipation swept through his body.

"How do you mean exactly? Are you saying that because abortion was illegal?"

"No. She was murdered."

Great. Here comes another wild theory.

"I'm listening," he said.

"I didn't know if I should tell you this story or not, but it's true."

Oh boy. I've heard that before.

There was a long pause.

"Do you have something you want to tell me?" asked Brad. "Are you still there?"

"I'm sorry. Yes. I was thinking. Can we meet?"

"Okay. Where?"

"The Decatur Library."
"All right."
"Can you meet me at 2:00?"
"Sure. I'll be there."
"I'll be sitting at a table on the second floor next to the mystery section."
Interesting that she picked that section. "Sounds good. See you then."

* * *

Shortly before 2:00, Brad entered the library and went upstairs. He saw a young woman with light brown hair reading a book, seated at a side table in the mystery section of books. He hesitated. There was a middle-aged woman with blonde hair seated at a table in the back of the room.
I bet that's her.
The first woman stood up and went downstairs. The second woman looked up from her book and smiled.
Brad took a seat at the table.
"You like mysteries, I see," said Brad.
"Yes, I do," she said. "I recognized you from your Facebook page."
Brad smiled. "So, you have some important information about Mary Faye? You don't think she died because of the abortion?"
"Oh, no, I didn't say that. I said she was murdered. But it was because of the abortion."
"What?" Brad was puzzled. The woman had said murder. Now she is saying abortion. Was she just some nut or what?
"It's all connected," she said.
"Okay. I need you to explain."
Jenny bookmarked her page and closed the book.
"I was told this several years ago by my father," she said. "He told me what really happened to Mary Faye. He

worked for a man who performed abortions."

"In Huntsville or Florence?"

"This was in Decatur."

Brad raised his eyebrows.

"So your father helped with abortions?"

"Oh, no...heavens no...never." The woman shook her head. "My father wasn't there. Neither was Mary Faye's boyfriend."

Brad nearly fell out of his chair. "Excuse me?"

"My father worked in carpentry, laying floors and such. He worked with this man named Rusty Cole."

Rusty Cole.

"Are you sure Adam Fletcher wasn't there?" he asked.

"Yes." She held up her hands as if to stop Brad. "Wait. Just listen." Jenny took a deep breath.

"This was in the early 1970s. My father was in a bar. One of the men struck up a conversation with him. They got to drinking and talking...you know how it is after a few drinks. The tongue becomes looser. They talked about work and soon realized that they both knew Rusty Cole. Then the man said..."

Brad sat in silence while Jenny told the story. After she finished, he shook his head slowly. Brad was astounded.

"Are sure about this?"

"Yes. I used to be married to one of Rusty's sons. Rusty decided one day that he would just show up on our doorstep and try to develop some type of relationship with my husband. That relationship destroyed our marriage. Let me tell you, Rusty Cole was an evil man who died alone in a hospital room. His heart, which I'm surprised he even had one, just stopped. I guess he had a heart attack, but I don't know and I don't care."

"Do you think your dad would talk to me?"

"Probably. I'll ask him." She took out her phone and dialed a number.

"Dad, there's a guy who is investigating the Mary Faye

Hunter case. I told him what you told me, and he wants to know if you'll talk to him." She waited. "Yeah. No, he won't use your name if you tell him not to. Uh huh. Okay. I'll tell him. Love you too." She ended the call.

"He said he'd talk to you. He figured since Rusty is dead that it would be okay."

"That's great! When?"

Jenny wrote down the number.

"Here. He said to call him whenever you're ready."

Brad stared at the number as if he was memorizing it.

"Yeah, I'll call him within the hour." He hesitated. "You got anything else you want to tell me?"

"What? Why I loathe Rusty Cole?"

"For starters."

She paused for a few seconds to gather herself. "He helped his son steal something very dear to me." She smiled. "But he lost."

Jenny proceeded to tell the story of how Rusty Cole helped her ex-husband kidnap their two-year-old daughter. It had taken two years, but her daughter was found unharmed in Kentucky.

"Now you see why I take pleasure in knowing that when Rusty died, he had no one. No one to hold his hand. No one to tell him he was loved. No words of comfort as he left this world."

* * *

As soon as he got home, Brad sat down at his desk and made the phone call to Jenny's father, Sam Weatherford.

"I'll never forget that night or what he told me," said Sam. "I can't remember his name, but his words have always haunted me. He died in a car wreck about a year later. But I knew not to tell. Rusty Cole was still around. You don't mess with Rusty Cole and live to tell about it. Now ol' Rusty Cole is dead too. Guess it's safe to tell the truth now."

Sam's voice dropped.

"Should have had the guts to tell this story before Rusty died, but how could I? It would have been my word against his. Rusty Cole, as mean and vile a man that has ever lived, still had friends in high places. I guess they knew his dirt, and he knew theirs."

"Exactly," said Brad. He waited, eager to hear more.

"I believe it was 1972. It was raining that night, just like it had been when Mary Faye Hunter went missing. At first, I thought this guy was just running his mouth, but he knew exactly what he was saying. I have no doubts about that. We were in a bar in Huntsville…"

Chapter 62

May 5, 1972

It was Friday night and payday. That combination always brought out the bar crowd to Nicki's Saloon in Huntsville. People had money, needed to unwind, and wanted to connect with people. Others wanted to relax in a place where the music was loud, liquor flowed, and attractive young women whirled around on the dance floor. There was a light rain falling outside, but inside it was dry and cozy with dim lights. The smell of burgers wafted from the grill.

Sam Weatherford walked through the door and wandered over to the bar. He didn't want to eat or dance, but he did want a drink.

"Jasper, give me a beer," he said to the bartender, who wasn't named Jasper. Sam called any man Jasper if he didn't know his name. He looked at the name tag on the bartender's vest. "Oh, lookie there—I mean, Bill, give me a beer."

With his beer in hand, he turned around and looked at the crowd. There was no one there he recognized. He turned back to the bar. A man stood by him and glanced in his direction.

"Howdy, Jasper," Sam said.

"Jasper?" The man laughed. "Are you drunk?"

Sam snickered. "Not yet. What about you?"

"Nope. It takes a lot to get me drunk."

"Me too."

The two men laughed and introduced themselves.

They finished their beers, then ordered a shot of Jack Daniel's, followed by another beer. As the evening wore on, the alcohol stole the discretion from their tongues. The subject of work came up. To their surprise, both men had been employed by Rusty Cole.

"C'mon, let's get a table over here," said Sam. "Rest our weary bones." The man followed him.

"So you worked for Rusty too," Sam commented as both men took a seat.

"Yeah, worked for him quite a while. He's a character. You better not ever cross him." He took another drink of his beer. "He'd get even with ya if he even suspected that ya crossed him."

"You got that right." Sam turned his beer mug up. "How long did you work for him?"

"Too long. Especially after what he did."

"He wasn't the best boss, that's for sure."

"Oh, you have no idea what that guy was capable of. It was scary."

"Really?"

The man hugged his beer close to himself. His eyes darted around. Then he spoke, his voice low, as if he was afraid that Rusty would hear him. "What I'm about to tell ya, can't ever be repeated. He'd kill us both."

"Who?"

"Rusty Cole! Who else!"

Sam Weatherford nodded in agreement. What was this man talking about? Did Sam really want to know?

"I saw her before Rusty did, walking down Johnston

Street, headed toward Second Avenue. She had on a light blue headscarf. You could tell she'd just had her hair fixed...the wind was tugging at it. She touched one hand to her head. In her other hand, was a little brown bag." He took a drink. "Then Rusty saw her."

The man stared into the beer. "And..."

Chapter 63

May 6, 1967 – Noon

A southwest wind picked up as Mary Faye left the A&P supermarket. The headscarf protected her new set. She looked toward the sky—dark storm clouds were moving in. She headed down Johnston Street toward Second Avenue. A brown paper bag with instant potatoes was in one hand. If Mary Faye had not been so nervous, she would have also bought a small bag of candy. No, today was different.

Mary Faye explored the downtown street. She had been instructed to walk slowly until he came along. She tucked her billfold and paper bag against her body. Her hands trembled. Mary Faye could feel her pulse racing. Never did she think she'd be—

"You lookin' for someone?" said a deep voice from the car that had just pulled up behind her.

Mary Faye jumped.

"I'm a friend of Dr. Carter. He said you might need some…help?"

"Yes."

So it was him. Rusty Cole.

"Hop in." A man on the passenger side opened the door for her. She slipped into the backseat.

"Whatcha got?" asked Rusty.

"What?"

"In the bag?"

"Instant potatoes."

"Oh, okay." Rusty glanced in the rearview mirror. "Been a while, huh, Mary Faye? You remember me? Probably not. I was a grade ahead of you at Decatur High. I remember seeing you in the hall."

"Yes, I remember." He was one of the nice-looking older boys whom she thought never noticed her. "I wasn't expecting there would be two of you."

"Oh, don't mind him," Rusty said, "He's just my helper."

"Helper?" she asked.

"Yeah, he just does little things."

She wanted to ask what exactly the man helped him with, but fear kept her mouth silent. The less she knew, the better. She just wanted all of this to be over.

"No reason to be scared. It won't take long."

Mary Faye nodded and forced a smile.

Silence fell between them. There was no turning back now. Mixed emotions surged through her, but she reassured herself that everything was okay. It had to be done.

She glanced out the side window. So far, no red lights had caught them.

What if someone recognized me?

Less than an hour ago she had left the House of Beauty on Grant Street.

Her mother would be expecting her at home in 30 minutes. If this took longer than expected, she might need to call home. Mary Faye always called if she was going to be late.

"You sure this won't take long?" asked Mary Faye. "Momma will worry if I'm late getting home."

Rusty grinned. Mary Faye wished he hadn't. A grin was the last thing she needed right now. She needed Adam's strong arms around her for support. The same arms that had held her just a few nights ago.

"Don't worry. This takes no time. No time at all."

She turned back to the window.

They left downtown, cut across several streets until they reached Sixth Avenue. The dread in Mary Faye's stomach grew. The cat-eye shades sat securely on her face, but she nervously pushed them up anyway.

"Momma," she mumbled to the window. "I'm sorry."

Just before they reached the river bridge, Rusty pulled into the Decatur Inn parking lot. They drove around to the back and parked in front of room 303. The motel was only a few blocks from Mary Faye's home. Rusty removed a little black bag from the back seat. He unlocked the door and went inside. Mary Faye and Rusty's assistant followed close behind.

"Just pull off your panties and lie down." He regarded the full-tailed skirt. "Go ahead and pull that skirt off too. Don't want anything to get on it."

He means blood.

She couldn't get blood on her orange skirt. Her momma had made it for her. Both men were turned away from her. Mary Faye unbuttoned the skirt and let it drop to the floor. The assistant placed three white towels on the mattress.

"Okay," said Rusty. "Just lie back and relax. This ain't no big deal. Be over in no time." Mary Faye laid on the three towels. Rusty picked up his black bag. Without looking at her, he asked, "You did bring the three hundred, right?"

"Yes. It's in my billfold."

Adam had given her the money. He had insisted.

The assistant handed Mary Faye the billfold. She pulled out three, one hundred dollar bills and gave them to

Rusty. He folded the money and put it into his pants pocket.

"Now, just relax. Like I said, no big deal."

Not to you.

Mary Faye closed her eyes. She silently asked God to forgive her for what transpired next.

* * *

Mary Faye's legs were up, but something wasn't right. The coat hanger wire should have gone in without any difficulty, but something in the cervix blocked it from entering the uterus.

That made no sense.

The hanger had always gone in smoothly. He pushed a little more. It wouldn't budge. Mary Faye moaned.

"Just hold on," said Rusty. "You're probably just too tense. It should go in," he said under his breath to himself. In frustration, he pushed harder like someone trying to pry open a door. Rusty shoved the hanger again, trying to break through with force.

Mary Faye shrieked. "You're hurting me!"

The assistant watched from the other side of the bed. The only thing he had done when he came with Rusty on these little jobs was to hand him hangers, suction cups, tubing, whatever. This time he just watched in bewilderment. Something was wrong.

Rusty tried again. Harder.

Mary Faye's moans grew louder. "Wait! No! It hurts!"

"Of course it's gonna hurt a little, baby. Be still…" He shoved the hanger again, breaking through the cervix and entering the uterus.

Mary Faye's shrill cry echoed against the walls.

* * *

The assistant caught her hand. "Hold on. It'll be over in just a minute. Just don't move. Lay still."

Her body was perfectly still. She had never endured such pain. Mary Faye moved her head side to side as the pain grew. She could feel the blood trickling from her body.

"There." Rusty removed the hanger. "It's over."

"What about all that blood?" the assistant asked.

"It'll be okay. Gimme some gauze."

Mary Faye moaned. She started to roll over, but Rusty stopped her. His assistant gave him the gauze.

"You got to be still. Can't be rolling around."

"It hurts…"

"It'll stop. Be still." Rusty packed the gauze into her vagina as deep as he could. "The bleeding will stop. When you get home, go straight to bed and rest. Stay off your feet."

She nodded and groaned.

"C'mon," Rusty said.

"You think we ought to wait a bit?" asked the assistant. "Give her a minute?" He glanced at Mary Faye.

"Naw, she'll be fine. She needs to be at home so she can rest. The bleeding will stop and so will the pain. Besides, she said her momma was expecting her." He looked at Mary Faye. "When you get home, don't take no aspirins for the pain. That'll make you bleed more."

Mary Faye did not respond. She could feel the blood pooling between her legs. The pain was excruciating.

Rusty helped Mary Faye to her feet and even helped her slip on her shoes.

"Okay. How're you feelin'?" asked Rusty.

Mary Faye's answer was another groan. She was terrified but didn't have the energy to express it. Oh, how she wished Adam was here with her.

The two men helped her to the car. She laid down in the backseat.

"Please," she whispered. "Help me. Please. You've got to help me. I'm...hurting so bad."

They didn't answer.

Rusty turned onto Lafayette Street. As the road curved south, it became Eighth Avenue.

"Okay, listen," said Rusty. "You're just a few blocks from home. You can walk from here, can't you? If we drop you off at your door, someone might see."

"Please, take me closer to my house. I...I don't think I can walk that far."

Rusty drove slowly down Eighth Avenue. After they passed Grant Street, he parked the car next to the curb.

"It's still half a mile to her house," said his assistant.

"Yes, I know that," said Rusty. "I want to see how far she can walk."

He opened the car door. Mary Faye sluggishly slipped out of the car. The pain was worse. Blood seeped through the gauze. Mary Faye stepped onto the sidewalk and hobbled down Eighth Avenue. Her steps short, and careful. She staggered a couple of times, but forced herself to stay on her feet. Guttural moans escaped her mouth as she crossed over Jackson Street.

"She's bad off."

"Yeah," said Rusty. "She probably can't make it home. Even if she did, she's gonna talk. She might name us." Rusty watched Mary Faye stumble on the sidewalk. "I know a snitch when I see one."

Mary Faye clutched her stomach and nearly fell.

"Get her!" Rusty yelled.

The assistant jumped out and rushed up behind Mary Faye. He grabbed her around the waist, then guided her back to the car. Her weak body offered no resistance. She laid down in the back seat. The brown paper bag rested under her.

"Please," she gasped, as the car pulled away from the curb. "Please take me to the hospital. "I'm...I'm in so

much…pain. Please."
They ignored her. Rusty glanced over at his partner with a cold, menacing glare.
"Rusty," said the assistant. "You gonna take her to a doctor?"
Rusty shook his head. "She'll tell. I'm not going to jail for anybody."

* * *

Mary Faye glanced up. They were on Prospect Drive, turning onto Somerville Road. She could see the water tower.
He was taking her to the hospital!
Relief spread over her. A doctor would give her something to end the horrible pain and stop the bleeding.
The blood seeped through her panties, slip, skirt and started to puddle on the seat. When the car turned, blood streaked down into the floorboard. Pain gripped her body. Mary Faye closed her eyes tightly as if she could stop the torture if she squeezed hard enough.
They should be at the hospital now. Mary Faye opened her eyes.
They had already passed it!
"NO!" she shouted. "Please. Don't do this. Please."
Where were they taking her? Maybe to Dr. Carter's home?
"Are you taking me to Dr. Carter?"
Rusty turned onto Country Club Road.
"Where are we going?" she demanded. "Please! I need a hospital…please…"
Rusty turned onto Highway 67 toward Priceville.
Tears embraced the pain. "WHERE ARE WE GOING?" Mary Faye screamed. Her voice became weak again. "Please, please, take me to the hospital. Please."
Rusty didn't answer. He turned left onto Hickory Hill

Road. The winding road led deep into the woods. Mary Faye attempted to sit up, but the pain caused her to double over. Blood gushed down her legs and slid across the seat. She was going to die if they did not help her. Is that what they were going to do? Throw her out and leave her to die?

"Oh, please, I beg you...please help me. Please don't leave me here...please..." She gasped as the pain stabbed her abdomen again and again. Something was terribly wrong. "Please..." Again she whispered. Then softer, she began to pray. Her words simple, asking God to forgive her of her sins, to help her.

"She's praying," the assistant uttered as he leaned toward Rusty.

"Shut up," Rusty hissed.

* * *

The assistant stared straight ahead, trying to shut out the moans coming from the back seat.

What was Rusty going to do?

He was afraid to ask.

Raindrops began to hit the car. Then several. Thunder rumbled in the distance as they drove deeper into the woods. There were no houses around now, just an undeveloped subdivision. To the left, another sharp, curvy road that led to the boat ramp. A secluded place that lovers used to their advantage.

Rusty scanned the area. The parking lot was empty. Dark clouds hung low in the sky. He eased the car through the foliage and into a wooded area near the water. He parked the car and turned to the backseat. She was hunched down sideways in the seat. Mary Faye's head rested against the door. Her face wracked with pain.

The assistant leaned over the seat to touch her. He flinched when Mary Faye moaned. She raised her head and peered weakly into his solemn eyes.

"Please...don't...I won't tell anyone your names. Please..." Her voice soft, childlike as she pleaded again for her life.

"Rusty?" He turned to his partner. What was Rusty going to do? Throw her out here and let her die? He hadn't signed on for murder.

* * *

Rusty stepped out into the drizzling rain. He glanced around and saw no one. The old fishing trail that went into the woods was located off to his right. People could follow it down to the river to fish. The path was also wide enough for the car. He could drive it close to the river—almost to the creek bank.

Rusty got back inside the car. He started the engine and turned the car down the fisherman's trail.

For a moment, Mary Faye thought Rusty had changed his mind and decided to take her to the doctor. When he instead turned onto the trail, Mary Faye's heart sunk.

The car slowed to a stop a few feet from the creek bank. Without a word, Rusty got out of the car again. He opened the back door.

"Get out," he said.

"Please, don't do this. I promise I won't tell anyone. I promise!"

Rusty grabbed Mary Faye's arm and pulled her forward.

"Get out!" he barked. He pulled on her, but she caught the back of the front seat. Rusty pried her hands away and dragged her out of the car. Mary Faye stumbled against him. She gripped the back fender for support.

"Don't do this...please. Rusty, I want to live...please!"

"So do I."

"I won't tell anyone! I promise! I'll—I'll say that it was someone else." Mary Faye slumped against the car.

She was too weak to stand on her own. Blood ran down her legs. "Please! I won't give them a name!" She wiped her leg with her skirt. "Please." Her bloody hand reached toward him. Mary Faye searched his eyes for mercy.

"C'mon, Rusty," said his partner. "She said she won't tell. Let's get her out of here."

Rusty eyed Mary Faye and sighed. "Do I have your word?" he said.

"YES! You have my word! I PROMISE!"

Rusty nodded.

Mary Faye released the fender. "Thank—"

Rusty grabbed Mary Faye's neck and squeezed her throat. She tore at his hands, but could not loosen his steely grip. Mary Faye thrashed violently against him, desperate for air. Rusty's grip tightened. Her legs folded. She could not utter a sound. The absence of air tormented her. Every blood vessel in her head swelled as if her brain would explode. When the darkness encircled Mary Faye, she embraced it. Her body went limp.

Rusty kept his grip tight. His fingers dug into her throat, crushing her larynx. Her slack body drooped in his hands like a rag doll.

The assistant stared frozen in horror. He hadn't done anything to stop Rusty's actions. He was still in the car. Fear trapped his body. Then, like a rubber band that snapped, his conscience rose to the surface. He jumped out of the car.

"Rusty! Let her go! Let her GO!"

His words fell on deaf ears.

He grabbed Rusty's arm. "Let her go, Rusty! Stop!"

Rusty released his grip. Mary Faye collapsed onto the wet ground. Rain streaked down Rusty's face as he turned to face his partner. They stared at the motionless body.

"What have you done?" he cried. He got down on his knees and checked for a pulse.

Nothing.

"C'mon," Rusty said. "We've got to get rid of the body. We can't just leave her here. Someone might find her."

His partner took several short breaths. "You gonna bury her?"

"What am I gonna dig a hole with, my hands?" Rusty glanced around. The dark clouds, trees, and rain covered them from view.

"We're gonna throw her in the river."

Rusty pulled Mary Faye up and threw her over his shoulder. "Let's go."

"But won't she come up?"

"Not if we weigh her down."

"With what?"

"I don't know—a rock. Something. C'mon."

Mary Faye's arms bounced against Rusty's back as they tromped through brush and young saplings. The area was still vacant. Rusty searched for any boats that might be headed toward the ramp. Nothing.

A fish sailed into the air then splashed back into the water. The assistant jumped, but Rusty ignored it.

"Rusty," his partner said as he walked a few steps ahead of him. "I'm not so sure you can keep her down."

"You better hope I do. Prison ain't a good place."

His partner stopped. "But I didn't kill her."

Rusty moved past him. "You didn't stop me either, did you? That makes you an accomplice."

His partner fell into step behind him. The sight of Mary Faye's bouncing arms disturbed him. He sidestepped Rusty then returned to the front. He couldn't believe what was happening. He was involved in the murder of a woman he didn't even know and had no reason to kill. He wasn't the one who performed the abortion. Rusty gave him ten dollars to go with him. Said he wouldn't have to do anything. Would they go to prison? The electric chair?

The questions exploded in his mind like fireworks.

Adrenaline rushed through his body. His knees were weak. His mouth dry.

They stopped at the edge of the creek, hidden by the trees. Rusty slung Mary Faye onto the soggy ground.

"Go down there and find a big rock," said Rusty.

"A rock? How can you keep her down with a rock? You got anything in the trunk of the car? And what about rope?"

Rusty looked at Mary Faye's clothes. What could they use? The headscarf wasn't long enough. There was no belt. He could use his own belt, but he didn't want to leave anything connected to him.

Rusty glanced at his partner. He didn't have on a belt.

His eyes turned back to Mary Faye. No belt, but she did have stockings. Perfect. Quickly, he removed one of the stockings, and tied it to one ankle.

"Get me a rock," he said without looking up.

His partner hurried to the shoreline. The rock he needed was on the bottom of the creek a few inches from the bank. A large, rectangular sandstone rock lay a few feet from him. He pulled the rock out of the sandy mud. It must have weighed 30 pounds.

"This what you had in mind?" He asked Rusty as he placed the sandstone next to the body.

"That should work out just fine."

Rusty took the other end of the stocking and constructed a bowline knot that he had learned in the Navy. He secured it around the center of the rock.

"C'mon," said Rusty. "Lift up her arms. I'll get her feet. We'll walk out a little piece in the water and swing her out."

His partner didn't want to touch a dead body, but he had no choice. He slipped his hands under Mary Faye's shoulders and lifted her. Rusty grabbed the rock. He put it on her stomach then lifted her legs.

The water was about three inches from the top of the

bank. They stepped into the creek.

"Okay, on the count of three," Rusty said as he gently began to swing Mary Faye's legs. "One...Two...Three." A high swing sent Mary Faye into the water. The men stood still and waited to see what would happen.

Mary Faye's skirt bloomed out around her for just a moment before it deflated like a balloon. Her body slowly descended as the rock and her own weight pulled her to the bottom of Flint Creek.

* * *

"See? Just like that, she's gone." Rusty clapped his hands together as if he was knocking off dust or dirt from his hands.

Just like flushing the commode to wash away evidence.

Rusty knew how to clean up a mess. He always stayed one step ahead.

His eyes drifted to his partner. Rusty didn't need him as another mess to clean up.

"Don't get any funny ideas," said Rusty. "Just remember, you're part of this too. If I go down, you go down."

"I won't say nothing, Rusty. You know I don't rat out my friends."

"Just make sure you don't. If the law don't get ya, I will." He winked. "Let's get out of here."

As they turned onto Highway 67, the rain picked up, as did the wind. The assistant stared out the side window, motionless.

"Relax," said Rusty. No one will ever know." Then he laughed. "No one will ever connect her to us. Who would believe Mary Faye Hunter needed an abortion!"

"The father of her child," said his partner blankly.

Rusty gave him a cold glare. "Did she say who he was?"

"Not to me."
Wonder if she did to the doc? But he couldn't ask him. If the subject ever came up, he would say that the woman never showed up.
But who was the father? He could be a problem.

Chapter 64

The man leaned in his chair.

"There you have it. That's what happened. It was the most pitiful thing I had ever seen."

He glared at Sam.

"But if you repeat this, I'd have to deny it, turn it around, and say you told the story to me." He took another drink and a draw off his cigarette. "Wouldn't matter though. Rusty would kill us both before he went to jail."

Sam nodded. His new friend was right. Rusty Cole always won—he made sure of that.

"Hey, man, you ain't got nothing to worry about from me."

The men continued to drink, neither mentioned Rusty again, but each was very much aware what had been said.

Chapter 65

"That's the story," Sam said into the phone.

"So that's why Mary Faye was seen so close to home," said Brad. "It makes perfect sense. Do you believe this guy was telling the truth?"

"Sadly, yes. The only reason I told my daughter was because I was concerned when she married one of Rusty's sons."

"I understand."

"But now it doesn't matter because Rusty's dead and so is the guy I met at the bar," Sam said. "Does this help your investigation?"

"Are you kidding? Yes. I just wish you could remember his name. If it's the same man that I think it is, I'll be completely convinced that what he told you was true. If you saw a photo of him, do you think you would recognize him?"

"I think so. I can still see him pretty clearly in my mind."

"Does the name Phillip Pierce sound right?"

"Hmmm. I'm not sure. He only said his name once and that was a long time ago."

"Okay. I think I can find some photos of him. He's got family on Facebook. If I find any, I'll call you back."

"Yeah, that'll be fine. You know, Miss Hunter's death has weighed heavy on my mind for years. Sorry to say, no one will ever pay for her death."

"No, but I'm grateful for the information. If the man in the bar was Phillip Pierce, I'll be celebrating. You see, he was Rusty's best friend. They worked together at the ambulance service. I was told they did pretty much everything together. It wouldn't be a stretch to think they had also killed together."

"Could very well be. I tell you, Rusty was pure evil. I think it was justifiable that he died alone after the way he killed that poor woman...and all those babies too." Silence fell between them. "Just an evil man."

"If you think of anything else please call me. I can't tell you how much I appreciate you sharing this story with me."

"Yes, sir. I'm glad I was able to bring some closure to it."

After he ended the call, Brad sat quietly for a few minutes thinking about what the man had just told him. Mary Faye Hunter had been murdered. It wasn't just a tragic accident. Rusty Cole got away with murder.

He picked up his phone and called Jamie Hunter.

"Hello."

"Hey. I have some news."

"Oh, really?" said Jamie. "What?"

"Mary Faye was murdered."

"I know that."

"No, I mean first-degree murder. Not from a botched abortion."

"I knew it!" Jamie slapped the arm of the chair he was sitting in.

Brad chuckled.

"Okay, okay. Before you get too excited, I want to

check something out first. Give me a couple of days, okay."

"Do I have a choice?"

"Not really. I need to verify something. If it's true, we'll finally have all the pieces to the puzzle. We've waited this long. A couple of more days won't matter."

"All right, but hurry. Patience is not one of my virtues."

"No kidding."

After the call ended, Brad started digging. He searched until he found what he was looking for.

* * *

The next day, Brad called Sam Weatherford.

"Can we meet tomorrow?"

"Yeah, sure. In fact, you're welcome to come to my place."

At 2:00 the following afternoon, Sam welcomed Brad into his home. The two men sat at the kitchen table. Brad had a glass of sweet tea. Sam sipped on a cup of coffee.

"Gave up the beer," Sam said as he pulled out a chair. "Decided my body didn't need to get drunk anymore." He laughed. "When you get older, you look at things differently."

Brad smiled. "I already do."

"Did you bring it?"

Brad removed a photograph from a small envelope.

"Is this the man you talked to in the bar that night?" The man in the photo was standing beside a black dog. He looked to be in his early twenties.

"I don't know," said Sam. "This man is younger and heavier than the one I saw in the bar. His face is too round."

Brad sighed.

Please don't tell me this is the wrong guy.

Brad thumbed through the stack and produced another

photograph.

"What about this one?"

Without hesitation, Sam said, "That's him."

Brad's pupils expanded. "Are you sure?" he asked, trying to contain his excitement.

"Yes, sir. This is a better photo. He's older and thinner in this one. That's the way he looked in the bar."

Brad leaned back and shut his eyes. A smile crept across his face.

* * *

That evening, Brad called Jamie.

"Please tell me something," said Jamie without saying hello. "I can't wait any longer."

Brad ran a hand through his hair and took a deep breath. "Jamie."

"Yes?"

"It's over."

Jamie Hunter erupted into triumphant cheers along with a few choice expletives. Brad went on to explain his meeting with Jenny and her father. He relayed the entire story that Phillip Pierce had provided to Sam.

"I knew that devil killed her! I just knew it! Mary Faye would have gone to the hospital and told my grandparents if she had been given the chance. They could have saved her life. May those devils rot in Hell!" Then he added, "And the man who got her pregnant."

"But he wasn't there. We were wrong about that."

"But he got her pregnant."

"Jamie, if we are going to be honest here, I know you want to think of Mary Faye as this poor girl that some married man led astray, and maybe to some extent she was, but Mary Faye was also a woman who fell in love. And who knows. Maybe he loved her. Actually, I hope he did."

"Why?"

"Because the case is already tragic enough. It would be even worse if Mary Faye went through all of that and Fletcher didn't love her."

Jamie did not respond right away. The silence grew. Finally, he said, "Maybe you're right. I would hate for her to lose her life for someone who didn't even care."

"Maybe Fletcher cared more than we know. He did kill himself. He wasn't there during the abortion. He just got her pregnant. Perhaps Fletcher killed himself because of his conscience. Or maybe he couldn't face life without Mary Faye."

"But what if the police were closing in on him and he was afraid that he would lose his job, wife, and children?"

"We will never know. Just because Mary Faye got pregnant doesn't mean the affair would have ended. Once the abortion was over, they still could have planned on seeing each other. Who knows, he might have even left his wife for her."

Jamie didn't want to think his aunt would be some man's mistress. No, it was better to think of her as the wonderful Christian woman that everyone had described. As far as Jamie was concerned, Mary Faye Hunter was an innocent woman who fell prey to evil men. They may not have met judgment on earth, but they were paying the price now.

"So you said they all died in horrible ways?" asked Jamie.

"Well, horrible might be stretching it, but Pierce did die in a car crash. He was 33. Fletcher, of course, drowned himself at age 34. Cole died an old man. I was told he was completely alone, not even a nurse in the room with him. No family, no one. So I guess you could say that it was horrible. Out of the three, Rusty Cole was the worst, but he outlived the other two."

"Maybe it's best that my grandparents never knew the whole truth. They knew enough as it was."

"Sometimes the truth can be worse than not knowing. So what do we do now?"

"We make a movie!" Jamie declared. "We tell the whole world what happened to Mary Faye and by whose hands. That's what we do!"

Also by Glenda Yarbrough

Ghosts, Ghosts, and More Ghosts
Aunt Phoebe's Valley
Liar
Petals of Deceptions
Back To Midnight
Under The Fish Pond
Little Things
What Happened Last Night
Thomas Matthew

ABOUT THE AUTHORS

Brad Golson is a broadcast journalist, specializing in television production and directing. Since 2003, Brad is responsible for producing a variety of local programs, commercial advertisements, and documentaries. Brad dedicates his spare time to assisting law enforcement in solving cold cases. He investigated the Mary Faye Hunter case for two years. Brad is currently the Facebook page administrator for The Morgan County Three: Hunter, Acker, & Drake, three cold cases in Alabama that were committed between 1967 and 1970.

Glenda Yarbrough is the author of several books, usually mysteries, but always set in the South. Many of her books are based on true stories. She has written plays for churches, meditations, and short stories for magazines. Glenda also has experienced having a book banned by a local court then have it overturned in her favor in the Alabama Supreme Court as she fought for the book, *Under The Fish Pond*. Glenda is currently working on the novel, *Killed 1928*, which is inspired by a true story.

Follow Brad and Glenda on Facebook

www.facebook.com/morgancounty3unsolved/
www.facebook.com/glendayarbroughbooks/

Made in the USA
Monee, IL
15 January 2022